AN AMERICAN
KILL

JOHN STONEHOUSE

CHAPTER 1

Webb County, TX.
May 1992

Through the night scope at Whicher's eye, the south Texas brush shimmers under a sweep of desert stars.

John Whicher. US Deputy Marshal. Lawman. Newly-badged.

He squints into the scope.

With his thumb, he flicks the upper of two lens-switches, turning on the illuminated reticle.

He rolls the knurled switch, bringing up the brightness, sighting the three-point cross hair on a bank of shale.

Blackbrush and guajillo move in the light wind. At five hundred meters, the outline of Spanish dagger is stark against the midnight air.

He sweeps the scope—right to left across the flats.

Along a fifty-mile front, law enforcement officers wait on the border with Mexico.

1

He searches the empty land, looking for a face, an outline. For the first sign of the ragged men that cross the river, to walk the brush, to stumble among the thorn and scrub. Illegal crossers—migrants. *Coyotes*; the guides that bring them in.

In his mind's eye he sees other faces—men with dirt-blacked skin; hands high, stepping from Iraqi trenches. No gun, no uniform. Glass eyed, full of animal fear. But it's twelve months since Desert Storm, a part of history now. The night scope is not connected to any weapon.

Lawman, he tells himself—what you are now. Who you are.

Mojados will cross tonight, just as every night. Wetbacks, a handful here, a handful there. Each band will follow a *coyote*, paid to get them through. Like Randell Creagan. Thirty-five. From Port Arthur, east Texas.

For two days, the Marshals Service have had a bench warrant for his arrest.

Creagan's a car thief, an ex-trucker. And according to Border Patrol, a part-time *coyote*.

Whicher lays the night scope on the passenger seat of his Chevy C/K truck. He pushes open the door with a boot. Steps out, stares into the darkness.

He thinks of the distance between patrol zones—a Dimmit County deputy two miles west—his boss, Marshal Reuben Scruggs, about the same again, east.

He takes out the Glock 19 from the shoulder holster. Lays it on the roof of the cab.

The list of units on duty runs to Dimmit, Webb and Maverick County Sheriff. Plus Border Patrol. But Randell Creagan or any other *coyote* could walk straight through the line. Unseen. Simplest thing in the world. In all that space.

Unless they got unlucky. Which case, things could turn fast. Get ugly.

Whicher takes off his Resistol hat. 4 and 5/8th crown, stone color felt. He wipes sweat from his brow, listening to the night sounds. Heated air moves against his skin.

The beat of cicadas slips in phase, then out again. He settles the hat back in place.

Wind stirs the brush, heat ticking off the truck.

From inside the cab is a burst of static.

He jolts, despite himself. Steps to the truck—stares in the open window.

The radio's silent.

He stands a moment. Thinks of countless night ops—3rd Armored Cavalry, leading a Scout Platoon. Then shrugs it off, no point calling brass over nothing. He slips the Glock back into the shoulder holster.

The smell of desert fills the air. Baked earth, hot sand, aromatics. In the far distance, heat lightning pulses, silent. He leans against the Chevy hood, steel warm from the big-block motor.

A white flash streaks into orange in the middle distance. A point of brilliant white. For a split second, then it's gone.

He stares at the spot, mouth open.

There's a second flash. A third.

He strains to make out a sound, reaches in the truck. Grabs the night scope, presses it against his eye. He scans the scrub, rolls the tube gain maxing-out the brightness. The image in the lens is meaningless, saturated. He snatches the scope away, fixing the position in his mind.

He jumps in the pickup—whips the radio transmitter off the dash hook. "Dispatch, this is Whicher. I have a sighting. Multiple gunshots..."

Three shots. Quickly taken. Muzzle flash, unmistakeable.

"Estimate, one to two miles north-west..." He turns the key in the ignition. No response from the radio.

He brings up the truck lights, hits drive, turning the Chevy in line with the fixed spot in his mind. Six months out of Glynco; new to law enforcement—not to this.

The radio crackles. "Dispatch. You see gunfire? Can you get there?"

He stomps the gas. "I'm in route..."

The truck tires bite into the primitive earth, brush screeching beneath the chassis.

He picks up speed—ahead is a gravel draw, a rise beyond it. The marshal floors it out, truck barreling into the depression. He swerves by a low stand of mesquite, steers across the scrub, ground rising to a sandy ridge. At the top, the Chevy's lights disappear into blue night. Whicher brakes to a stop, dust billowing.

Below is a flat plain—ranch land, cut with shallow arroyos. Dry grass, thorn brush. A light is showing. A moving light.

He stares at twin beams, less than half a mile off. A *coyote* like Randell Creagan would be on foot—the lights ahead were a vehicle.

He nudges the front axle over the ridge, steering down a dirt bank. Through the windshield, he sees the vehicle lights change direction—turning, stopping.

Another light shows, a flat beam, moving across the scrub.

It's tracking the ground like a searchlight. Shining straight out from the vehicle.

Whicher stops. He puts the night scope to his eye.

A man is running through the brush.

Range indicators in the reticle show him at roughly three hundred meters. The vehicle's just visible, a pickup—out at eight hundred plus.

The marshal steadies his breathing, watches the beam of light. A cop's flashlight? It's super bright. The scope bursts into blinding green—a split second, before the gain auto-compensates.

A shot.

Whicher searches for the running man—spots him. The lens pulses green again. The man staggers, changes direction. He doesn't stop.

The marshal grabs the radio transmitter. "All units, who's firing?" Another shot lights up the scope. "*Repeat*—who's firing?"

A burst of static. "This is dispatch—marshal, nobody's firing, what's going on?"

Two more shots, Whicher hears the faint crack of the rounds. He sees the man hit in the back, impact pushing his body ahead of itself, legs flailing like a child.

He drops the transmitter, floors the gas. The truck bounds forward into the brush—lights picking out the stumbling man.

And then he's vanished.

The searchlight beam from the shooter vehicle snaps out.

Whicher grabs the transmitter, holding it close. "I've got a gunshot victim ahead..."

The radio crackles. "We're sending the nearest unit; Marshal Scruggs—he's about three minutes behind."

The pickup's headlights are moving, turning away.

"I see the shooter leaving."

"Check the victim..."

"I need to pursue..."

"Check the victim first. Put on all your lights—next unit needs to see you."

Whicher turns the truck in an arc—watching the re-treating pickup, trying to memorize the line. Ahead is a clearing—a stand of trees, a stock tank. From an iron windmill, fence posts stretch away, smooth wires shining in the Chevy beams.

A figure's lying at the edge of the brush. He's on his side, black hair, rag-like clothes, knees drawn up toward his gut.

Whicher brakes to a stop. He pulls the Glock from the shoulder holster.

The man on the ground is Hispanic, late-twenties—around the same age as Whicher.

The marshal jumps out, runs crouched, army habit. "Speak English?"

The man's eyes are round with fear, blood leaking out of him, pooling in the dirt.

Whicher squats, heart racing. *"Habla inglés?"*

The man's head rolls back, one bloody hand dropping from his shirt.

"Alright." Whicher reaches out, touches him on the shoulder. Every muscle in the young man's body slackens—he's sinking into the earth. "It's okay," the marshal breathes. "Alright. It's alright..."

The young man twitches, shakes against the ground. Then the twitching stops, he lies inert—light gone from his eyes.

Whicher stands, swallows. Stares out across the scrub.

In the distance, pinpricks of red show—tail lights on the shooter's pickup.

He runs to the Chevy, climbs in the truck bed, flipping open the tool chest. From inside, he picks out a road flare. He rips off the cap, striking the flare against the friction surface—it sparks, catches, starts to burn.

He jumps from the truck, sets the flare in the ground. It lights up the windmill, the stock tank, the fence wire. Twisted branches of a plateau oak flick shadows on the dead man's body.

Whicher climbs in the cab, swings the truck around.

Ahead is broken country, dipping, rising. Brush and cactus choke the land. He grabs the radio. "Dispatch—this is Whicher. Gunshot victim is a male, Hispanic. Injuries fatal."

"You're there with him?"

"I've marked the position with a flare. I'm in pursuit of the shooter."

There's a pause on the radio. "Marshal, you need to wait for back up..."

"He's getting away, we're going to lose him."

The Chevy bucks and kicks over the worsening ground, tire noise rising to a pummeling drone. He bursts through a tangle of thicket—drops three feet into a dry creek— back end rearing as the front wheels dive.

He gets off the gas, bracing, head snapping forward. The chassis grounds, veers right—he points the hood to where the creek bank's fallen.

The truck climbs, powering up the bank. He searches for the pickup—no sign of lights. The brush is dense, grown to head-height. He turns left then right, scouting out a way forward.

In the Chevy beams he sees the broken wall of an abandoned house. Roof fallen, one wall robbed out to knee-height for the stone.

Something catches the marshal's eye, he stands on the brakes.

He stares, reaches for his weapon. Sees an arm, a shirt-sleeve draped across the wall.

"Dispatch?"

The radio hisses. "Go ahead."

"Think I got another body..." He scans the building, Glock sweaty in his hand.

"Marshal, say your position?"

"Mile and a half from my patrol sector. North-west. Some abandoned house."

"Anything else? You see any landmark?"

"Black as hell out here. I just crossed a dry creek..."

"A creek?"

"You need to get somebody down here."

"Alright, marshal. We're checking against the map."

Whicher eyes the property from the driver window—motor rumbling beneath the hood.

"Marshal? We think you're near the old Channing place."

"Channing?"

"It's a disused ranch. There's somebody not far from you..."

"Be advised there's a shooter making his way out."

"We'll alert all units."

"He's in a regular-cab pickup, dark in color, black, maybe. I didn't get much of a look. He was headed north-west..."

"We'll handle it, marshal. Stay with your vehicle."

Whicher stares at the house, thinking of the thin-skinned Chevy. Anybody inside looking to shoot, the truck wouldn't stop any round. He cuts the motor, snaps off the lights. Steps out, holding the compact semi-auto.

He runs to the near wall. *"US Marshal,"* he calls out. *"Anybody in there?"*

No sound, no movement. He takes a breath, steps along the line of the wall, scanning left and right. He can see part-way through the interior—bare walls, no plaster, roof beams hanging down. One wall is soot-blacked from a fire.

The body of a man is laid across the broken wall. Two dark stains at his back—head slumped between his shoulders. Enough times he's seen it, in Iraq.

He climbs the wall, moving into the building. *"Anybody in here?"*

Another pace, another step. Earth underfoot iron-hard. He reaches a door to a derelict room, a kitchen. Inside are four bodies. Two young women. Two men.

Touch nothing, he tells himself.

He sweeps the space—walks through to an exterior doorway. Steps outside. At the back of the house, the ground is churned up, tire tracks everywhere. He sees the line of a dirt road running north.

The brush is silent. There's just the sound of his own breathing. He steps back in the house, shutting down something inside—a lesson learned; self-protection.

He stands a moment, eyes adjusting in the dark, starting to make out some detail. Strewn around are bags tipped out, clothing, food, plastic water bottles.

The two women are crumpled at the foot of a wall, shot multiple times. They're fallen in opposite directions.

A Caucasian male is laying on his back. Hispanic male, face down in a corner.

The Caucasian is young, skinny. Camo shirt pulled up over his ribs. He's shot in the head, staring open-mouthed at the remains of the roof.

The Hispanic looks like a *campesino*—country boy, judging from the clothes. His face is pressed to the dirt.

Whicher turns to the women, they're early twenties, pretty, fine-boned. No field hands. One has black hair to her shoulders, very straight. The outline of her face graceful, even in death. Her arm is caught in a long necklace; it's broken by the weight of the fall, the beads scattered. On her bare shoulder is a small tattoo—a bird in flight.

The second woman is darker, hair short, a slight curl in it. The blood stained shirt she's wearing is buttoned to the throat.

He takes a pace from the room, retraces his steps. Checks the first body—the man draped across the wall. He's Hispanic, twenties, a farm hand. The long-sleeved canvas work shirt is bulging; extra layers—typical of an illegal crosser. From the way he's fallen, he was trying to get out of the house.

The marshal stares out into the dark beyond the wall.

He hears the sound of a motor. Thinks of the dirt road coming in at the rear. He jumps the wall, runs along the outside of the house. At the end, he squats.

Shafts of light are turning through a stand of trees.

Whicher edges back, finger on the trigger guard of the Glock.

Beyond the trees, a pickup truck's moving fast. It swings out from the end of a thicket, headlights sweeping the abandoned house.

It pulls up, the driver door springs open.

A man steps out. Tall, thin, back-lit in the headlights. He's carrying a pistol-grip shotgun.

"*US Marshal*," Whicher shouts.

The man holds the shotgun level.

Whicher stares down the front sight.

"*Border Patrol*," the man calls back. "Agent Talamantes. Carrizo Springs."

Whicher gets to his feet. "US Marshals Service," he says. "Out of Laredo."

Talamantes turns toward him. Hispanic, gaunt face. Collar-length hair.

"Name's Whicher. You see any vehicle just now? A pickup truck, headed out?"

"No, *mano*." Talamantes lets the cut-down twelve-gauge swing at his side.

Whicher fits the Glock back in the shoulder holster.

The Border Patrol agent steps to the doorway of the house. "Dispatch said you have a body?"

"Five bodies." Whicher jerks a thumb over his shoulder. "Inside."

Talamantes eyes him, running his hand over a thin mustache. He crosses the threshold. Whicher follows.

Neither man speaks.

Talamantes takes a flashlight from a cargo pocket in his fatigues. He shines it at each of the bodies in the derelict room.

"There's a fifth body back there," Whicher says.

The Border Patrol agent steps to the interior door frame, staring through, leveling the flashlight. He turns to Whicher. "It's not your sector, *mano*."

The marshal looks at him.

"This sector," Talamantes says. "The Channing Ranch."

Whicher reaches in his shirt pocket. He pulls out a pack of Marlboro Reds. "Smoke?"

Talamantes shakes his head. "Who's guarding your sector, *compañero*?"

The marshal lights up—drawing deep. He steps out the door, doesn't answer.

The Border Patrol agent follows. He crosses to his truck.

Above the noise of the pickup idling, both men notice the sound of another motor.

Talamantes raises the pistol-grip shotgun. Whicher thinks of drawing the Glock.

A light is coming from the north-east, a vehicle, it's headed out of the brush. They track it clearing the last of the high scrub—a white Ford Bronco.

The marshal sees the black lettering on the door as it pulls up—*Dimmit County Sheriff's Department.*

A uniform deputy gets out. "Hey, Raul. That you? Y'all have a body out here?" The deputy steps toward them. Heavy guy, tan shirt, a Western hat.

"There's five dead in there," Whicher says.

"*Five?*" The deputy looks at Talamantes.

"I just got here, *mano.*"

Whicher reads the name on the deputy's shirt. *R. Hagen.* "You see any vehicle?"

"Who are you?"

"Marshal's Service. Out of Laredo. You see a pickup truck, headed out?"

Talamantes shoots Hagen a look.

"If I would've seen something," the deputy says, "I would've stopped it."

From inside the Bronco is a burst of radio chatter. Hagen hitches up his duty belt. "Dispatch are saying a bunch of wets just got roped, up to Maverick county. They're taking 'em to jail in Eagle Pass. Supposed to be a gunshot victim in Webb—just across the county line..."

"There is," Whicher says.

"How you all know that?"

"I just came from there." The marshal takes a pull on the cigarette. "Injuries were fatal."

The deputy pushes back the hat on his head. "Somebody want to tell me what in the name of hell is going on?"

Chapter 2

Eagle Pass. Maverick County, TX.

Three o'clock in the morning. The Maverick County jail facility is full to capacity. Every cell filled with illegal crossers out of Mexico—the interview rooms, all the holding areas, corridors teeming with law enforcement personnel.

Whicher leans against a marked up wall in reception—a brace of sheriff's deputies hustling by.

There's men in all variety of uniform, he thinks of an army command post—an edge in the air, catch of inter-unit friction.

At the main counter Reuben Scruggs, his boss, waits. Whip-thin in his dark suit. He tilts the black brim of his Ridge Top hat forward, studies the officer on reception. "What time you think we can get in?"

The desk man, Hector Medrano, pushes a pair of metal-frame glasses onto his bald head. "Soon as they tell me it's okay."

Scruggs eyes him under the strip light. "Damn near waited half the night..."

Medrano leans in to the counter. Blue uniform shirt bulging."They were arrested in Maverick—the county has jurisdiction. INS are running all the interviews."

"Who's in for INS?"

"Carrasco."

"Miguel Carrasco?"

The officer nods. "Border Patrol's coordinating for Immigration & Nationalization Service."

"I got a bench warrant out of the Laredo court," Scruggs says. "And federal authority to serve it."

Medrano bounces a pen against a note pad. "I can't get you in. Not till they tell me it's okay."

Scruggs drains the last of a cup of coffee. Rangy. Ramrod straight. At forty-one, he's a career lawman—criminal investigator for the US Marshals Service. From Sonora, out in the hill country. Southern Baptist, tough as teak. "You can't find out if my bird is here? They picked up some *coyotes*, along with the *pollos*—I know they did."

Medrano shakes his head.

"Come on. The guy's name is Creagan. Randell Creagan."

"Can't do it."

"He's one of the *coyotes*—am I right? Just tell me, yes or no?"

"Miguel Carrasco's calling the shots. Or you can take it up with Sheriff Owens."

Whicher steps from his place at the wall.

Scruggs cuts a look at him—eyes black as jet in the leathery face.

"We've got a multiple homicide," Medrano says. "Body count running at *six*."

"How come we can't take a look?" Whicher says.

Scruggs tosses his empty cup in the trash. "Informants. People need protecting."

Medrano nods. "How a sweep for wets escalates to this, I don't know. But everything needs to get done right."

Scruggs stoops to a briefcase at his boot. He pulls out a sheaf of written notes. "I lean on this here counter?"

"Be my guest," the deputy says.

"Alright. Might as well do something useful." He takes out an A4, Xeroxed map. "You were on post, here." Scruggs looks at Whicher. Pointing to a numbered patrol sector.

Whicher leans in.

"You're there four hours, doing squat. Then you hear shooting."

"I saw flashes."

"How far you figure?"

"Mile. Maybe more. I called dispatch."

"You were closest unit, you high tail it out there, see a bunch of lights. Then you use that night scope." Scruggs turns to Deputy Medrano. "Man has a night scope from Desert Storm..."

"It work?"

Whicher nods.

"You're looking through the scope, you see a guy running from a pickup truck. Then you see another light."

"Yes, sir. Hunting light. Fixed to a rifle."

"A jacklight. Somebody jacklighting the guy..."

"They were shooting at him but he kept on running, they couldn't drop him."

Scruggs checks his notes. "You said that earlier."

"Who has the body?" Medrano says.

"Webb County Sheriff," Scruggs says. "I got there, the guy was dead. Webb County had a justice of the peace on call. Their officers took him."

Medrano peers at the map. "Sounds like he was shot in Dimmit." He looks at Whicher. "Your patrol sector was right up on the county line, there. Mile north, you're across it."

"The guy was running," Scruggs says. "Maybe they started shooting in Dimmit—he ends up dying in Webb. Don't make a whole lot of difference."

"Not to him," Medrano says. "But on the legal end."

In back of the reception counter, a door opens.

Whicher sees a tall guy, six-five, carrying a gut in front of him like a fridge full of beer. He's wearing a high crown hat, Boss of the Plains. He's strong-looking, built like a tackle. Bad-tempered face of a catch dog.

"Jim Gale," Scruggs says. "Bless my soul."

The man stomps forward to the counter, sport coat tight over his bulky frame.

"I thought you was up to Los Angeles, California?" Scruggs says.

"I just got in."

"Didn't know you were here tonight?"

"You neither," Gale answers, none too friendly.

"We got a bench warrant to serve. Feller named Randell Creagan. Boosts cars out of Laredo, you know him?"

Gale's face is blank.

Scruggs rubs the back of his neck. "The man works *coyote* now and again. We heard he could be into this thing tonight." He turns to Deputy Medrano. "He gets to go in, we don't?"

"He's western district," Medrano says, "it's his beat."

Gale grins. "Haul your skinny ass back to southern, you don't like it."

Scruggs glances at Whicher, then back at Gale. "Did you meet my new partner?"

Whicher takes off the Resistol. Puts out a hand.

Gale takes it, grips it, squeezes hard.

"John Whicher."

"How come y'all ain't down in Laredo, bustin' drunks?"

Whicher fits the Resistol back in place. "Mostly go where I get told…"

"What you do before? Let me guess—a cop? Laredo police department?"

"3rd Armored Cavalry."

Gale looks at him, surprised. "Army. Up to Fort Bliss?"

"Man ain't long back from Desert Storm," Scruggs says.

Gale folds his arms over his big gut. "You kick some ass out there?" He bunches his shoulders under the sport coat.

Whicher stares at him, saying nothing.

Medrano takes down his glasses.

Scruggs eyes the pair of them. "How about LA?" he says. "Them riots."

The big man twists his mouth.

"I seen the coverage on my TV."

Gale grunts. "Never known a thing like it."

"They say the city damn near lost control."

"National Guard couldn't stop it, what the hell were we supposed to do? I say shoot the sons of bitches before they shoot you."

Scruggs clears his throat. "Tell you what, John?"

Whicher nods.

"Whyn't you take a ride back out to that ranch house? No sense the both of us waiting here. See what you can find at the scene, talk to folk. Then meet me back here, don't look like we're going home any time soon."

Whicher buttons his suit jacket over the shoulder holster.

"Do me one thing?"

"What's that, sir?"

"Don't be finding no more dead people..."

The desert sky is tinged in the east—a faint cold light of coming dawn. Whicher steers the Chevy down the pitted track. Stomach churning with the bite of hunger.

The truck rumbles over hard packed dirt. Dense brush spreads in all directions; ranch land, grazed out—through south Texas, down into Mexico.

Ahead, he can just make out the house, the Channing Ranch, what's left of it. A darkened mass above the uniform gray.

He reaches to his shirt, pulls out his cigarettes. Takes one, tossing the pack on the seat.

He pushes in the lighter on the console center.

The jail at Eagle Pass had been a waste of time. He thinks of tac-op centers, forward posts—men in desert cam, night cam, nomex. No cohesion. Everybody with an axe to grind.

The lighter springs back. Whicher touches the end of the cigarette against the red hot coils.

He thinks of the bodies up ahead. Memories of desert villages flicker. He draws the burning glow up the cigarette—paper and tobacco crackling. Images flash in his mind, mud brick rooms, bodies, all ages, indiscriminate. He pushes the thought away.

At the far reach of the headlight beam is a stand of trees, a thicket.

He searches for any vehicle—law enforcement, crime scene. The clearing at the back of the house is empty.

It should be full of vehicles.

He drives in, brakes the truck to a stop. Rolls the window, cuts the motor. He stubs out the cigarette, flipping open the glove box. Inside is a flashlight, he takes it out.

Adrenaline's running, he can feel it, though he can't say why. He opens the door of the truck, steps out. Night air a living mass.

"Anybody here?"

He walks across the churned up dirt to the doorway. Switches on the flashlight.

The room is clear. Empty. No bodies, nothing from before. There's no way a crime scene should be finished, it's the site of a multiple killing, no way the bodies should be gone. He sweeps the beam of the flashlight across the dirt floor. Winged insects scatter in the glare.

On the wall, blood is splattered. A dark pool at the base. Across the beaten earth floor, he remembers tipped-out clothing, water bottles. He picks his way across the room.

He shines the light through the interior doorway, onto the broken outer wall. The *campesino* in the long-sleeved shirt is gone.

He stands inside the broken ruin. The silence numbing. Thinks of five young people shot to death. If they put up any fight, it hadn't amounted to much. They must have died within seconds of each other, died ugly. He stares up through the gaping roof of the house. Black wings dart in the space above him. Bats. Gorging on insects.

He turns, runs the flashlight beam over the dirt floor. A glint of color winks back. A turquoise bead is wedged at the foot of the wall. Whicher thinks of the young woman, arm caught in the broken necklace, beads scattered. He kneels. Picks it out. Folds it into his hand.

In his mind's eye he sees the running man, sees him tearing through the brush. He pushes the thought down, the moment it's formed.

It falls to you.

He sees the clearing—the man, knees drawn up. His own hand laid upon his shoulder.

He thinks of the blood red of the road flare. Windmill and the stock tank caught in its angry light.

It falls to you.

CHAPTER 3

Eagle Pass, TX.

Caught between sleeping and waking, Whicher feels the jolt against his boot.

He opens one eye, wary.

In the waiting room at the Maverick County Sheriff's Department, Marshal Reuben Scruggs is standing by him. He's holding his hat in one hand. He swipes it again at Whicher's boot.

"Come on. We got to haul ass."

Whicher eases a leg off the chair in front. He pushes himself upright.

"It's nearly eight o'clock. We got to go."

"Eight?"

"Randell Creagan's not here."

Whicher puts a hand to his own hat. It's tilted forward, he sits it back level, throws his boss a quick glance.

Scruggs's face is pinched-looking. Half the night out in the desert, the rest hanging round waiting on interviews, trying to sleep on hard-backed chairs.

"They tell you he's not here?"

"Finally," Scruggs says.

"What now?"

"We're going to roust this little prick, Creagan. Or get the hell out of Dodge."

"He wasn't anywhere among the group arrested last night?"

"Nope."

"Did they let you in to see anybody?"

"If you're fixing to use the bathroom, make it right quick. I want out of here."

Whicher nods. He strides from the airless waiting room—sun already streaming through the blinds.

In the bathroom, he hangs the Resistol on a coat hook. Stretches out his six-one frame. He runs the faucet, throws a handful of water on his face. Grabs a bunch of paper towels from the dispenser, dries himself off.

The light in the bathroom shines harsh across his broken nose. Wide set eyes—hazel to green. At twenty eight, the bags are just starting to show from lack of sleep. He runs a hand through his short, dark hair.

He buttons his shirt, pulls the rolled tie from his pocket. Fixes it in place around his neck.

He takes the hat from the hook. Out in the waiting room, he scoops his suit jacket off the seat back.

"Ready?" Scruggs says. "Grab your keys. You're driving."

At the junction with east Main, Whicher makes a right—heading south on the four lane.

In daylight, the town of Eagle Pass is spread out over wide-spaced lots. A mix of scattered housing, scrub-filled building plots.

"I head south—down the highway?"

"Head down it," Scruggs says. "I'll tell you when to turn."

Whicher eases the Chevy through the light traffic. Past the fast food joints, the big-box stores.

"I spoke with Sheriff Owens last night."

"About Creagan?"

"Owens didn't know squat about him."

"He too much of a low-life?"

"For the Sheriff of Maverick County?" Scruggs says. "Maybe so." He scowls out the window. "Anyhow, I kept my foot in. It turns out somebody in the sheriff's department heard of Creagan. Man has an address here."

"He's living here?"

"Not living—he keeps an address in town. Son of a bitch has rat holes all over the damn place. Don't live permanent any one of 'em."

Whicher stares out at the brittle light of a late spring morning. Mid-May—the whole of summer still to come, with all its oppressive, primal heat. "If Creagan likes to move around, what are the odds he'll be there now?"

"One way to find out..."

The younger marshal hits the blinker, switching lanes, passing a slow moving eighteen-wheeler. "Anything come back on the pickup—the shooter's pickup from last night?"

"Not a thing."

"It can't just disappear."

"South Texas is a big ol' place."

Whicher chews on his lip. No license plate, not even a make.

Scruggs sits up straight in the passenger seat. "Let's get this business with Creagan squared away, we already spent too much time on it." He points through the windshield. "Get in the turn lane—make a left."

Whicher steers the truck into the center of the highway. He makes the turn by a gas station, into a smaller road. The lane is beat up asphalt, one-floor houses, aging cars.

"You okay?" Scruggs says.

Whicher hears the note in his boss's voice.

"I mean, after last night. Finding all the victims, and such. Not easy, sometimes."

"I'm okay."

Scruggs puts a hand to his collar, pinches the skin between a finger and thumb. "I have a hard time believing some of what happened last night. Removing five bodies. Just like that..."

"We know where they were taken?"

"Carrizo Springs. According to Sheriff Elwood Owens."

Carrizo Springs—forty miles away, the Dimmit County seat. Whicher thinks of it, he'd been through a handful of times. Local sheriff was a man named Cole Barnhart. Big political operator. The place itself was small, an outpost town—a fraction of the size of Eagle Pass.

"I reckon Dimmit got 'emselves a problem," Scruggs says.

"How's that?"

"No way the bodies should have been gone. County don't run to a medical examiner. They're supposed to wait on a justice of the peace. In place of the coroner."

"They didn't do that?"

"Not according to Sheriff Owens." Scruggs leans forward in his seat, reading numbers off of mailboxes. "See that house there? Near the intersection..."

"Twin porches?"

"That's the one. Single house divided into two apartments. Creagan has one of 'em. Pull over, let's take a look."

The marshal slows the Chevy to a stop at the curbside. He eases the strap of the shoulder holster against his shirt.

"That thing bothering you? Why you want to wear it, anyhow?"

"Habit, I guess. Riding tanks."

"Don't look real comfortable." Scruggs stares out the windshield at the house.

"Faster if you need it in a hurry."

"Nothing parked outside," Scruggs says. "I guess he could be inside."

Along the lane, across from the intersection is a sedan. Garnet red Caprice. It's parked beneath a bunch of live oak set back from the road.

"See that?" Scruggs says.

The car stands out—sleek among the weed filled lots. Light reflecting off the windshield, no seeing inside.

"Something don't look right."

Scruggs opens the door, steps down in the roadway.

Whicher follows, pulling his jacket across his shoulders.

Beneath the live oak, the door of the Caprice opens. A man in a city suit steps out. Dark glasses. White blond hair. He reaches for something inside a pocket.

Whicher's hand moves toward the holster.

"*Name's Vogel,*" the man calls out, "Dane Vogel." He pulls out a leather badge-holder.

"Reuben Scruggs. US Marshals Service."

The man named Vogel moves forward from the car—light on his feet, faint grin at the edge of his mouth. He holds out the badge.

Whicher sees the brass eagle and shield.

"FBI?" says Scruggs. "You looking for Randell Creagan?"

"Are you?"

Scruggs folds his arms over his chest. "Don't think I know you. You're not out of the Houston office?"

"No, marshal."

"San Antonio?"

The grin stays in place. "I didn't say."

"Well," says Scruggs. "I guess you didn't."

Whicher takes a step to the Caprice.

"I'll tell you what," Scruggs says. He turns—looks at the house. "I have a bench warrant out of the Laredo court. For Randell Creagan." He taps the breast pocket of his jacket. "So, me and my partner are going on in there. And see if we cain't find the son of a bitch." He grins back at the FBI agent. "What do you say to that?"

"No need."

"No need to serve a warrant?"

"No need to go in. Nobody's home."

"Y'all been watching the place?"

"I didn't say."

Scruggs compresses his mouth, looks down at the ground.

Inside the sedan, Whicher sees a second guy, Hispanic, chewing on a stick of gum. His hair is long, curled, pulled back in a pony tail. Gold rings hang from both ears.

"Nobody home, huh?" Scruggs says.

Agent Vogel stares from behind the dark glasses.

"If it turns out, I could've served this here warrant, and y'all got in the way of my doing that, I guess the Laredo court can get its explanation from you."

The FBI agent inclines his head a fraction.

"Good," says Scruggs. He turns, starts to walk back toward the truck.

Whicher follows, lengthening his stride.

They reach the Chevy. Climb in. Whicher settles at the wheel.

Down the lane, Vogel eases back into the Caprice.

"Head back to the jail," Scruggs says, "I need to pick up my truck."

Whicher twists the key in the ignition. He drops into drive, pulls out from the curb, steering a U.

"We'll stop by the Sheriff's Department in Carrizo Springs. Then get back to Laredo."

"What was that all about?"

Scruggs doesn't answer.

The pickup rumbles back down the lane, sun lighting up a row of battered agave.

Scruggs crosses a shined boot over one knee.

Whicher pulls out into traffic, heading north on the highway.

"The guy inside the Caprice," Scruggs says. "Hispanic—looked like a pirate? Can't recall his name but I reckon I seen him before. San Antonio office."

A stop light ahead flicks from red to green.

Scruggs sits back in the passenger seat. Tapping a hand on one knee.

"There something I'm not getting, sir?"

"How's that?"

"You don't seem too concerned."

"You think Creagan was back there?"

"They told us no."

"Well then."

Whicher dips his head. "It felt like they kind of bounced us out of there."

"Reckon they were watching the place?"

"I'd say so."

Up ahead is the turn for the Maverick County Sheriff's Department. Whicher checks the rear-view, switches lanes.

"I'm a criminal investigator," Scruggs says. "The job you're training for. I don't like chasing bail skips. Nickel and dime no-shows..."

"Like Randell Creagan..."

"I'm in the middle of two major cases—up to my ass. I get a job like Creagan, I'm not real interested. I do it, best I can. But like I said—I'm not real interested."

Whicher throws a sideways look at his boss.

Scruggs is leaning all the way back in his seat, a light in his eyes.

"A lot of strange things are going on," he says. "Six people shot to death. Five of 'em in one house. Their bodies taken up, like that..." He snaps a finger and thumb. "Top it all, the fence I'm trying to bring in turns out to be under surveillance by the FBI."

Whicher powers the Chevy across the on-coming lanes of traffic. The Maverick County Sheriff's Department up ahead.

"So, what now?"

"*Now?*" Scruggs says. "Now, I'm interested..."

⅄

Carrizo Springs. Dimmit County, TX.

In Carrizo Springs, the courthouse square is full of trucks and cars—Border Patrol plus two sheriff's departments, Dimmit County and Maverick. Whicher pulls in off the highway running through the town, swings around back of the square, finds space by a store-front bail bond office. He grabs his jacket, sets his hat straight. Locks the truck, heads for the courthouse building.

It's two-story, stone built, classical revival—straight out of the nineteen-twenties. Watered-green lawns surround the place, sabal palms tall as the roof.

He crosses a path beneath the shade of a hackberry. Heads toward a set of scrolled, stone columns framing the door.

Inside, there's a square lobby—central reception. Scalloped-back lights reflect on the polished floor. Law enforcement people are standing around talking—uniform, civilian, there's a headquarters buzz. Deputy Hagen, from the Channing Ranch is near the counter. Beside him, the six-five frame of Marshal Jim Gale.

Whicher sweeps an eye over the gathering, looking for Scruggs. Driving down, they'd separated.

Gale catches sight of him. "Sheriff Barnhart be wanting to talk with you..."

Whicher steps to the counter.

"Seeing how y'all found the bodies," Gale says.

"They have them here?"

"Two blocks south. Over in the hospital morgue."

Whicher takes in the assembly, maybe thirty people. "Any word on the pickup? The shooter?"

Gale shakes his head. "Nothing I heard."

Two Border Patrol agents are at the side of the lobby. In dress uniform—olive-green shirts and pants. Whicher recognizes the tall man in the campaign hat—Raul Talamantes.

"Why the circus?" Whicher says.

"Sheriff's looking to brief the press. Everybody wants a piece. Like they done in LA."

Marshal Scruggs steps in view from a corridor in the rear. He's moving fast, black hat jammed down on his head.

He reaches the counter. Looks at Gale. "What are you doing here?"

"Dimmit County's part of my district," Gale answers. "'Case you all forgot."

"Sheriff Barnhart here?" Scruggs cracks the knuckles in his right hand.

"Got a bone to pick?"

Scruggs stares around the lobby "You familiar with the Texas Code of Criminal Procedure?"

Gale squints at him.

"On moving a body," Scruggs says. "There wasn't a damn thing left, the time my deputy went on back to that ranch. I intend to hear why."

⋏

Inside Cole Barnhart's private upstairs office, Whicher sits by a dark-wood Spanish bookcase. He reaches for a cigarette. Taps it on the pack.

A twenties-era ceiling fan turns smoke from the sheriff's cigar.

The sheriff himself leans against the sill of an open window. King Cole—Whicher takes the man's measure.

He's the top side of two hundred fifty pounds—dressed in a billowing white shirt, Western cut slacks. He wears a Mexican palm straw cowboy hat. His face is freckled, hair sandy, eyebrows pale.

Raul Talamantes stands at the rear of the room, dress uniform stiff. Deputy Hagen sits watchful at a corner of the sheriff's desk. Scruggs is in the middle of the room.

"Maybe it's only me loses sleep over a phrase like '*inadmissible evidence*'."

The sheriff looks at him.

"None of them victims should've been moved."

Cole Barnhart brings the cigar to his mouth. Allowing Scruggs center stage. Knife thin, sober-sided. Isolated.

"Any defense attorney is going to jump all over it."

The sheriff dips his head. "Marshal, I want to thank you for raising this."

"Evidence from a scene can get thrown out, this kind of slack procedure."

The sheriff crosses his arms, resting them on his gut. "Man of your standing," he nods, "federal investigator. I take it very serious."

"Don't matter who's saying it—it's written into the laws of this state."

"Exactly right, marshal. Of course."

Whicher studies the sheriff—four times elected, sixteen years with his boots under the table. Time enough to root out every skeleton, every corner of the county, in politics, in business, all walks.

"Who sanctioned the removal?" Scruggs says.

Talamantes speaks up from the back. "We had to move them, marshal. It wouldn't wait."

Scruggs catches the sheriff with a look.

"Let me tell you how it stacks up my side of the table." The sheriff tips his ash against the window ledge. He leans his big bulk forward. "We've had twelve cases of rabies confirmed this year..."

"Rabies?"

"A bunch of others suspected."

Scruggs looks at him.

"Across the whole of south Texas, we've seen over a hundred cases—this year alone."

"Rabies in animals," Scruggs says.

"Two human fatalities," the sheriff counters.

"That land is full of it," Talamantes says, "that ranch land. They got coyote, fox, skunk, wild dog. Plus the house is crawling, *mano*. It's crawling with bats."

Whicher pictures standing in the abandoned house—wings cutting, swirling above his head.

"Agent Talamantes knows that acreage better'n anybody," the sheriff says. "Border Patrol are in and out of there all the time."

"Rabies in animals don't mean people are going to get it," Scruggs says.

The sheriff nods. "But anything gets bit, there's a possibility of transfer."

Scruggs flicks a hand against the edge of his suit jacket, dismissing it.

"Infected animals bite," the sheriff says. "Hell, they'll bite anything. We don't know how long the victims were out there. Small bites or scratches, can be hard to see. "

"It's really that big of a deal?"

"I got a bunch of public health veterinarians lecturing me." The sheriff waves his cigar in the air. "Anybody handling them bodies is exposed, the virus stays active. Any exposure, the county has to monitor, vaccinate, isolate. Till we find out there ain't no infection."

"You mean, they'll take people out of circulation?"

"I have a county to cover. Not enough folk to do it."

Whicher takes out a lighter. He sparks up the cigarette.

The sheriff turns to him, pale eyes blinking slowly. "You were first on the scene?"

Whicher nods.

"How long you figure they'd been there?"

"Not long."

"Hours? Minutes?"

"Not as long as an hour."

"You touch any of 'em? Did you check for a pulse?"

"No, sir."

"You didn't?" The sheriff hutches his shoulders. "Alright, then. We might not have to quarantine you."

Color's rising in Scruggs's face.

The sheriff clamps the plug of cigar to his mouth, whips it away again. "If word got out we let a bunch of dead wetbacks lay around half the night, a place condemned with rabies—I'd have a riot on my hands. I need to respect the dead, and comply with the public health obligation."

"And compromise a major homicide investigation?" Scruggs says.

Deputy Hagen rises from the desk. "Everything got done right, marshal. We collected evidence with due diligence, photographed it all." He turns to Sheriff Barnhart. "We took good care of it, Raul and me."

"What about the victims?" Whicher says. "Have any of them been identified?"

"The Hispanics could be from anywhere," the sheriff says.

"There was no ID?"

"Not a thing," Hagen says.

"What about the Caucasian?"

"That one we do know," the sheriff says. "Local kid, late of this county. Name of Todd Williams."

"How about the runner?" Scruggs says. "The man shot out in the brush?"

"Webb County officers took the body to Laredo. You need to check with them." The sheriff watches from the window. Cigar at his mouth, blue smoke curling.

"I'll tell you what," Scruggs says. "I'd want a whole lot tighter grip—an investigation big as this thing's going to be."

"Hold your horses, marshal." The sheriff steps from the window. He leans over the desk, stubbing out the cigar in an antique brass tray. "Before any investigation, I have to balance resource against the likely outcome."

"Meaning?"

"I'm about to go brief the radio and newspaper folk. But y'all might as well hear it now. I'll put together an investigation—but only so far as it concerns the death of Todd Williams. As to the rest..."

"You won't investigate?"

"We'll look into the death of Williams—we find out who killed them wetbacks, so much the better. It's likely the same killer, so the chances ain't bad."

"But?"

"We may never find out who any of them wets were. With no ID. They could be from anywhere—and I do mean *any*where."

"I can't hardly believe I'm hearing this."

"I cain't do a tenth of what I'd like to do, marshal. If it ends up an open verdict, that's just the way it's going to have to be."

"There must be some way to ID the Hispanics." Scruggs looks to Hagen and Talamantes in turn. "Y'all are certain there was nothing out there, nothing at the scene?"

Both men shake their heads. Talamantes runs a hand across his mustache.

Whicher thinks of the turquoise bead. Winking out of the dark at the foot of the wall. He puts a hand against the leg of his pants—it's still in there, he can feel it at the bottom of his pocket. Preserving evidence was the crime scene priority, everybody at Glynco told him that. Did they miss it, or leave it?

Hagen and Talamantes cleared everything from the ranch in double-time.

He stares out the window at a brick cantina across the square.

What else happened?

What else did they miss?

CHAPTER 4

Back outside in the courthouse square, Whicher leans against his truck.

Scruggs is making his way over, dust blowing, palm fronds twisting in the hot wind.

At Sheriff Barnhart's window there's no sign of the man himself, King Cole with the big cigar—he'd be briefing the press.

Whicher takes the truck keys from his pocket. They could head south, regroup, maybe get home an hour. He'd catch a shower, get a change of clothes.

Scruggs slows as he approaches. "I just spoke with Laredo Coroner's Office."

Whicher pushes up off the side of the Chevy.

Cars and trucks from the sheriff's department are starting to pull out—the square emptying, town returning to a regular tempo.

"They found a match, a fingerprint match on the runner. FBI database came up with a name—Alfonso Saldana."

The younger marshal watches a Border Patrol truck pulling out onto the two-lane highway—into a steady mid-day flow. "They think they know who he is?"

"Alfonso Saldana. Arrested and printed around a year ago. Subsequently deported to Mexico. Looks like he came back."

"Did you tell the sheriff?"

"Man's real busy." Scruggs cuts a look at the upper floor window.

"You didn't tell him."

The older marshal doesn't answer.

"So what now, we head back to Laredo?"

"Not you," Scruggs says. "I want you to head back into Eagle Pass. Park your ass at the jail, or at INS, or wherever you need to be to get an interview with that group of *mojados* from last night. We have a name now," Scruggs says. "One of them wets might've known Saldana."

"Alright, sir."

"Talk to Carrasco, Miguel Carrasco—he's lead intel, it was his sweep, he coordinated the whole deal. I'll head on down to Laredo."

"Are we investigating Saldana's death?"

A cloud passes behind Scruggs's eyes. "I'll see what I can dig up in Laredo. If the guy was deported last year, there ought to be a record on it. Find Miguel Carrasco. Stick with it, get in his face."

Eagle Pass, TX.

Reception at the Maverick County Sheriff's Department is practically deserted—compared with the scene the night before.

At the main counter, Deputy Medrano watches the marshal coming in—metal-frame glasses resting on the top of his head. "Back again? I do something for you?"

"I'm here to see the detainees," Whicher says. "Everybody from last night."

Medrano leans his shirt front against the counter top.

"We have an ID on one of the shooting victims. I need to get in, with an interpreter."

The deputy shakes his head. "They all VR-ed."

"They did what?"

"Voluntarily returned."

Whicher's face is blank.

"They waived their right to a hearing in a US immigration court. We put 'em on a bus back to Mexico," Medrano says. "Couple hours since."

"Is Miguel Carrasco here?"

The deputy searches through the piles of paper on the counter, finds a list, traces a finger down it. "He didn't sign out of the building yet." He picks up the phone, keys in a number.

Whicher runs a hand across the stubble at his chin.

"Miguel? I have a deputy from the Marshals Service at the front desk…" Medrano listens to the response. Puts down the receiver. "Down the hall. Fourth door on the left."

Whicher touches a finger to his hat. He strides by the counter, enters a door into a featureless hall. Strip lights. Gray carpet. A feel of stale air.

A short Hispanic man is standing partway down the hall. Early-thirties, cropped hair, flattened nose like a boxer.

"You're not with Jim Gale?"

"No," Whicher says. "I'm out of southern district. Laredo."

Carrasco leads him into a small office, no windows, a desk strewn with carbon-backed paper forms. There's a telephone and three plastic chairs.

Carrasco's tough-looking, wiry. Ink-black eyes of a Mexican-Indian.

"I came to see the detainees from the sweep. Deputy Medrano says they're not here?"

"Why'd you want to see them?"

"I witnessed a murder last night. Man named Saldana. One of the people in the jail might have been able to help."

"You serious?"

Whicher holds the man's gaze.

"You want to fill me in, *ese*?" The INS agent points at one of the plastic chairs.

Whicher sits.

Carrasco settles at the desk.

"Last night," Whicher says. "I was working one of the zones—on the sweep."

"Didn't know we had any marshals out of southern..."

"Late addition, my boss volunteered. We were down in Webb County, southern end of the line."

"This is about the ranch shootings?"

"About a mile and a half from there. A guy out on his own, running."

Carrasco picks up a pen. "The *pollos* we brought in were arrested in Maverick County. That's like, ten, twelve miles from Webb."

"Somebody might have known Saldana. But you let 'em all walk."

Carrasco flashes his teeth. "You think Sheriff Owens wants to house them, *ese*? Feed them? In his county? These are farm hands—entering without inspection."

"No Caucasians?"

"A few OTM. Other-than-Mexican. No Caucasian."

"You get names?"

"I have a list of names," Carrasco says. "Whether any of them are real..." He spreads his hands.

"We waited half the night, how come we couldn't get to see them?"

"Not your business." Carrasco watches from across the desk.

"You always let 'em go?"

The INS agent turns the pen in his hand. "You new to the border, *ese*?"

"How about DEA," Whicher says, "were they part of this?"

"We weren't looking for *narcos*."

"Just illegal crossers? Now everybody's gone."

"They were *pollos*—no *coyotes*. We drive them back, give them to the *Municipales*."

"We formed a patrol line fifty miles long—for that?"

Carrasco doesn't respond.

"You guys were looking for somebody you didn't get?" Whicher sits back in the chair.

"Tell me about the shooting at the ranch?" Carrasco says.

"So far, we have the name of a local kid, Todd Williams. And a single ID—on the runner, Alfonso Saldana."

Carrasco clicks the pen, scrawls it down. "Why you want to know if we picked up any Caucasians?"

"We're looking to serve a bench warrant," Whicher says. "A man named Randell Creagan."

"What you want with him?"

"Laredo court wants him. Charge of felony auto theft."

"You think he would've been with a bunch of *pollos*?"

"That's all we heard."

"Well. I'm sorry you had a wasted trip, *ese*."

"I'd like a copy of that list of names, all the same."

Carrasco looks at him.

"The detainees. From last night."

"They're most likely all fake." Carrasco regards him a moment. Then he opens up a folder, picks out a typed list—twenty to thirty names. He hands it over, flashing the grin. "Let me know if you find any of them, *ese*."

"Count on it," Whicher says.

⋏

Out in the parking lot, Whicher starts the Chevy, cranks the A/C. Then stands by the cab, studying the list from Agent Carrasco.

None of the neatly-typed names mean a thing.

He reaches in the truck—grabbing a leather tote from the passenger seat. Takes out a copy of the file on Randell Creagan. Plus the bench warrant still sitting in the plastic jacket. Two days old.

The photograph of Creagan shows a rough-looking guy, bearded, heavily tattooed. Thirty-five years old. Former truck driver from Port Arthur—east Texas.

The marshal stares across the parking lot. Stuffs the file back in the tote, tosses it on the seat. Creagan was a waste of time, waste of space. Flea on the dog.

A man like that, base-level criminal, was depressing to pursue.

Scruggs said FBI tipped the Marshals office about him. Why would that be? They had somebody watching the place in Eagle Pass—Dane Vogel, with the white blond hair. The garnet red Caprice.

The marshal feels the afternoon sun on the back of his shirt. He reaches for the pack of cigarettes, lights one. Climbs in the truck, cold air streaming.

He drops the truck into drive, turns out onto the highway, scowling at himself in the rear-view.

Ever since arriving in the town of Eagle Pass, a feeling's been nagging at him, no sign of letting up. No matter how he tries to ignore it.

He steers the truck south, reaches the four-lane, headed down town.

Driving on. Grim faced, toward the heart of it.

⋏

Way down Main, past the county lake and the rail tracks, past the gas stations and the grocery stores—almost to the river itself, Whicher sees the little street between the loan company and the liquor mart—he turns down, into not much more than a lane running parallel with the river.

Junk-filled plots are set among the skinny trees. He drives a block to a wood-frame house, a Trans-Am parked in the yard.

A man sits in the shade on a front porch.

Whicher pulls over at the curbside.

The man finally looks up, notices him. He's wearing board shorts, a crumpled vest. Hair almost down to his shoulders. Sipping on a long-neck bottle of beer.

Lieutenant Eric Kessler. 3rd Armored Cavalry.

Whicher steps from the Chevy, looking up from the street.

The man puts the neck of the bottle to his mid-length goatee.

Whicher crosses the little yard.

"Holy shit, Which. I don't see you in six months, you turn into fuckin' Wyatt Earp."

Whicher takes off the Resistol. "What do you think?"

The man looks him up and down. "Shoulder holster don't look right on a cowboy."

The marshal spins the hat on a finger. "Everybody says that."

He mounts the steps to the porch. Stands awkward.

Eric Kessler pushes up out of the seat. "What's going on, what you doing here?"

"I was in town."

"Working?"

The marshal nods.

"You a regular lawman, now?"

"Finished training a couple of months back."

Whicher studies the man in front of him—M1 tank commander, a man who went to war at his side. The change is deeper than the long hair, the beard, the clothes. His face is someone ten years older.

"You want a beer?" Eric says.

"I could use something to eat?"

Eric crosses the porch, pushing open a screen door. "Come on inside."

Whicher follows into a kitchen—dishes piled in the sink, empty bottles crowding the drainer.

"Kind of a mess. Sort of just me right now..."

"Karen not around?"

Eric pads to the refrigerator in his bare feet. He yanks it open, bottles clink in the door. "I can fix a chili dog. Some nachos, jalapenos..."

"You want a cigarette?" Whicher takes out two from the pack, lighting both.

Eric finds a plate, shakes out a couple of hot dogs from a pack. Slow—like he has to think about it. He spoons chili sauce and jalapenos over the dog, sticks the plate in a microwave oven. "I quit a whole month. Smoking two packs a day now."

Whicher grabs an overflowing ashtray, knocking it empty in a garbage can.

Eric opens a beer—fumbling the bottle opener. Puts out a bowl of nachos, spilling half. "Don't mind the mess. Remember how we used to get the guys to clean out latrines, end of a day?"

"Mix it up with diesel fuel, set fire to everything."

"Sometimes I think it could work for this."

"Check your house insurance," Whicher says.

Eric smokes on the cigarette. The microwave dings, he takes out the plate, grabs a bag of Wonder Bread from the side.

The two men step back out on the porch. They sit at a little table. Whicher scarfs the food.

"You lost some weight," the marshal says.

"Man, let's not talk about me." Eric takes a slug out of the long-neck. Gaze shifting to stare across the lane.

"Pretty good view of the river."

"Ain't it?"

"You like being this close? It don't flood?"

"Sometimes it floods." Eric swings the long-neck side to side between his fingers. "I grew up here, I like the border. Guess sometimes I feel like taking off."

Whicher looks at him. "You all done? Finished with the army?"

The man nods. "Active service obligation, I'm done."

"Thought you still owed 'em?"

"Couple years I could do with the reserves. If I could do any damn thing of use."

Whicher finishes up the chili dog. Picks out a handful of nachos from the bowl. "You had any more of them tests?"

His friend slumps lower in the chair, eyes dull as he answers. "Couple of specialists reckon exposure. Some kind of toxin. We breathed some shit out there, fires burning all the time, weapon dumps, all kinds of things..."

Whicher mops up the last of the jalapenos with a corner of bread. "I remember."

"How you like being a marshal?" Eric says.

"We got to sleep at the sheriff's department, in a bunch of chairs."

"Here—in Eagle Pass?"

"Supposed to be picking up a *coyote*."

"Come back any night of the week, man. You'll hardly move for 'em."

Whicher nods.

"This somebody important?"

"Wouldn't know."

"You didn't get him?"

The marshal shakes his head. "A bunch of people got killed, though."

Eric stubs out his cigarette. He sails the butt end across the burnt brown scrub of grass in the yard. "Soon get enough of that," he says. "Dead people."

Whicher pushes away the plate. "How's Karen?"

Eric's face changes, expression hardening.

A young Hispanic in an El Camino rolls by. Chopped suspension. Body work painted up in primer.

"She's hardly ever here. She's working all the time."

Whicher studies the table.

"She thinks I'm gone in the head."

Wind is blowing from the river, heat pressing in the late afternoon. Eric wraps his arms about himself, as if from the cold.

"I have to call my boss," Whicher says. "I use your phone?"

"In the kitchen."

He picks up the empty plate, carries it inside.

The phone is on the back wall, Whicher dials the office number in Laredo. On a cork-board, among the bills and letters is a photograph of Eric with a bunch of grunts, in front of a Bradley. Whicher in a corner of the picture. They're dressed like guerrilla fighters, not one of them had a full set of anything. It'd rained the night before the picture, he remembered. *In the desert.* A hard February rain. Fog set in that morning, visibility was terrible. They had new phase lines to reach, they didn't look worried. They all looked so sure.

The phone's ringing at the office in Laredo. Scruggs picks up.

"It's Whicher."

"You still up to Eagle Pass?"

"All the prisoners were..."

"Voluntarily returned, I know."

"You want me to get back down there?"

"Matter of fact, no. I don't. There's somebody I need you to go find..."

CHAPTER 5

Amistad Reservoir, TX.

An hour and a half north, past the border town of Del Rio, Whicher sees the great expanse of lake—a vast oasis in the bleached-out scrub.

The road starts to dip toward a gravel shoreline—low sun picking out steel struts of a railroad bridge.

Boyd Harris. Known as 'Jug Line' Harris. From Quemado, north of Eagle Pass.

Someone from the sheriff's department reckoned Harris an associate of Randell Creagan. Harris was operating a hunting, fishing concession seventy miles north. Shooting deer and turkey, hooking Gaudalupe bass and catfish out at the lake.

The battered highway mounts a concrete pontoon. The road crossing a stretch of water, wind picking up. Surface of the rippled lake like molten steel.

An hour till sunset. If he could find Harris, maybe there was still a chance with Creagan.

He steers to the end of the bridge where the road makes landfall on a scrubby headland. Railroad kicking out on a bank of stone.

Whicher follows the highway into low hills of brush and mesquite. He checks the note from the sheriff's department, sees the shack, the bait fish sign—beyond it, an unmarked turn.

He steers from the highway, shifts to low, tires kicking up dust.

The lake is barely visible, the land stretched out in long grades. The rough track passes solitary trailers till it's nothing but faint marks in the hard packed sand.

Whicher slows the truck. He stops where a rail-tie marks the end of the line. He cuts the motor. Steps out, straightens his hat.

A path snakes into the brush, he sets out down it, smell of the lake water in the air, grit lifting in the wind. The path descends, scarcely more than an animal track. The marshal works his way down—a hundred feet, all the way to the water's edge.

Inlets cut in and out of the shoreline. He stares at a crude boathouse made of painted ply and tin sheet. In back is a steel cage filled with propane cylinders. There's no sign of any fishing skiff or bass boat.

He circles the place, it's locked, deserted. He takes off the Resistol, runs a hand through the sweat in his hair.

Cooled air moves off the surface of the lake. He stands a moment—scanning the inlet.

The channel curves back into the headland, sides steep, the creek flanked with rocky cliffs. He re-fits the hat, takes a few paces. Picks a way along the creek—pushing through a tangle of reed.

Set high in the face of the rock, maybe fifteen feet above the ground is a hollowed out-bowl—a natural overhang.

He stops. Stares at it. A ledge runs beneath the overhang, he looks around for a handhold. He pulls himself up into a cave overlooking the creek. On the walls are faint carvings, painted symbols, animals in a red stain, dark as blood. He studies them a moment. Turns to survey the creek—a view straight up and down the inlet.

A man is watching him.

A man standing entirely still.

He's in the reeds at the side of the creek, holding a shotgun. Dressed in camo pants, a worn denim jacket, ball cap over straggling hair.

Whicher drops to his haunches, edges over the lip of the overhang. He scrambles down, jumping the last few feet to the ground.

He straightens up. "Looking for a man name of Harris..."

No response.

The marshal steps in closer. "Your name Harris?"

"You ain't supposed to be up there. This here is private land."

"I'm a law officer. US Marshal." Whicher eyes the shotgun. "Hunting season's over. What you doing out with that?"

"After rabbit and hare."

"That right?"

"Ain't no closed season on them." The man squares his chin.

"Well," says the marshal. "I guess you must be Harris."

"What if I am?"

"You know a man name of Randell Creagan?"

Harris swallows. His eyes slide away.

"Not many people seem to know the guy," Whicher says. "But your name came up."

"What do you want?"

"You do know him?"

"Might have met him."

"He come out here to hunt and fish?"

Harris stands hunched over the shotgun.

"I'm going to need an answer."

"I've met him a couple of times, what of it?"

"You know where he's at?"

Harris shakes his head.

"Know where I might find him?"

"I don't guess." He stares over Whicher's shoulder.

The marshal wipes a line of sweat from beneath his eye. "So, you're out here with a shotgun. You follow me here?"

The man says nothing.

"Getting dark. Not easy, shooting at night. You hunt deer?"

"In winter I'll hunt 'em."

"Got a rifle as well as the shotgun? I guess you do. Where were you last night?"

"I camp out," Harris says. "I got the boathouse yonder."

"Anybody see you?"

Harris shifts his grip on the gun, eyes quick in the failing light.

"Well," says Whicher, "maybe it ain't going to matter."

The man steals a look at the marshal, despite himself. "What ain't?"

"Last night, down river," Whicher says. "Had a multiple homicide, a bunch of wets. Looking like a high-powered rifle was used. Hunting rifle. Sure hope it don't turn out to be a problem. You being here." Whicher nods. "If I need to take a look at any rifle, or any other gun you might have. This be the best place to find you?"

Jug Line Harris only stares back. Mouth working. No sound coming out.

ᴬ

Laredo. Webb County, TX.

Three hours later, Whicher leaves the Chevy at the back of the district courthouse in Laredo, the night still warm, wide streets busy with traffic, downtown brightly lit—the white limestone of the courthouse glowing.

He crosses the sidewalk, enters the building. Takes the terrazzo stairs two at a time.

On the second floor is the US Marshals Office. Inside, Scruggs is seated, straight-backed, behind a wooden desk.

He glances up from his writing. "You find Harris?"

"I found him." Whicher pulls out a chair.

Scruggs puts down the pen.

"He claimed he didn't know anything."

The older marshal studies his face. "Does he know Randell Creagan?"

"He knows him. That's it."

Whicher takes off his jacket, slips it on the back of the empty chair.

Scruggs's desk is covered in typed pages, hand written notes. A Xeroxed photograph—the runner, Alfonso Saldana, on a mortuary slab. "I'm putting together a report. For Marshal Lassiter."

Whicher knows the name, he tries to place it. "Lassiter?"

"Head of Marshals Service, western district. Channing Ranch is in Dimmit County—that's part of western jurisdiction. He wants to know what went on."

"Is he coming out here?"

"Already in the building." Scruggs leans forward in his chair, eyes sharp beneath the thick black brows. "He stopped by Laredo Coroner's Office. There's been word on Saldana. Turns out he was arrested in Brownsville, attempted break-in at the hospital. Before he was deported, last year."

"I had him pegged as a regular *campesino*. He after drugs?"

"I don't know. Border Patrol took custody, kicked his ass out back to Mexico." Scruggs looks at the notes on his desk.

"What are we telling Marshal Lassiter?"

"What we saw, what we know."

"I think Jug Line Harris knows something," Whicher says. "I leaned on him, asked where he was last night. Told him I saw a man shot dead with a hunting rifle, asked him did he own one. He said he owned a bunch."

"Man runs a hunting concession," Scruggs says. "Don't be getting ahead of yourself."

"Saldana was hit multiple times at four hundred meters. Running. In the dark."

Scruggs turns the pen in his hand. "Coroner's office confirm Saldana was shot with full-metal-jackets." He clears his throat. "Anyhow, it ain't our case. We find Randell Creagan—that's it."

Whicher slips off the shoulder holster. He crosses the room to a steel gun locker. Hangs the weapon inside. Through the half-open window the sound of a siren carries in the night air above the noise of the city.

"I called Houston this afternoon," Scruggs says. "FBI. Account of that guy Dane Vogel—out at Creagan's place."

Whicher looks at his boss.

"I spoke with a guy I know—name of Gerry Nugent. Asked him did they have the place under surveillance? He said he didn't know a thing about it."

Whicher closes the door on the gun locker.

"Nugent reckoned Dane Vogel works some kind of IA detail. Internal Affairs."

The younger marshal pictures the big Caprice beneath the trees. Hispanic, with two gold earrings. Vogel fronting it out behind the shades.

There's a knock at the office door. A man enters—lean, wiry, the classic build of the cowboy. He's wearing a bootlace tie, a cowhide waistcoat. In one hand he holds the crown of a fine gray cattleman hat.

Scruggs pushes back his chair. "Marshal Lassiter."

"Reuben," the man says.

Lassiter's good-looking, craggy—a kink in his silvered hair. At sixty-something there's not an ounce of fat.

Scruggs gathers the papers on his desk, placing them in a cardboard folder. He tucks in the photograph of Alfonso Saldana. "I'm just finishing up the preliminary report, marshal."

The tan skin around Lassiter's eyes crinkles. "District likely won't investigate. But best I know what went on."

"We wouldn't have been anyplace near that ranch," Scruggs says. "Except we were manning a couple of the sweep zones."

"Looking for some *coyote*—according to Sheriff Barnhart."

"Yes, sir—a man named Randell Creagan."

Lassiter nods, reaching for the folder. He turns to look in Whicher's direction.

"This here's my new assistant," Scruggs says. "Deputy Marshal Whicher—my new trainee."

"Quinton Lassiter." The man offers his hand. Blue eyes piercing. "You be sure and listen to Marshal Scruggs, he's one heck of a criminal investigator." He squints. "You the ex-army feller? I heard about you, you were out in the Gulf?"

Whicher nods, flattered. "With 3rd Armored, yes, sir."

"Korea, my day, 6th Tank Battalion. *Semper in Hostes*. Know what it means?" He looks the younger marshal up and down.

"Always—something?"

"Into the enemy..." The district marshal cracks out a laugh. "We need more grunts in the service. How you like being a US Marshal?"

"Just fine, sir."

Lassiter glances at the folder in his hand. He turns to Scruggs. "This Saldana guy sounds like a serial border-jumper."

"Yes, sir, marshal. That's what they say."

"The other shooting victims, there's only one ID. According to Cole Barnhart, in Carrizo Springs."

"We were up there earlier."

"I heard." Lassiter shakes his head. "Five dead in one night is a hell of a thing for the county. Hell of a thing."

"My concern is over the bodies getting moved. Any case they want to bring..."

"Nobody's happy about it," Lassiter cuts in. "Way I heard it, Border Patrol insisted, account of the rabies risk."

Scruggs nods, a little stiff.

"A thing like this is going to run its course," Lassiter says. "They're just getting started. Cole Barnhart will see it done right, give him a chance." He turns to Whicher. "Sheriff reckoned you got a pretty good look at what happened in Webb?"

"I had a scope," Whicher says.

"What kind of scope?"

"Image intensifier."

Lassiter sits on the edge of Scruggs's desk. He places the hat crown down. "This a military thing?"

"Yes, sir."

"Hot damn."

The younger marshal glances at his boss. "The shooter had a hunting light. And a rifle."

"A jacklight?"

Whicher nods. "He was firing from a pickup, the rounds were full-metal-jacket—passed clean through. The victim kept on running, I've seen it before, out in the Gulf."

Lassiter sucks air over his teeth. "Hell of a time finding any lead. Webb County took possession of the body, they run any kind of search?"

"Basic search," Scruggs says. "They didn't find a thing."

"The rounds would deflect," Whicher says. "They could be anywhere."

"How about the vehicle?"

"I couldn't get an ID."

"You get a look at the shooter, with that scope?"

"No, sir. I couldn't see that kind of detail."

"Well," Lassiter says. "It's a strange one." Turning to Scruggs. "Ever hear of one like that?"

"Not that I recall."

Lassiter looks at Whicher. "Marshal Scruggs been bustin' heads here since the seventies. Been here myself since '58." He picks his hat off the desk. Flips it over. "You don't have a cigarette?" he says. "I know your boss don't."

Whicher stands awkward. Scruggs gives the faintest nod.

The younger marshal breaks out the pack of Marlboro Reds. Lassiter takes one. Whicher lights him.

"Ain't you having one?"

Scruggs looks over. "Go ahead," he says.

Whicher takes another cigarette from the pack. Lights it. Steps to the half-open window, opens it wide.

Lassiter takes a draw, holds it. Lets it out. "Ain't supposed to do this no more. According to Mrs Lassiter. And the doc. But what's a feller to do, he cain't have a little something?"

Scruggs sits at the desk organizing his papers.

"Used to be a whole lot more fun," Lassiter says. "The job, the border. Back in the old days." He grins, eyes far away. "Place for wild men, it was then. Wilder women, y'all know what I mean?"

Whicher smokes silent by the window.

"It's changing," Lassiter says. "Changing fast." He looks at Whicher. "You're not from around here?"

"North Texas."

Lassiter angles his head.

"You wouldn't have heard of it..."

"Try me."

"Briscoe County."

"In the panhandle?"

"Quitaque, there's nothing to it."

"Say, you want head out, find some place to get a drink?"

Whicher doesn't answer. He looks at his boss.

"Feeling alright, army?" Lassiter says.

"Yes, sir. I think we have an early start in the morning..."

The district marshal shakes his head, grinning. "Alright. Well, I guess I have to head on back to San Antonio." He stands. Turns to Scruggs, taps the folder. "'Preciate you all doing this, short notice."

"Not a problem, marshal."

Lassiter settles the hat over his silver hair. "Good meeting you, army," he says to Whicher.

"Yes, sir. Thank you."

He taps his hat rim. "I'll say goodnight fellers." He steps from the room.

Whicher grinds out the cigarette on the window sill.

Scruggs sits. Back flat as a board. He opens another folder on his desk.

The younger marshal studies the street, noise of the city rumbling. "Do we start over in the morning?"

Scruggs searches through a folder, taking out a plastic jacket. Randell Creagan's bearded face stares out from a photograph on the first page.

"Right now," Scruggs says, "we need to find this son of a bitch." He compresses his mouth. "While you were up at the lake I made a bunch of calls trying to get this thing to roll. I spoke with Border Patrol here in Laredo. Somebody put up another name—someone else linked to Creagan. Merrill M. Johnson. A customs broker. Freight forwarder."

"What's the connection?"

"Creagan's a former truck driver—Merrill Johnson handles freight, he's a middleman. The freight business is how they know each other."

"How come he's known to Laredo Border Patrol?"

"Johnson organizes a lot of cross-border transactions."

Whicher looks at his boss. "Cross-border..."

"Yeah. Could be of interest. You want to go take a look for him?"

⋏

All the way down Matamoros Street, Whicher follows the LPD cruiser—light bar flashing, no siren.

They pass Santa Rita Avenue, the cruiser signals, pulls over. Whicher follows to the curb in front of a small cantina—lit with blue and white neon.

The driver of the cruiser, Martinez, steps out. He walks the few paces back along the sidewalk to the Chevy.

Whicher rolls the window.

"A lot of the rail guys hang here," Martinez says. "I'll go ask inside."

"You want me to come?"

Martinez shakes his head. "Might as well wait. If Johnson's in there, I'll bring him on out." He hitches the belt on his uniform. Steps toward the entrance of the cantina. A guy on security raises himself from a bar stool by the door.

Whicher leaves the engine running in the truck.

He slips a cigarette from the pack, lights it. Across town, traffic's still moving, the sound of music drifting from inside the cantina. Tall palms wave in the night air. Ragged fronds rippling above the sidewalk.

The people out are loose and loud. Groups of young girls, college kids, a few drunks.

The marshal checks his watch. Eleven-thirty.

Merrill M. Johnson.

Jug Line Harris maybe knew something. But a freight guy—what were the odds?

According to Officer Martinez, Johnson was known to work late—irregular hours a normal part of organizing loads at the switching yard. Whicher takes a pull on the cigarette. Thinking on trains. Freight loads moving back and forth in and out of Mexico. He feels the emptiness in his stomach. When did he last eat? Up at Eric's place—in Eagle Pass, six hours back. Seven?

He stares down the street, blows a stream of smoke out the open driver window. Thinks of Alfonso Saldana. The murdered *mojados* at the Channing Ranch, the long haired girl against the foot of the wall.

Martinez is walking back out of the cantina. He stands in the doorway—speaking with security. Then crosses the sidewalk, back to Whicher. "He's not here, marshal."

"Anybody know where he's at?"

"No, sir. You could try at the switching yard, he could still be there. You want me to ride along?"

The marshal shakes his head. "It's just a few blocks down, right?"

Martinez nods. "The rail spurs will still be working. They'll be loading at the cross docks, off the main line. There's a few of them. He could be anyplace around there."

"I'll take a look before I turn in."

Martinez touches the peak of his cap.

Whicher clamps the cigarette in his mouth. He sticks the truck in drive, pulls out into the street. Johnson wouldn't be there. If he was, the most he'd get would be another address. He takes a last pull on the cigarette, flips the butt end out the window. A shower of sparks burst in the rear-view.

Six people shot to death. Close on midnight—chasing a guy on a stolen vehicle charge.

He reaches the end of Matamoros Street. The far end of town, older houses give out to down-at-heel warehouse units—motels, dispatch offices. Sand blown lots.

At the intersection, he drives over to a parking lot, barely lit. Tractor-trailer combos are locked up side to side. The rail lines stretch north-south across the hard pan.

Whicher parks beneath a solitary overhead light. He steps out, locks the truck, surveying a line of flatbeds full of steel plate, pipes and beams.

Nothing's moving. There's the smell of thick oil, burnt grease. Noise of the city faint. He walks toward the tracks, they're open, unfenced. Primer red box cars stretch off into the darkness—the cars covered in graffiti.

He picks his way across the polished rails.

The track's lined with old brick and cinder block rentals. Dumpsters, used tires, general garbage. He thinks of night scouts on Iraqi soil, oil installations—factory grounds; places fast abandoned, an edge in the air.

At a raised platform he spots a brick office, a metal hangar, sodium lights. A forklift is on the platform, swinging a giant sack. The driver's a black guy, two-hundred pounds. He's backing the forklift from the side of an open box car.

Whicher steps along the sharp gravel. *"Merrill Johnson,"* the marshal calls out.

The driver sits, not reacting.

"Looking for a guy named Merrill Johnson," Whicher shouts.

The driver takes a hand off the wheel, pulls an orange foam plug from his ear. "What you want, man?"

"Trying to find somebody called Merrill Johnson. You know him?"

The man shakes his head.

"Anybody around here I can ask?"

The driver jerks a thumb over his shoulder. "Down there..."

Stretching a quarter-mile is a row of dirt-streaked rail cars, painted green and yellow. Another set of buildings beyond them, half lit.

Whicher follows along the track, noise of the forklift receding. Light from the town is blocked out by the high-sided cars—to the west it's dark, a mess of unused, weed-filled lots.

He passes a row of hopper cars. Tube-steel ladders welded to their sides. He grabs one puts a toe on a rung, pulls himself up. At the top, the rim of the hopper's lined with steel lugs to sheet off a load. It's empty, an open container. A dark, rusted hulk.

He peers down into it, just enough light to see. Dust is powdered in the corners and sides. He runs a finger round the top rim—holds it up. White gray dust, some kind of mineral. Plus a finer, red powder. He wipes it off against a lug. Notices the red stain on his skin.

He climbs back down the ladder, moves down the track, listening to the sound of the city, voices shouting in the distance—raucous, indistinct.

Lights show across the river in Mexico—from the sister city, Nuevo Laredo. He thinks of moving in urban areas, dismounted from the tanks.

He walks along the line of hoppers, silent now, aware of something, breathing shallow.

A feeling is on him—a familiar feeling. Sixth sense.

He stops—scans around in all directions.

Somebody's close by.

He can feel it, can't explain it, but it's there. He stands a moment, stock-still. Staring along the edge of the hard pan—at the unlit buildings, block walls, fences, private yards.

Somebody's watching. Maybe following.

He moves to the end of the nearest hopper, steps through the gap, jumping the hitch.

The track fans out into a dozen lines; more. There's a noise—dull, metallic. As if something's been struck.

Dark spaces wait ahead between the lines of box cars—ambush country. Maybe it's just some hobo, some kid out tagging with a spray can? He climbs back into the shadowed side of the track. Looks along the line toward the lit-up office.

A man steps from the end of a hopper. Two feet of steel hanging at his leg. He's Hispanic, hair cropped, a canvas jacket, engineering boots. He moves the length of steel—an over-size wrench. "What's going on, *mano*? What you doing up in that container?"

"Looking for somebody."

"Looking inside of hopper cars?"

The man takes a step forward.

Whicher stands his ground.

"You need to get your ass out of here." The wrench moves against the man's leg.

"Looking for somebody name of Johnson."

"This is private property. Got no business sneaking around this yard, *ese*."

"I'll go when I'm done."

The man raises the steel. Holds it flat between both hands. "You need to listen up, *mano*."

"Tell you what I'm going to do. I'm going to take a walk on down to that office there. And see if I can't find this guy Johnson."

The man doesn't answer. He stands directly in the path.

Whicher faces him down—reckless streak oozing out the bottle. He makes to step by, head for the office.

A hand flies to his shoulder, grabbing hold of his jacket.

The marshal hits him side-on—driving him hard into the box-car, both hands on the wrench-arm—weight on the elbow, forcing it back.

The Hispanic twists, hooks a fist to the side of the marshal's head.

He staggers. Hears a shout close by.

Someone's running with a flashlight.

The Hispanic rolls off the hopper—kicking out a steel-cap boot to Whicher's hip.

The beam of the flashlight hits the pair of them. Whicher holds the wrench-arm in one hand, whipping his balled fist to the man's gut.

The Hispanic doubles up, pulls loose—breaks free. He scrambles to the gap between the hoppers.

"*Hold it right there,*" the man with the light shouts. "*I called 9-1-1, police are going to be here any second...*" He raises a black baton; a night stick.

"Law officer," Whicher says, "US Marshal." He straightens, takes out his badge.

The man's in an ill-fitting uniform. "What the hell's going on?"

Whicher runs for the gap at the end of the hopper car, leaping the hitch.

No sign of anybody on the other side.

The guard follows behind him.

"Looking for Merrill Johnson," Whicher says, short of breath. "You know him? He working here tonight?"

The guard stares, light reflecting in his thick glasses. "Yessir, I know him. But he's not slated tonight, not on my list."

Whicher rubs his swollen jaw, hawking excess spit. "I want to know everybody that is..."

Chapter 6

Laredo, TX.

Morning sun falls on the grass in front of Whicher's con-do apartment. The eastern division of Laredo, by the airport and Lake Casa Blanca, it's new build, functional, anonymous—like living on an army base.

In the yard there's nothing but dry grass, a couple of earthen pots, dead plants hanging over their sides.

A section of panel fence blocks the view of the road. Sliding glass doors look out on a flat sky, an untended world.

Maybe it was time to look for something better? He could do something about it, but what would be the point? A rental place, he wouldn't be there long, the lease was six months. It was close to work, it had everything. He could focus on the new job, his new life.

He sips on a cup of coffee, chewing on a piece of rye toast. Jaw stiff from the blow the night before.

Briscoe County feels a long way—the home he grew up in, a one-time farm. He studies the turquoise bead on the table, the bead from the broken necklace.

He stares out the window again—thinking of the Caprock Canyons, the view from his boyhood yard.

Alongside the turquoise bead is a list of names. Furnished by security at the rail yard. Sixteen names, ten of them Hispanic.

He'd left the rail yard, called Scruggs, let him know he couldn't find Johnson. His boss told him to go home. He'd swung by the office, retrieved the Glock. Then headed for the apartment to stare at the list, fall asleep, rise at six, still dark outside.

The phone starts to ring.

Whicher puts down the piece of toast. He checks his watch, not yet eight. He sits straight, whips up the receiver.

"This is Scruggs. Downtown. Thought I'd start early. There's a message on my desk. Laredo Police say they got a call last night."

The marshal stares at his reflection in the double pane of glass.

"You got into some kind of incident—at the rail yard?"

"Somebody picked a fight," Whicher says. "Yard security didn't much like it."

"The rail company's less than happy," Scruggs says. "They want to know how come their site manager wasn't informed of your presence?"

"Don't want to tip off the enemy."

"How's that?"

"Reconnaissance, sir."

Scruggs is silent a moment. "That's just it," he says. "There's ways of doing things. Don't let it happen again."

Whicher doesn't respond.

"And listen, don't come in to the office this morning. I need you to head to Brownsville."

"What's going on?"

"This hospital break-in, Alfonso Saldana—I want you to take a look at it. There'll be a guy there, name of Vic Delossantos."

"We're not investigating Saldana..."

"We're trying to find Randell Creagan, a *coyote*. Saldana might have been one of his clients. You have a pen?"

Whicher grabs one from the table.

"Vic Delossantos is a friend of mine, from Border Patrol. I asked him for a contact at the Brownsville Station, he offered to meet you there, hook you up. I'm headed out to Carrizo Springs, Sheriff Barnhart's asking to see me."

"You know what he wants?"

"He wouldn't say. Call me later," Scruggs says. "And stay the hell out of trouble." He hangs up the phone.

Whicher drains the last of the coffee, staring at the shoulder holster on the table. In the bedroom is a regular holster. He could wear that. Act like a cop.

He steps from the kitchen, aware of the neatness of the apartment, the bed already made, years of army life he can't shake. He takes out the regular holster from the closet. Clips it to his belt.

In the kitchen, he transfers the Glock 19. Picks up the truck keys. Fits the Resistol.

λ

Brownsville. Cameron County, TX.

Rain is swirling in the Brownsville sky—ocean rain, straight off the Gulf.

At Border Patrol in Olmito, Whicher leaves the Chevy in the station lot, eying the lowering cloud.

A storm coming off the Gulf could bring a lot of water—put it on the ground fast. The sabal and palmetto are full of movement, gutters overflowing on the station roof.

He crosses the parking lot, thinking on Alfonso Saldana. He'd be one among hundreds—arrested, processed, shipped back. What would anybody know here?

He ducks under a porch roof, sheltering from the rain. Last hand on Saldana had been Whicher's. He thinks of the shutting-down sensation.

He pushes open the station door, walks into reception. A Border Patrol agent sits in the waiting area, reading a newspaper—dress uniform, olive green, dark blue stripe along the pants. He's Hispanic, well-fed, early-forties. He looks up from the paper, broad smile across his face.

"Agent Delossantos?"

"Call me Vic," the man says. He stands. Offers his hand. "I spoke with your boss." Delossantos shouts over his shoulder. "*Arturo?* You in there?"

A young man dressed in olive fatigues steps from an ante-room. Sunglasses on the top of his head.

Whicher reads the name on his shirt. *Agent Barajas.*

"This is the marshal from Laredo."

Whicher and the young agent exchange nods.

"About the deportee?"

"Alfonso Saldana."

"Not much of a case," Barajas says. "He was arrested at one of the hospitals. Brownsville Police brought him over. We put him in the dog pound. Sent him back across the river."

"Anything we can find out could help."

Barajas holds a typed sheet of paper. "Log report says the guy that handled the transfer was Agent Aguilar. He's on station at the new bridge."

Delossantos puts on his campaign hat. "You want to take a ride downtown?"

Whicher follows the two agents outside, across the lot to a green and white Ford Taurus, rain falling steady.

Barajas takes out a set of keys, opening the driver door. Delossantos and Whicher climb in the rear.

Barajas starts the motor. "What's the Marshals Office want with a *bracero* like Saldana?" He shifts into drive, pulls out of the lot.

"We're looking for a suspected *coyote*. We've got a warrant, but we can't find him. There might be some connection with this guy Saldana."

Barajas steers out of the side road onto the highway. "Vic says the guy's dead now?"

"He was murdered. Night before last."

"Out in the *monte*," Delossantos says to Barajas. "Up near Carrizo Springs."

"Not much to go on," Whicher says. "If we could catch a break, find out how he entered last time, who helped him, who he might have met..."

"What's the name of the *coyote*?"

"Creagan. Randell Creagan."

Barajas shakes his head. "Don't know him." He puts on the blinker, steers onto a concrete ramp to enter the freeway. "Most likely way your guy would have come in is the bus station. Over the river, in Matamoros. He probably crossed the river with a *patero*—a little guy with a boat. Cheapest way, man."

"I thought they paid *coyotes* to get them north?" Whicher says.

"Yeah, but that's if they have money."

Delossantos nods. "If Saldana was picked up in Brownsville a year back, he probably couldn't pay to get further."

Whicher gazes out the windshield as the wipers flick rain. "Y'all don't think there's going to be much of a trail, do you?"

Barajas cuts in and out of the flow of cars and trucks. "A *pollo* hooked up with an organized *coyote*," he says. "If he can pay, he'll end up on a freight train north. Or in a taxi, or in somebody's truck, under a tarp. He won't end up in Brownsville, man."

"How about the people that walk?"

"They cross far away from any town," Delossantos says. "They'll walk for days out in the brush. The *coyote* will arrange to get them picked up, some little place."

"Like Carrizo Springs?"

"Exactly like that."

Whicher thinks it over.

Out the window of the Taurus, lush green stretches either side of the freeway. Sub-tropical, a different country, rain sweeping on gusts of wind.

"Don't miss the exit," Delossantos says.

Barajas cuts across a lane, maneuvering down an exit ramp.

They're downtown, getting close to the river, traffic thick, cars and trucks queuing both directions. Whicher spots the hangar-like roof of the crossing station.

A sign hangs over the roadway—warning against the carrying of firearms or ammunition into Mexico. Barajas drives down a separate lane for law enforcement vehicles— pulling up outside the main checkpoint building.

The three men step out, Barajas taking the lead, hurrying under the hangar roof. A supervising officer directs him toward a US-registered Toyota pickup. It's parked in an inspection bay, a Hispanic couple beside it, young child hanging off the mother's arm.

Whicher follows Barajas and Delossantos. A Border Patrol agent is talking with the driver.

"That's Aguilar," Barajas says.

The pickup driver's holding a red baseball cap. Turning it and turning it in his hands. The child, a girl, maybe four years old, is crying—the mother wide-eyed, looking sick.

Agent Aguilar reads the documentation in his hand. Hi-top boots planted on the oily concrete.

"Just let us go back, *hermano*..." the driver mumbles.

Barajas steps toward the little group, lowering his sunglasses, despite the rain. "I take a look?" he says.

Aguilar turns, greets him. Passes over the documents.

"Let us go back—that's all we're asking...."

"Those are not your papers," Aguilar replies.

Barajas quickly skims the paperwork. "Impersonating a US citizen is a felony under US law..."

"Five years prison," Aguilar says. "Plus a lifetime ban on legal entry." Specks of rain glisten on his shaved head.

Whicher takes a half-step forward. Delossantos places a hand on his arm.

Barajas looks up from the paperwork. "Where did you get the truck?"

The woman's legs look about to give out under her. The child bawls, pulling at her mother's arm.

"This goes down as an apprehension, you'll be straight back," Aguilar says. "You know it..."

"No, *señor.*"

"Whose is the truck?" Barajas repeats.

"We borrowed it, *señor.*"

"Take it," the woman says, "keep it, *por favor,* just let us go."

"I have a family, *señor*—a little girl to feed..."

Barajas raises the sunglasses back up onto his head. He looks at Aguilar. "Got a minute?"

The two men step away—to the far side of the inspection bay. Whicher and Delossantos following after them.

Barajas takes a folded sheet of paper from the pocket of his shirt. "You remember anything about this? It's a case from last year. Alfonso Saldana. Apprehended and deported." He passes the paper to Aguilar.

The shaven-headed agent reads the short report, edges of his mouth down-turned. "Maybe. What about it?"

"Brownsville police picked him up on a B and E? You remember anything about it? Breaking and entering at the hospital?"

Aguilar stares out into the rain sweeping over the queue of cars. "Like what?"

"Like how come he didn't get charged?" Barajas says.

The man frowns. "I don't think he broke in. I think it was a 910."

"A prowler?"

Whicher looks at Agent Aguilar. "This was here at the hospital—that right? At the pharmacy?"

"No," says Aguilar.

"No?"

"It was on campus at the university."

"Sure about that?"

"Yeah. Pretty sure."

Whicher looks at Barajas.

The agent shrugs.

"It was the medical research place," Aguilar says. "The bio-med facility. I think. That's the way I remember it."

"That's a half mile from here," Barajas says to Whicher.

"What's up?" Aguilar says. He looks to Barajas. "The guy come back again? You looking to put him away?"

The marshal shakes his head. "Not this time."

⋏

Outside the window of the cubicle, rain's still falling. Whicher listens to the hum on the line for Carrizo Springs.

The front desk at the courthouse is bouncing the call around the building—looking for Scruggs, somewhere with Sheriff Barnhart. The marshal thinks of the white shirt, the straw cowboy hat, stub of cigar.

Agent Aguilar stands by the US registered Toyota—going through the set of faked papers.

The Mexican family huddle beneath the dripping hangar roof, future hanging by a thread, a picture of misery.

There's a click at the end of the line. "Scruggs."

"Sir—it's Whicher, I'm down at the port of entry in Brownsville."

"You with Vic?"

"I'm with him down at the check point."

"Y'all getting anywhere?"

Whicher stares out the cubicle window. "I've been talking with the agent that handled Saldana. He says Saldana was arrested prowling. At the university."

"Not the hospital?"

"No, sir."

"I thought the pharmacy." There's a pause as Scruggs thinks it over.

"You want me to go over there?"

"To the university?" Scruggs says.

"Doesn't sound real promising. Maybe I ought to head on back?"

"Long as you're there you could check it out. See if you can speak with somebody."

Whicher nods. "What's going on with Sheriff Barnhart?"

Outside, in the inspection bay, Agent Aguilar signals to the couple to remain where they are. He walks to a small office at the back of the inspection area. Delossantos steps forward, smiles, kneels. Tries to talk to the little girl.

"We've been asked to take over the investigation. Todd Williams—the American kill at the ranch."

Whicher puts a hand to the brim of his hat. He tips it back, not sure of what to say.

"The whole thing's toxic to the sheriff," Scruggs says, low-voiced. "Man has to run for office. We don't."

"That's it?"

"We have federal jurisdiction," Scruggs says. "It makes sense we coordinate the other services."

"Are we going to take it?"

"I have to clear it with Buddy Riggins at district."

Whicher thinks of their boss—the southern district marshal. He feels a quickening; aware how much he'd want it, if Riggins said yes. A major case, something big, it'd be his first—a homicide. "You still want me to go ask at the university?"

"Might get us somewhere," Scruggs says. "You get done, head back to Laredo. We'll talk later." He puts down the phone.

Whicher stares at the family by the pickup. The little girl has her hands on the truck sides, she's climbing the wheel—the parents drained, their bodies stooped.

Aguilar steps from the supervisor's office. He walks back, starts talking with the driver, pointing his finger at the man's chest.

The man and woman stare back. Mouths tight.

And then Aguilar turns.

The couple stand a moment. The man replaces the red baseball cap on his head. The mother catches hold of her daughter's arm, pulling it sharp. They climb into the pickup.

Whicher watches them start it up, drive from the inspection bay, cross into the check point lane.

He feels an unexpected relief in the pit of his stomach.

As they turn around. Headed back into Mexico.

⋏

Fort Brown Campus. Whicher waits by the green and white Taurus in the parking lot, Agent Barajas behind the wheel.

A pale sun reflects off the ornamental lake in the university gardens. The rain has stopped. Wind disturbs the surface of the water. Another world, a lifetime from raw nerves and gasoline fumes at the port of entry.

Along a wooden bridge across the lake, Agent Delossantos approaches, a woman beside him—a black woman, wearing a business suit.

The marshal walks from the lot, crossing a rectangle of grass to wait by a picnic table.

A quarter-mile south, the Rio Grande twists and turns, the air filled with a distant hum—two cities alive and heaving. Brownsville. Matamoros on the river's southern bank.

Delossantos steps from the bridge with the woman.

She adjusts her glasses. "Joyce Kinley," she says.

"Deputy Marshal Whicher."

"I'm not sure I can be of much help."

"Professor Kinley's head of bio-medical research," Delossantos says. "The facility that had the problem."

"There's really not much to tell..."

"What can you remember about the incident?" the marshal says.

"This man, Saldana," she looks at Delossantos. "He's dead now, you say?"

"Yes ma'am."

She takes a breath. "Well. It was last year. He was spotted in the parking lot by the old cotton press."

"This was daytime, night time?" Whicher looks at her.

"Around lunchtime. One of the lab technicians noticed him hanging around."

"What happened?"

"Security came down. They asked him to leave."

"Did he leave?"

"He did, but he came back. He was spotted again, later. The second time, he ran off before security could get there."

"How'd he end up getting arrested?"

"He was bothering one of the students, inside the research building."

"He came back a third time?"

"Yes, he did."

"But he didn't break in?"

"No, it was nothing like that. He just wasn't supposed to be here." She spreads her hands.

"And you called the police?"

"I called them, yes."

"This was late?"

"Early evening."

Delossantos looks at the professor. "Did he show up anyplace else on campus? So far as you know?"

"No, I think it was just us."

"You have anything he might have been interested in?"

"There's nothing of value, no drugs, no equipment. Nothing worth the trouble to steal."

Whicher notes the few details in a pad. "What kind of research work goes on in the department?"

"We're studying NTDs."

The marshal stops writing.

"Neural tube defects," Professor Kinley says. "Birth defects. In babies."

"How about back then? Last year?"

"We were working on it then. We'd just started on it."

Whicher looks at Delossantos. The Border Patrol agent shrugs.

"Can you tell me anything about the work?"

The professor looks at him a moment. She settles her glasses. "At the start of last year several babies at the hospital were born with fatal birth defects."

"Here? In Brownsville?"

She nods.

"Several?"

"Three. Within thirty-six hours. That's rare," she says. "It's extremely rare to get a cluster like that. Rare even to get a single case."

Across the campus grounds, groups of students lounge among the outdoor sculptures. A faint sun struggles to emerge from behind a cloud.

"Can you tell me anything about the babies?"

"Not specifically. I can tell you that neural tube defects are most common among the Hispanic community—least common among African Americans. And most common among families with low income." The professor regards him steadily.

"You're telling me these were poor Hispanic families?"

She doesn't respond.

"Ma'am." Whicher fixes her with a look. "Was one of the infants Saldana's child?"

Her face is blank.

"I'm going to need to know."

A moment passes. She shakes her head.

"Are you sure?"

She nods.

"Did you check?"

"Right after it happened," she says. "Right after he was arrested."

"None of the infants had the name Saldana?"

"No. But I really can't tell you more, all of this is private and highly confidential."

Delossantos hunches his shoulders. He gazes out across the wide green lawns. "Do they know much about it? The doctors and such?"

The professor folds her arms on her chest. "Current thinking is it's related to elevated levels of pollution, pesticide use. All the assembly plant industries along the border, the *maquilas*, that kind of thing."

In the shallows of the lake a cattle egret stands. Ragged feathers. Stick thin legs. Whicher taps the pen against the pad, thinking of Eric, in Eagle Pass. "There a lot of work on that?"

"On chemical toxicity?"

"It's well documented, understood?"

"It's not well understood. Pollutant effects on human health can be very complex."

Whicher closes the notepad. Puts away the pen.

"May I ask why you're investigating this now?" the professor says. "Considering this man's dead."

"I'm trying to find somebody that might have helped him enter the country."

"Would he need help?"

"There was an outside chance," Whicher says. "Thank you for your time, Professor Kinley."

"Is that it? I'm sorry I couldn't be more help. I did tell your colleague…"

From the parking lot, there's a blast on a vehicle horn.

Agent Barajas is standing by the Taurus, door wide. "*Radio call*," he shouts. "*For the marshal…*"

The professor takes out a business card. "If you think of any other questions…"

Whicher takes it, jabs a thumb toward Barajas. "I better get that…"

Delossantos ushers the professor back toward the bridge.

At the Taurus, Barajas passes over the radio transmitter.

"This is Whicher, go ahead…"

"Marshal, this is the sheriff's department in Eagle Pass. We've been trying to get a hold of you for half an hour."

"What's going on?"

"It's Randell Creagan."

"Y'all find him?"

"Your boss says he wants you up here, immediately."

"Did somebody find him?"

There's a pause from the operator. "They found him. That's all I can tell you."

Chapter 7

Eagle Pass, TX.

Five hours later, three hundred miles north-west, it's almost sundown as Whicher steers the Chevy onto waste ground at the back of an industrial lot.

Police department cruisers are parked by an empty-looking warehouse. He can see Scruggs's blue and white Ford Ranger, plus a county sheriff's truck.

At the eastern edge of the flattened ground is a rail line. Scrubby trees, scattered housing. Along the track a group are standing close to a tarp screen, Scruggs among them.

Whicher parks, steps from the truck, notices patrol officers searching the waste ground. Scruggs sees him, he takes a couple of paces from the assembled group.

A civilian male in a suit is kneeling by the tarp.

"*Looks like we won't be needing to serve that warrant,*" Scruggs calls.

A bearded man turns to look. Broad-brimmed hat, a black sport coat. Whicher recognizes Elwood Owens, the local sheriff—from his picture in the Eagle Pass station.

"It's Creagan," Scruggs says. "He's been dead a while. They're just about to move him. Doc's about finishing up."

Whicher scans up and down the track, glances at the man by the tarp—white-haired, gaunt, well into his sixties.

"Couple of kids found him," Sheriff Owens says.

"Looks like he was tied to a freight car," says Scruggs.

"Tied on?"

Scruggs nods. "Or chained. He fell off, ended up here."

Whicher steps to the tarp screen. He takes a look around the side. Creagan's a mess. The face recognizable— beard caked in blood, skin grazed off along one cheek. He's stretched out, elongated, one foot crushed flat. Covered in dirt and grit, like he rolled in it. "He was already dead by the time he ended up here?"

"So far as we know."

"Where's the rail line go?"

Sheriff Owens points along the hard pan south, toward the outskirts of town. "We're just up the track from a main junction. There's a line comes in across the river from Mexico. A bunch of other lines from the south. If he was chained to a train, there's no way to tell where it came from. We're checking with the freight companies."

"He might have been killed anywhere?" Whicher says.

"It wasn't here," the doctor says.

"Definite?"

"He was shot multiple times with hollow point rounds—there'd be blood everywhere."

Whicher steps from the body, eyes the thin trees at the side of the track. "How you figure he was attached to a freight car?"

"There's tissue damage," the doctor says, "staining, probably from rusted metal. Plus the postmortem lividity." He eases back the shirt from Creagan's wrist. Against the reddish-blue are stand-out white marks where a chain link's compressed the skin.

Whicher nods.

"The blood's pooled face down. But he was found on his back. There's the foot, too," the doctor says.

"Looks like a train wheel went over it."

"Train wheel would do it. We'll check the grease and oil on him. Looks like the kind of thing you'd find on the underside of rolling stock."

Whicher takes a long look at Creagan's lifeless body. Feeling nothing.

"What's the TOD window?" Sheriff Owens says. "I know y'all don't like to say."

"Sometime yesterday. In the morning."

Scruggs steps toward the tarp. "Any chance it could have been earlier? The night prior to that?"

The doctor shakes his head. "Far too early to say."

Scruggs scowls. He shoves his hands into his pockets. "We need to find out where he was killed." He looks at Whicher. "So far, we're focused on the rail line—locations adjacent. There's a bunch to go at."

"You ask me," Sheriff Owens says, "it could've been over the river, in Mexico. If he was chained beneath a freight car, nobody would've spotted it."

Whicher thinks of Owens's reputation, what little he knows of it—a hard-liner, critic of border security, in favor of much tighter control.

"I called Laredo police," Scruggs says. "The detective working the stolen autos case against Randell Creagan was a guy called Simms—I let him know what happened. Told him to get a search organized at Creagan's place in Laredo."

"Did you hear back yet?"

Scruggs nods. "He wasn't killed there."

"They're sure?"

"The place was clean. Simms is going to have them go through his stuff, see if there's anything. He didn't sound real hopeful."

The sun is almost down now, sky bruised over the track.

"Take a walk with me," Scruggs says. He steps from the tarp, starts walking to the north, toward the highway.

Whicher follows. "What happens now?"

Scruggs continues further up the line, out of earshot of the group at the tarp. "Tell me about Brownsville, y'all come up with anything?"

"We got some detail about Saldana being arrested. I'm not sure it's going to get us anyplace."

"Sheriff Owens is asking us to investigate," Scruggs says, his voice low.

"This?"

"Randell Creagan's murder." Scruggs stops. Rests a boot on the track. "Sheriff of Dimmit wants us investigating Todd Williams. Sheriff of Maverick wants us for Creagan. We cain't do squat till I talk with Buddy Riggins."

Whicher stares back down the line. "What do you think he'll say?"

"I don't know. I'm headed out to see him after this. But I want you here, in case he says yes. Get a room tonight, keep the receipt."

"Alright, sir."

"Sheriff Barnhart's offering space at the courthouse in Carrizo Springs—if we take it. Base to work from. If Riggins tells me yes, I want you to get set up in the morning."

Across the lot, an ambulance is pulling in behind the warehouse, come for the body.

"They have to be connected," Whicher says.

"I'd want to know the time of death on Creagan."

"You think it could have been the same night?"

"Two *coyotes* get burned?"

Whicher studies his boss's face. The black eyes hooded, deep in thought. "Two *coyotes*," Whicher says. "And five *mojados*..."

Scruggs pins him with a look. "Something I need you to do. Head on over to Creagan's place, the apartment..."

"Nobody checked it yet?"

"We been waiting on the key-holder, property guy, name of Brady Iverson." Scruggs looks at his watch. "He ought to be there by now."

"If it turns out to be a crime scene?"

Scruggs shakes his head.

"You don't think it will?"

"That little place ain't the scene of any murder. Not with Dane Vogel watching over it."

"If Vogel's there what do I tell him?"

"Tell him Creagan's dead. If he don't already know."

"Do I let him into the apartment?"

"You can let him in."

Across the rail tracks, wind is moving in the thin trees. Whicher stares out into the growing dark. "What do you think they were doing there?"

"FBI?" says Scruggs. "I don't know."

"Am I looking for anything in particular?"

"Take a look at the apartment. Then we can strike it from the list..."

⊼

The house at the end of lane, is deserted. Twin porches empty, no light. Beneath the trees, across from the intersection there's no Caprice.

Whicher searches the road for the property owner, Brady Iverson. He leaves the Chevy at the curbside, checks for vehicles on the main strip.

A mid-eighties Lincoln Town Car is parked up—middle-aged white male behind the wheel. The driver rolls the window.

"Mister Iverson, Brady Iverson?"

"Yessir."

"I'm Deputy Marshal Whicher."

Iverson's balding, slight, sporting a mustache. "I been here near an hour."

"I'll make it quick."

"You can have the key." Iverson reaches into his shirt pocket. "I have to be someplace, 'less you're going to need me to wait?"

"That's alright. I just need to see inside."

"Y'all have my number if you need to call. Has something happened to Mister Creagan?"

Whicher looks at him. "They didn't tell you what this was about?"

"Sheriff's department just said to haul ass over here. The guy was paid up on the rent. Has there been some kind of trouble?"

"I'll see the key gets back to you." Whicher steps away toward the house.

Behind him, he hears the man start the engine in his car.

The marshal studies the front door—nothing seems out of place.

He takes out a cotton handkerchief, inserts the key in the lock. Nothing's been forced, he turns the key, pushes open the door with an elbow.

Inside, the apartment's completely dark.

Whicher presses the handkerchief against the light switch. An overhead bulb illuminates an open-plan room, a kitchen in back, bathroom off to one side. It's sparse, barely furnished. Undisturbed.

He walks to the kitchen, the counter tops dusty, no dishes, no pans. He opens a cupboard with the handkerchief, it's empty. He tries the refrigerator—nothing much inside; a few beers, half-empty bottles of sauce. No supplies.

Stepping back in the main room he spots a closed door. He opens it—it's a bedroom, the bed unmade. A rain jacket hangs in an open wardrobe. Pair of work boots, nothing else.

Why keep a place and never use it? Whicher stares around the main room—a couch, no TV, no stereo. There's a telephone on a low table, a bunch of notepaper by it. Couple of pens.

Randell Creagan wasn't killed in the apartment, that much is clear. Multiple gunshots, hollow points—nobody could clean it up like this.

He steps to the little table. Looks at the phone, picks up the sheets of paper torn from a pad.

There's numbers, makes and types of cars. Prices, license plates.

He flicks through, recognizing nothing. It's just bare details—cars the man must've been buying, selling, stealing, who could say?

Along with the numbers are a few names. He could call—see if anybody would talk.

Nobody was going to kill Creagan over a couple stolen cars.

Whicher eyes the last sheets of paper, scribbled, barely legible.

A name and number stick out. He reads it over, stock still in the empty apartment.

⚓

Outside on the lane there's barely a light in any of the houses. Whicher sits in his truck.

Scruggs would already be gone, headed out to Houston to see Marshal Riggins in the morning.

Maybe Riggins would say no?

If the southern district marshal decided they couldn't take it, it'd never come up, it wouldn't be a problem. Scruggs already had a ton of work, he was due in court to testify, there were ongoing cases for the Laredo office, all kinds of stuff.

Say nothing. Get a room for the night, get some rest, think it over.

Leaning back in the driver seat, he lets out a stream of air.

He could tell Scruggs, if he had to—tell him he'd missed it, that he couldn't make it out. He opens the glove box, places the sheet of notepaper inside.

He scans the deserted lane.

Law enforcement was meant to be straight-up, black and white, clear-cut decisions.

He fires up the truck, pulls out from the curbside.

Tread careful, he tells himself.

The name on the sheet of paper sits suspended in his mind's eye.

He turns the thought over, tries to work it through some other way.

A local area code, an Eagle Pass number.

Two short words. *Jim Gale.*

CHAPTER 8

In the motor court room in Eagle Pass, Whicher blows on a scalding hot cup of coffee, trying to shake the tiredness from his body. On top of a veneered night stand is a napkin and a half-eaten doughnut.

A cigarette burns in the ashtray, the marshal watches blue smoke curling in the morning sun.

Beyond the window, traffic's rolling on the highway. He hadn't slept, the bed too small, light from the court outside too bright.

He stares at the slim file on the bed—Randell Creagan's jacket.

From the next room a TV blares behind thin walls.

Outside, out the window, the Chevy's nose is tight to the room, twin light-clusters staring in. He thinks of the note inside the glove box. Law officers had informers— could that be it? He should have left the note in the apartment, some impulse made him take it—he picks the Marlboro out of the ashtray, takes a drag.

Focus on Creagan.

He lifts the topmost sheet out of Creagan's file. Sips his coffee, checks the time, it's after nine.

He picks the phone off the night stand, dials a number from memory.

At the Laredo Police Department, an operator patches through a call to the auto theft unit.

Whicher stares in the bathroom at the bleached towel hanging from a hook.

The line picks up. "Detective Simms."

"This is Deputy Marshal Whicher—I'm calling about Randell Creagan. Found dead yesterday, up in Eagle Pass."

There's a pause on the end of the line. "I spoke with somebody from the Marshals Service yesterday."

"Marshal Scruggs, my boss."

"We already searched in Creagan's apartment," Simms says. "There was nothing there. Is the Marshals office investigating?"

"This is just preliminary." Whicher takes a pull on the cigarette. "Can you tell me anything about the stolen vehicles charge?"

"Like what?"

"Like what kind of numbers, was it serious?"

"It was plenty serious," the detective says. "He was fencing vehicles out of state, so it got federal real quick."

"Okay."

"FBI thought he might have been moving vehicles back and forth across the border."

"Say again?"

"I don't know what evidence they had—we weren't party to it."

"FBI suspected Creagan of cross-border work?"

"Like I said, we weren't aware of any corroborating evidence."

"You know which office was handling it?"

"Houston, I think."

Whicher makes a note. He stands, stretches out the phone cable. "You think of anybody that might have wanted Creagan dead?"

Detective Simms cracks a laugh. "A dirt bag like him?"

"Specifically?"

"Not specifically, you'd have to dig. You could try in Port Arthur, I daresay the cops in his hometown knew him."

"Right," Whicher says. "If we get this, I'll probably want to come back to you."

"You know where to find me." Simms clicks off the call.

Whicher makes a brief note, stubs out the cigarette. He takes a turn around the room.

If Creagan was running cars across the border, he could've been killed in Mexico, maybe Sheriff Owens was right? He didn't seem to live at any of his addresses, maybe he spent time down there. So how come Dane Vogel had been watching the apartment in Eagle Pass? Vogel was IA, not connected to the Houston office.

In the mirror he eyes his freshly-shaved face, runs a hand through his wet hair.

He reaches to the night stand, picks up the Glock, clips the holster to his belt.

He grabs the phone, dials another number.

Above the TV is a shelf with the ornaments—a lone star, a plastic horseshoe. Glass bottle filled with colored sand. The sand is layered, one color on top of another. Rust red, brown to black, burnt yellow. He thinks of the hopper car in the Laredo yard. Raises his finger—the stain on his skin is still there.

At the end of the line, the phone picks up. "Scruggs."

"Sir, it's Whicher. I thought to call, see if you'd had word from Marshal Riggins?"

"We got it. He spoke with the county attorneys. Everybody's agreed."

Whicher reaches for another cigarette.

"Dimmit and Maverick don't have money to burn for homicide cases. Webb County don't mind, so long as it's on the federal tab."

"We handle both Todd Williams and Randell Creagan?"

"The both of 'em."

Whicher lights up, takes a hit off the smoke. "How about Saldana? The other deaths—at the ranch?"

"Nobody's asking us to investigate. The four Hispanics at the ranch we have no ID, no place to start."

Whicher stares at the bottle on the shelf. "But Saldana?"

"Webb coroner contacts the embassy, they find his family, they'll let 'em know. We can't expect anybody to come forward, the county will likely bury him. That's just the way it is. It goes on."

A beat passes. Whicher lets the silence grow.

"How you make out last night?" Scruggs says. "At Creagan's apartment, you didn't call."

"It got kind of late..."

"You think we need a thorough search?"

"Didn't seem like it." The marshal snatches up the note from the bed. "I was just on the phone with Detective Simms. At LPD..."

"Oh?"

"He reckons FBI had intel Creagan was fencing cars into Mexico. Houston office, what he said."

Scruggs grunts.

"You had a guy there—Gerry Nugent?"

"I'm coming up to Carrizo Springs," Scruggs says. "Ought to be there in a couple hours. I'll call the sheriff, let him know we'll be needing that office space. Get over there, get things set up. We got plenty to look at on Randell Creagan, nothing yet on this other feller; Todd Williams."

"You want me to start on that?"

"He's local, somebody in the county ought to know him."

"I'd like to talk to Harris again, Jug Line Harris. Out at the lake."

"I will lead the blind," Scruggs says, "by ways they have not known."

"Say again, sir?"

"*Isiah 42:16.* If you want to go talk to Harris, do it. Make sure you're back in Carrizo Springs this afternoon..."

ᛉ

Lake Amistad Reservoir.

Scrub and mesquite are high to all sides at the reservoir, birds wheeling over the low hills.

Whicher passes the few trailers, the route giving out to hard packed sand. Harris was nervous as hell the day they'd spoken, the day after the ranch murders. He'd admitted knowing Creagan, hunting with him at least.

He sees the rail-tie up ahead—the marker at the end of the track. A truck is parked there—a half ton GMC pickup, painted black.

The marshal draws alongside it, parks, cuts the motor. Steps out in the bright, midday heat.

The truck's about an eighty-nine, regular cab, on a Maverick County plate. He tries the door—it's locked. It could belong to Harris. How come it wasn't there before?

Whicher steps over the rail-tie, heads for the narrow path in the brush.

He works his way down the twisted trail. Below, he sees the tin-roofed boathouse. A figure is standing near it, a man, his back to the hill—looking out over the lake.

Big guy, not Harris.

He turns from the water's edge, toward the boathouse.

The marshal lowers himself in the scrub, till he shows no outline.

※

Carrizo Springs, TX.

Two hours later, Whicher sits parked by the bail bond office in the courthouse square; Marshal Scruggs's blue and white Ford Ranger in his sight-line.

Inside the courthouse, Scruggs would be working, straight-backed, sober-sided. *What to tell him?*

Two times, Gale had come up now.

Two times and he couldn't explain it.

Across the square he sees the window to Sheriff Barnhart's office. It's open. No sign of the boss man in the white shirt.

Whicher steps from the truck, shields his eyes from the glare. Crosses the street beneath the shade of the palms.

In the lobby of the courthouse, Raul Talamantes is sitting in a steel-frame chair.

He's wearing an olive fatigue shirt—sleeves rolled, pipe veins standing on his arms. "Vic Delossantos said you went to see him, *mano.*"

Whicher nods.

"Yesterday. Down in Brownsville."

"He said that?"

"Looking into that death in Webb County?" Talamantes crosses one laced boot over the other.

"I believe that'd be right."

From the corridor at the rear of the lobby, Marshal Scruggs swings into reception.

A female deputy is with him—Hispanic, good-looking, handsome face, a tough streak in it.

Talamantes sits up straighter, slicks his mustache.

Whicher takes in the deputy, swept-back hair, high cheekbones, eyes the color of molasses.

"Marshal," Scruggs says. "This here's Deputy Alvarenga. Sheriff assigned us a liaison."

"John Whicher, ma'am. Pleased to meet you."

"Benita Alvarenga," she says.

Talamantes lets his eyes linger on the woman. She's late twenties, around Whicher's age, not real friendly.

"You find Harris?" Scruggs says.

"No sir, no sign of him out at the lake. I thought to get back here...."

"Sheriff made good on his promise," Scruggs says. "We got us an office, right enough. Along the corridor yonder."

Whicher looks at Talamantes, still staring at Benita Alvarenga. The man finally breaks off.

"We head on down there?"

Alvarenga leads the way, a half pace in front.

The corridor is dim—at the end is an exit door to the courthouse square, to the right an opening onto a cramped office.

The office has a desk, shelves, a metal file cabinet, a phone. There's barely enough room for three. In the close space, Whicher feels Benita Alvarenga's physical presence, the curve to her body pronounced, despite the uniform.

"Deputy Alvarenga has some background," Scruggs says.

"The Caucasian victim at the ranch," she says.

"Todd Williams?"

"We found the mother, Reba Williams. I have an address."

Whicher looks at her.

"You need to head out, take a look," Scruggs says.

"She lives not far from here," Alvarenga says. "In Catarina."

"'Less you're fixing to stand around like a dogie all day, you best get her interviewed, get a statement."

"Did you speak with Gerry Nugent?" Whicher says. "Up in Houston? About Creagan, about what Detective Simms had to say?"

Scruggs's face darkens.

Whicher senses a mistake; that he's been too open.

Deputy Alvarenga regards him, self-contained.

"You want to give me the address?" Whicher says. "For Williams's mother. Or do we head out there together?"

"Marshal?" She looks to Scruggs.

He waves a hand, sits at the desk. "Go ahead and show him."

"You want to drive?" Whicher says.

"As you like."

He grabs the Chevy keys. "Let's take mine."

A

Catarina, TX.

Twenty miles south of Carrizo Springs on US 83—the brush scrub opens out onto a clearing. In its center a double-front brick building stands half abandoned, studded with palms. Whicher runs an eye across it—it's grand and squalid in equal measure.

Deputy Alvarenga follows his gaze.

"Quite the place."

"It used to be," she says. "Way back. In the nineteen-twenties. The old Catarina Hotel."

The brick is scorched by years in the sun and wind. Colonnades and cornices, windows rotted out, boarded up. There's two long floors, multiple rooms, palms in a court-yard, grown immense. A few stray vehicles are parked in the clearing—old trucks and cars. "It still open?"

"Hunters use it," Alvarenga says. "It's pretty rough in there. Haunted, too."

Whicher cuts a glance at her.

There's no smile at her wide mouth.

"Strange country," he says. "For a hotel."

"For a while, it was something."

Past the hotel, the view from the Chevy is a sea of brush and low mesquite. The land pinned beneath a brutal sun.

"Grandfather's time, cattle was booming," she says. "They had the railroad. Once the wells played out, there was no water—no way the place could survive."

"What they have around here now?"

"A lot of poor folk."

"That go for Todd Williams? His family?"

"If they're from anyplace around here."

She leans forward in the passenger seat, looking for something down the road. A radio mast stands tall in the brush at the south. He glances at the shape of her back, soft skin at the nape of her neck.

"We're not far from the turn," she says. "Make the next right."

Whicher slows, signals. Turns the Chevy down a metaled road blown with dirt. Shack-like properties are dotted in the brush. Built years back, surrounded with rusting junk.

Alvarenga studies a sheet of paper printed in the sheriff's department. She points to a shack painted dull blue— a lean-to at one end, wire fencing surrounding the place.

Whicher pulls over, shuts off the motor. "How far you figure this from the Channing Ranch?"

She checks the map. "Twenty something."

"Twenty miles? What's between there and here?"

They step out of the truck. Cross to a twisted wooden gate.

"There's nothing," she says. "Just the *monte*—the brush." She takes the lead across a beaten-earth plot. Raps at the door.

Beyond the shack, scrub stretches, unending. An air of decay is on everything, paint peeling from the rough board walls, windows thick with dirt, the drapes bleached out.

The door opens.

A thin woman in her fifties stands before them.

She's wearing a patched denim dress, hair wild. Reek of nicotine from the house.

"Reba Williams?"

The woman squints at the uniformed deputy. "What do y'all want?"

"It's about your son, ma'am," Whicher says.

She glares at him.

"Can we come inside?"

There's a look in her face he's seen before. Bombed out places, Gulf places, reduced to mud.

"Y'all fixing to bring him back?"

Whicher looks over her shoulder into the shack's main room—a sagging couch, a cluttered table, stacks of cheap magazines.

Reba Williams slumps. She turns back inside.

Deputy Alvarenga steps through the door, Whicher follows, taking off his hat.

In one corner of the room is an ancient-looking TV. A hunting bow, unstrung. Faded photographs—Todd Williams as a kid, a teenager. Ink tattoos, broken teeth, skinny.

"What y'all want?" She lights a cigarette from the butt end of another, holding it with yellowed fingers.

"US Marshals office is investigating the death of your son, ma'am."

She draws the smoke deep. "It ain't nothing more to say on that."

"I'm sorry for your loss." Whicher studies the thread-bare rug on the plank floor.

"Todd's all I had." She puts the heel of a hand to her eye.

"Ma'am," says Deputy Alvarenga. "Your son was unlawfully killed. We're here to help."

"Well, you cain't."

"He was found with a group of non-documented illegal aliens," Alvarenga says.

"Mexican trash." She glares at the deputy.

The marshal glances at the pile of fabric on a hard-backed chair.

"That's all I got, now," Reba Williams says. "Sewing bitty dresses to keep me alive."

"Did Todd live here with you?" Whicher says.

"Sometimes," she shrugs. "Sometimes not."

"Did you know what he was doing lately?" Alvarenga says. "In the weeks before his death? Was he working?"

Her face is bitter. "Only regular job he ever had lasted six months. Six God damn months…"

"What kind of work?" Whicher says.

She flicks the cigarette. "Some ol' warehouse."

"It didn't last?"

"Chicago it was, up to Chicago. I like to died and gone to heaven, he tol' me that. He finally went someplace, only place he ever did went, only time he ever sent me money. He got homesick." She throws out an arm. "For this…"

Whicher looks out the window into the dirt yard— thorn and scrub beyond it. "Did Todd know a guy named Randell Creagan?"

She nods.

"He did know him?"

"Randell, yeah."

"What was their relationship?"

She tilts her head to the side—as if at some insult. "Todd used to clean cars an' such. Randell had a bunch on 'em."

Whicher glances at Alvarenga.

"Where would that have been?" the deputy says.

"Up to Eagle Pass."

Whicher takes out a notepad. Writes down the detail. "He work regular for Creagan? Like that?"

Reba Williams scoffs. "God, no."

"How well did they know each other?"

She takes another pull at her cigarette. "Todd used to stay up there, time to time. Randell had a auto yard. Todd be fixin' up cars."

"Out at the yard?"

She nods.

Whicher rolls the pen between his finger and thumb. "You know where?"

"Monroe. South Monroe. I went up one time, seen him."

"What else?" Alvarenga says. "What else did he do around here?"

"Todd. He'd be huntin', or fishin'."

"He work as a guide?" Alvarenga says.

Reba Williams nods.

"For groups? The kind of people that camp out at the hotel, the old hotel?"

Whicher stares at the hunting bow. "I guess Todd knew this ground about as well as anyone?"

"Only thing he did know..."

Whicher checks the last page in his notepad. "Did Todd know somebody by the name of Merrill M. Johnson?"

She looks blank.

"How about Boyd Harris? Jug Line Harris?"

"Yeah. Jug Line."

"He knew him?"

"Bunch of 'em used to hunt together. Todd. Randell. Him."

"Where would that be?"

"Out in the brush."

"Here?"

"Here," she says. "Them ol' river camps."

Whicher writes fast in the notepad. "What camps?"

Deputy Alvarenga catches his eye. "There's hunting camps out at the river, along the border."

Reba Williams stabs out her cigarette.

"These camps, ma'am?" Whicher holds the pen above the notepad. "Where exactly might I find 'em?"

CHAPTER 9

The Rio Grande. Maverick County, TX.

At the river, the sun is low behind the trees—honey mesquite and blackbrush block the way. Seeing more than ten yards is next to impossible, there's no sign of any hunting camp.

The Chevy's parked a mile back, where the last track gave out. In one hand, Whicher holds the scrawled map drawn by Deputy Benita Alvarenga.

In Carrizo Springs, at the courthouse, Scruggs had been happy—the interview with Reba Williams linked Todd Williams, Randell Creagan and Jug Line Harris. Plus they had word of an auto yard. Scruggs had to head south, in the morning there was testimony to give, an appearance in court in Laredo. Whicher said he'd stick around, catch another night at the motor court.

Deputy Alvarenga told him about the hunting camps, she'd sketched out a rough map. Then finished her shift.

The map was laying on the table in the office. After everybody'd gone.

He folds the paper sketch, puts it inside his jacket. Pushes back the Resistol, wiping a hand across his forehead.

In the scrub there's signs of foot traffic—signs of people passing through.

He turns in the direction of the river, picking out marks in the earth.

The vegetation is dense green, strips of fabric tied in some of the trees. He follows the trail along a thin track through the brush. Till he's standing at the river bank in a muddy clearing—staring at a flow of fast, brown water.

Scores of footprints line the bank on both sides. There's pieces of old tire, an inner tube, worn out shoes abandoned in the grass.

He stares across at the other side. Mexico. In twenty eight years, he's never been over.

The water's deep-looking, the river current swift. He rubs at his chin.

People passed through, a lot of people. A stream of human traffic. He thinks of hunting camps, men like Creagan and Harris and Williams, with rifles. How long would it take them to think of money to be made? A guy like Todd Williams knew every inch of country, every piece of the ground.

He takes out a Marlboro, lights it, walks along the bank, staring at the river. Checks his watch—it's coming on seven. Hour and a half till full dark.

Did they move in daylight—the people crossing? Would they always wait for night? He stands, smokes. Stares at a clump of spiny hackberry. Looks up and down the river, listening for any sound.

He slips off his jacket, unclips the Glock, pushes it beneath the spiny hackberry. Then places his jacket and hat over the gun. Strides to the river in his shirtsleeves.

He waits at the water's edge, cigarette trailing from his hand. Not the first time he's crossed lines he shouldn't. He thinks of Iraq, the ground war, scouting ahead of an armor column. Puts a boot in the water, another. The current pulls at his feet.

He takes a hit off the cigarette, throws it upstream, watching the speed. Then launches himself into the river, cold weight dragging.

He kicks hard, swimming fast, adrenaline flowing. Working to keep his head high, boots like weights. He gulps down air, reaching through the racing water. Pushing down primal alarm.

His foot hits something—soft mud, the bank. He scrambles out to his knees, lungs heaving.

He stands, lets the water drain from his shirt and pants. Pulls off a boot, then the other. Tips them out.

Everywhere there's scraps of clothing, plastic bags, empty water bottles. Trails lead to the river, coming from a big track in the brush. He pulls his boots on, moves toward the opening in the scrub. The same thick vegetation is everywhere, tangled willow and mesquite.

He follows the track twenty yards back from the river, through a bank of lotebush. Something catches at the back of his throat—a sick smell, high and rancid.

He stops. Looks around in the shade-dappled light. Another waft hits him—he recognizes it from boyhood trips in the canyons. An animal must be laying someplace nearby. Decomposing in the heat.

He pushes down a side trail, toward a thin-grown copse. Light streaming through the canopy of branches.

In a small clearing is a sight that makes him stop in his tracks. The body of a man lies bloated, clothes tight on his swollen limbs. His skin is blackened, face crawling with flies.

The stench hits him. Whicher steadies, puts a hand across his mouth.

He scans the shadow-streaked clearing, nobody around—not another living soul. He's out of his legal jurisdiction, no telling where the nearest village might be.

Days the body must've lain there. Why had nobody come?

He thinks of all the empty land, hundreds, thousands of square acres, the vast deserted space. The US side, Carrizo Springs must be thirty miles away—the Mexican side, he can't think of a single place worth the name.

He stares out, motionless, across the clearing. At a man left to rot in plain sight. Like garbage. Unheeded.

He lets some time pass, breathing shallow. Birds rustling in the trees. And then he backs out, moving slow, mind turning, retracing his steps. All the way to the main trail, till he's at the river. Staring at the flow of water.

For a moment he stands—light fading. Wet clothes clinging to his skin. He sees himself as a boy, eleven years old—walking down to the Brazos River, sun high in the sky—to be immersed in the water, *los Brazos de Dios*, the arms of God. To be baptized. He thinks of smiling faces, songs, the water green between the banks; coming up for air, sky like fire, exhilaration, confusion.

He steps forward. Launches himself at the water—cold shock on his body. He kicks hard, swimming with all his strength.

At the far bank he scrambles out. He stumbles to the clump of spiny hackberry, reaches in, pulls out the hat, the jacket, the gun. He sits, takes off his boots, empties them.

He turns back into the brush, along the trail north—an ember like a hot coal in his chest.

He moves through the matted brush, twisting, turning. Sees black flies on a dead man's face. Alfonso Saldana in the light of a road flare, bleeding out by a cattle trough.

Ahead is an open place, a game trail. An animal sensation grips him, he stands dead still.

Stepping from a copse of chittamwood is a man in a bush hat—he's carrying a scoped rifle.

He swings the barrel.

Whicher draws the Glock. "US Marshal. Get that thing off of me..."

The man swallows—lowers the barrel, eying Whicher's soaking clothes. "This private land here."

"Put down the gun."

The man lets the butt swing out. He props the rifle against a tree. "I ain't broke any law."

Whicher moves from the brush, around the man, catching hold of the rifle—a Browning A-Bolt. Walnut stock.

"You come a-stepping out on me, I ain't done nothing."

"You threatened a law officer."

"Got no right to hold a gun on me..."

Whicher flicks the barrel of the Glock. "You hunting out of one of the camps?"

"What if I am?"

"Show me."

The man takes a step. "How about I get a look at your badge? If you're a marshal..."

"Just get walking."

The man stares at him. Then turns for the scrub.

Whicher follows him a hundred yards along a game trail west—Glock in one hand, rifle in the other. The brush is thickening, the trail leading toward a grove of elm. He sees the outline of a metal shipping container—one end fitted with a door.

There's a water tank, a bunch of chairs, an earth bank levee. Two men are standing in a clearing, one short, balding, in a wife-beater vest—the other wearing a ball cap, a denim jacket.

"Whoa," the short man calls; "what the hell's going on?"

"US Marshal..." Whicher holds the Glock out, where everybody can see. He fixes a look on the man in the ball cap. "You're a hard man to find, Harris."

Jug Line Harris peers through narrow-set eyes.

The marshal scans the clearing—no plan, just a fuse inside burning.

"He come out of nowhere," the bush hat man says. "Pulled a God damn gun. Took my rifle."

The short man turns to Harris. "You know him? The hell is this?"

At the back of the camp Whicher sees a rusted frame for dressing out deer.

He steps to the far side, climbs the dirt levee. Behind it is a pile of heads—animal heads. There must be thirty, maybe more. Long jaws, sharp teeth. *Javelina.*

Whicher swings the barrel of the Glock round to Harris. "Get walking," he tells him. "You and me are taking a ride."

Carrizo Springs.

Twenty minutes later, lights show in the Dimmit County courthouse as Whicher pushes Harris along a path toward the main door.

Harris has his hands out front, a pair of silvered cuffs at his wrists. Head down, he's barely spoken.

In the lobby, Deputy Hagen's eating a burrito—napkin at his collar.

They step to the counter. "Who do I need see to book a man in?"

Hagen lowers the burrito. "He's under arrest?" He looks to Harris. "What's the charge?"

"Illegal hunting. Shooting javelina out of season."

"You moonlightin' for Fish & Game?"

"Can you take custody?"

Hagen puts the half-eaten burrito on the counter. "I done picked the wrong week for night detail." He pulls the napkin from his collar. "You want to speak with an attorney?" he says to Harris. "You get one phone call."

"I don't got no lawyer."

"The court can appoint one. You'll have to wait till tomorrow."

Whicher passes Hagen the key to the handcuffs. "You got this? I need to make a call."

"I got it."

"You have a number for Border Patrol here?"

Hagen scratches his head. He writes a number on a square of paper. Whicher takes it, turns from reception, heads down the corridor to the back of the building.

At the office, he shuts the door. He picks up the phone, dials the number.

"Border Patrol. Carrizo Springs station."

"My name's Whicher, I'm a US Marshal. I need to talk with Raul Talamantes."

"I'm not sure Agent Talamantes is here. I can check?"

"I'm over at the Dimmit County courthouse. I need him to call if you can find him. Tell him it's urgent. Whicher's the name."

"Alright, marshal. Let me see what I can do."

Whicher puts down the receiver. He stands pulling the damp shirt from his chest. The hunting camp would fall in one of the Carrizo Springs sectors, Talamantes knew the area—he had to know what was going on.

The marshal steps from the office, walks the corridor to reception. The place is empty, a janitor mopping the floor.

Hagen would be processing Jug Line Harris. Harris wouldn't talk, not till morning, not before he lawyered up. But he could keep him in jail, turn the screw.

He steps out of the building, crosses the square. At the highway, a few store lights still show.

Half a block down is a Western wear outfitters. He walks fast along the sidewalk, reaches the store, it's still open.

Inside is an old guy in a saw-tooth pocket shirt. Hair like wire across his balding head. "Evenin'."

Whicher nods. He walks by a rack of boots to a display of plaids and checkers. He spends a minute, picks out a shirt. Blue and white window-pane. With pearl white snaps.

"We got that in your size," the man says. "Large to extra."

"I'll take it."

"Thirty-five bucks." The man finds a wrapped shirt from a hardwood rack behind the counter.

The marshal pays him. Steps back out.

Opposite the store is a roadside eatery. He heads over to the take-out window, buys a couple of hard shell tacos. He finds a bench, scarfs them down, salsa, meat and beans. Then crosses the square, re-entering the courthouse.

Back in the office, he strips off the damp shirt, hangs it on the seat back. He unwraps the new shirt, slips it on. It fits good. He tucks it in the dark gray suit pants.

He stares at the phone. Takes the pack of cigarettes from his jacket. Sticks them in the new shirt. Heads to the lobby.

Deputy Hagen is back.

"You lock the man up?"

"In the holding cells," Hagen says, "upstairs." He hands the marshal's silvered cuffs back to him. "Nice shirt."

Whicher sticks the cuffs in a pocket. "Anybody call from Border Patrol?"

Hagen checks the log, shakes his head. "Everything alright?"

The marshal doesn't answer.

"You seem a little—agitated." Hagen puts a pen to the corner of his mouth. "Hunting out of season, that's what you want the charge sheet to read?"

"Harris is a guide, I found a stack of javelina heads at a river camp, he knows it's against the law. I want to see him."

Hagen takes out a key. "Up the stairs in back. Last cell on the row." He hands the key to the marshal. "You take it easy, bud. You got that?"

⅄

Jug Line Harris sits on the edge of a fold-out cot, staring at the concrete floor.

Standing in the corridor, door open, Whicher takes out the pack of Marlboro Reds. He flicks one loose. "Sooner or later, you're going to have to talk to me." He lights up. "Start with those two guys you were hunting with. They're legit? They're regular customers?"

From the cot, Harris turns his head a fraction to look at him. "They're out of El Indio."

"They're what?"

"Up river, it's a place. They just a bunch of ol' boys I know."

"What are their names?"

Harris turns his face back to look at the floor. "I'd think I need to get me a lawyer."

Whicher pulls on the cigarette. "They shoot them java-lina?" He steps into the doorway, filling it.

"It ain't me shot 'em."

"What do you know about Todd Williams?"

The man's head sinks an inch.

"Reba Williams says the pair of y'all spent plenty of time out at the river. Out at the camps." Whicher takes another hit off the smoke. "Three nights back, Todd was shot dead in the brush. You know that."

"I don't know nothing..."

Whicher shakes his head. "You ain't going to lie to me a long time."

Harris stares at his boots.

The marshal smokes the cigarette down.

Harris turns, looks at him. "The hell you want with me?"

"You were buds with Todd Williams, he was a hunting guide, same as you. We found him with a bunch of illegal crossers. Randell Creagan, another friend of yours..."

"I done told you..."

"The only name came up in two days looking for him was your name."

"That don't make us friends."

The marshal leans against the frame of the door. "Creagan was found dead yesterday afternoon—at the rail yard in Eagle Pass."

Harris flinches, his eyes cut away. He sits on the edge of the cot—shrinking inside the denim jacket.

"You didn't know?"

From the corridor is a noise of footsteps in the stairwell.

Deputy Hagen emerges at the top, one hand held to the side of his face. "Phone call—from Border Patrol. Raul Talamantes..."

Whicher glances at Harris, still motionless on the cot.

He swings the cell door shut. Locks it.

In the downstairs office, he grabs the phone. "Yeah, this is Whicher..."

"Hey *mano*. You needed me to call?"

"I just arrested a guy name of Jug Line Harris. Boyd Harris. A hunting guide—you know the name?" Whicher puts his back against the office door.

"I don't think."

"I picked him up at a camp ten miles west of the Channing Ranch. By the river. That be your sector?"

No response

"There's evidence of people coming through there, lot of people. I wanted to speak with you about it."

"You wanted to speak?"

Whicher searches the desk, finds a block of notepaper, a pen.

"You're not from the border, *mano*? You new to this work?"

"What if I am?"

"*Es bien sabido*," Talamantes says. "Everybody knows. There's no way to stop it."

"There were trails everywhere. I crossed the river, I found a body."

"You crossed?"

Whicher jams the phone against his neck.

"Did you tell anybody? Let me give you some advice, *mano*. You don't cross the border..."

"Anyone can cross."

"Not you, not law enforcement. You break the law, you do that."

"There's a body in a copse near the river. It's by a crossing place..."

"Listen, *mano*..."

"No, you listen. That body's been laying there days, you call whoever you need to call on the Mexican side, you tell 'em it's there, you tell 'em to get the hell out and recover it. Or do it yourself. You hearing me?" Whicher stares at the wall.

The Border Patrol agent's voice is cold when he speaks again. "I'll do what I can do."

Whicher nods.

"But you better hear this," Talamantes says. "You tell no-one. Nobody."

"That's it? That's all you got to say?"

"Tell nobody. Don't think of doing it a second time. I'm putting down the phone now, *mano*. Don't call me again."

✦

Back upstairs in the holding cell, Harris sits with his boots on the edge of the cot, his knees drawn up. "You fixin' to charge me?"

Whicher leans against the wall. "Those heads weren't taken from any animals killed in winter."

"Who says I shot 'em?"

"That's your defense?"

Harris yanks the ball cap down. "Fuck it, man. I'm a hunting guide—ain't up to me what folk do. They get to drinkin', and foolin'..."

"I'll keep you here on the hunting charge. Look for vehicles, anything you drive, anything Creagan might've supplied. I'll check every federal firearms licensee..."

"I can buy a gun anyplace..."

"And I can ask the judge for time."

"Y'all cain't keep me in here."

"You're not afraid?"

"Of what," Harris says, "you?"

Whicher steps from the wall. "Not me." He grabs the cell door. "Afraid of ending up like them."

Harris stares.

"First Williams. Then Creagan. You next?"

⤳

Whicher stands by the Chevy outside in the square. He stares back at the courthouse—uplighters streaking the block stone walls.

Harris would sit tight, he'd be arraigned in the morning, enter a plea.

The men back at the river camp would likely ditch everything in the Rio Grande, he should've taken the heads as evidence. All he'd wanted was Harris—all he'd felt was anger. He pictures the body of the dead man in the copse.

He leans on the cab roof. Wind ragged. Talamantes under his skin. Watches the highway, ink sky arching overhead.

A half-ton GMC pickup turns into the square. It pulls in to the curbside at the end.

Marshal Jim Gale steps out. He sets his hi-crown hat—strides across the strip of watered grass.

He stomps fast, reaches the courthouse, shoulders open the door.

Whicher feels a tightness at his scalp. He crosses the dark square, enters the courthouse. Inside, Deputy Hagen and Gale are speaking—their conversation stops.

"I need to speak with Harris." Gale tries a grin—like a dog fixing to bite. "I heard he was here. Been looking to find him."

"You heard?" Whicher glances at Hagen.

"This here county is part of my jurisdiction. I've been looking to take Harris in for questioning."

"Well, you can't. I just arrested him, I'm investigating two homicides."

"I'll take custody in Eagle Pass," Gale says. "You can question Harris, after I'm done."

"That's not going to happen."

Gale's arms are out at his sides, barrel chest huge. "You're charging Harris?"

"Shooting javelina in the closed season."

"That some kind of joke?"

"It's not a joke."

Gale draws himself to his full six-feet five. "Alright. You and me need to step outside." His eyes are dark with anger. He stiff-arms the door.

Whicher feels his blood rise. He follows the man out.

Gale's walked to the center of the square—to stand in the shadows. "The hell's your problem? Where's your boss, where's Scruggs?"

"Laredo."

Gale steps his feet wide. "I'm going to say this one time—I need to speak with Harris. And you can talk to him. After I'm done."

"Harris stays in my custody."

"Listen you little pissant..." Gale's hand is balled into a fist. "You need to get your head out of your ass. I bring you out here, it's so the sheriff's department don't get to see you make a God damn fool of yourself..."

The younger marshal cuts a look across the square, at traffic in the street.

"You get cross-wise of me, you're going to wish you didn't."

"That it?"

Gale's hand opens and closes. "God damn, boy..."

Whicher steps forward. "The answer's no."

He stares at Gale, feels the boiling power, the big man itching to take a swing.

"Your truck is over yonder," Whicher says. He touches the brim of the Resistol. "I'll say goodnight. We're all done."

CHAPTER 10

Dimmit County Courthouse. Carrizo Springs, TX.

The ceiling of the holding cell swims into focus. All night Whicher's lain there—in an unused unit. He sits up on the fold-out cot, staring at the bare painted walls.

Jug Line Harris is next door.

Did he really think Jim Gale would come back?

Whicher stands, stretches. He steps out into the corridor. He peeks through the observation slit in the next cell. Harris is laying there, same as before, like a drunk on a bench.

He checks his watch—almost eight. Then walks fast down the corridor, finds a bathroom, hangs his hat.

At the wash basin he runs the water, cups his hands, drinks a little, washes his face. Last night, he'd been toe to toe, with Gale. He stares at his reflection in the mirror, rubs his eyes.

Putting on his hat, he steps out, heads down the main stairs, two at a time.

Along the corridor in back he thinks of Todd Williams, his mother Reba. She said Todd worked for Creagan fixing up autos.

At the end of the corridor, the door to the office is wide open. Inside, Benita Alvarenga's reading a file.

The sight of her stops him in his tracks.

She looks up, laundered uniform creased sharp. "Late finishing?"

"I brought in Harris last night..."

"I heard."

Whicher hesitates in the door frame.

"Like the shirt."

He glances at the mismatch, the blue check shirt, disheveled pants. "We need to keep Harris here long as we can. Yank his chain." On the desk he spots his notepad. "Reba Williams talked about some auto yard." He finds the page. "South Monroe. In Eagle Pass."

"I made a start compiling names and addresses," Alvarenga says. "I need to add that."

"I'm thinking to head up there."

"To Eagle Pass?"

The telephone rings. Whicher picks up.

It's Scruggs.

"Jim Gale is looking to kick your ass, when he sees you."

"Sir?"

"I'm in Laredo. You arrested this Harris character last night? On a hunting charge? What the hell for?"

"I wanted to bring him in, put the squeeze on him…" Whicher shifts the earpiece away from Alvarenga.

"This here's Gale's backyard," Scruggs says, "Dimmit's part of western district, same as Maverick."

"I made the arrest, I thought it proper we hold him. I can't arrest him one minute, give him up the next."

"Listen," Scruggs says, "I got to be in court to testify else I'd be headed up. But let me make something real clear—you don't antagonize Jim Gale, nor anybody else in this investigation. You hearin' this? Just one time I'm going to cut you slack. But there ain't going to be a repeat."

Whicher feels color rising in his face.

"What the hell does Harris have to say, anyhow?"

"So far, nothing."

"Nothing? Has he seen a lawyer? Listen, leave it alone till I get there. I've put the word out on Merrill Johnson, the freight guy," Scruggs says. "Merrill M. Johnson's somebody we ought to be talking with."

"You want me to go look for him?"

"Do nothing till I get there."

Scruggs hangs up.

Deputy Alvarenga's eyes are on him.

"You mind passing me that shirt?"

She leans forward, slips the plain white shirt from the seat back.

He takes it from her. Starts to strip off the blue.

She turns away, studies her fingernails. Hint of a smile.

"You want to come? To Eagle Pass."

"Not my county." She shakes her head.

"Want to take a run at Harris? Start looking for background."

"What kind of background?"

"Anything against his name, anything recorded, I'm thinking guns, vehicles..."

"There may be no record on any guns."

"Cars we could check. He might've got something off of Creagan."

She looks at him. "What do you think Harris knows?"

Eagle Pass, TX.

A dusty single lane runs parallel with the river, a quarter mile south from the main highway through Eagle Pass. Among the warehousing and disused lock-ups Whicher slows the Chevy, checks the road sign—*South Monroe*.

A forty mile run between Eagle Pass and Carrizo Springs, he can make it back in time.

He studies a run-down brick garage, graffitied—a cinder block wall. He parks the truck in an alley that runs to the side. He cuts the motor, climbs up in the truck bed. Over the top of the wall he sees six vehicles—a couple of sedans, a minivan, two pickups, a suburban.

Among the debris in the yard there's oil drums, hoses, tires, a pressure washer. If Todd Williams was fixing vehicles, ready to move, this had to be the place.

The garage is closed up, padlocked. If Creagan was killed in there, crime scene would have to search it, turn it upside down. He could speak with Scruggs, let him know he found the place. Eagle Pass auto-theft unit would want in.

From across the river is the sound of a train horn drifting—the rail line couldn't be far. He stares at the minivan parked by the near wall. Inside on the seats are plastic bags, water bottles, discarded clothing. It's like looking at the brush trails down at the river.

The same people have passed through.

A mile away at a gas station on US 57, Whicher feeds quarters into a wall-mount payphone. He glances at headlines poking from a newspaper rack. The phone rings at Carrizo Springs. Benita Alvarenga picks up.

"I found the yard. On South Monroe."

"Did you go in?"

"Creagan might have been killed in there, we need to let Scruggs know, get a crime scene tech."

"He called again, he's coming up soon as he gets done in court. I think you ought to be here..."

Whicher stares across the station forecourt, toeing a broken piece of asphalt. "I want to talk to INS, Miguel Carrasco, here in Eagle Pass. I'm going to call him, go see him. I think Creagan might've been moving illegals up country. Providing transport."

"If you're not here it's on you."

"You find anything on Harris?"

"He has an eighty-eight Super Duty registered."

"Legit?"

"Looks like it."

"Nothing on him?"

"Nothing yet."

"Keep looking."

At reception in the Maverick County Sheriff's Department, the tough-looking Mexican-Indian is already waiting for him. "Back again," Carrasco says. He runs a knuckle over his boxer's nose.

Whicher follows the INS agent down the corridor to his small, windowless office.

They step inside. Carrasco sits behind the desk.

Whicher pulls out a chair.

"You don't have enough to do, *ese*? All that killing at the ranch?"

"We got ourselves another homicide; Randell Creagan."

"I heard. From Sheriff Owens."

"I'd like to know did he have a file here? Creagan. Was he of interest—to Immigration and Nationalization?"

The INS agent gazes at him.

"Was he known?"

"Not by me."

"I think he might've been running people upcountry." Whicher pushes back his chair. "How do wets get away from border towns?"

Carrasco shrugs. "A lot of times, a family member. A brother, a cousin. They'll pick 'em up, somebody already working here."

"*Coyotes* don't take 'em north?"

"Some will. Depends on the money, *ese*."

"But there is money—in moving them north?"

"Jobs are in the cities, no? Plus it's dangerous here, the Patrol's always on the look out."

The marshal takes off the Resistol.

Carrasco looks at him. "You think Creagan was running wets north?"

Whicher nods.

"If he was low-level, we might not know about it."

The marshal stares at the stone-colored felt hat. "We got Creagan shot dead, somebody went to a bunch of trouble, chaining him to a train. Nobody seems to know nothing, it comes to him. But add in everything at the Channing Ranch..."

"You find anything yet?"

"US victim looks to be a low-grade *coyote*. One of the Hispanics, we got a name..."

"Saldana—I remember. How about that list of names I gave you, all the people we VR'ed?"

Whicher shakes his head.

"The names will all be false, *ese*. I told you."

"The rest of the Hispanic victims we have no idea."

Miguel Carrasco leans his head to one side.

"What I can't figure is, why they all were killed? I mean, is it normal? For people crossing to be murdered?"

The INS agent looks at him a long moment. He leans forward. "No," he finally says. "It's not normal." He folds his hands together on the desk. "The most likely scenario? They were OTM, the stakes are higher. There's multiple borders to cross, one country after another..."

"Other-than-Mexican?"

"Right."

"They pay higher?"

"Five times, ten times higher."

Whicher slips a notepad from his jacket. "You mind?"

"Go ahead."

"So there's a difference, depending on what country they're from?"

"A Mexican *pollo* will cross with somebody known, somebody who made the trip before. If things goes wrong, they never give up the *coyote*. Most of them make another run the next night. They give up the *coyote*, how they going to get across? Plus, they paid out all their money, last thing they want is the guide thrown in jail. They don't have money for a second shake."

"I heard *coyotes* run out on the crossers, that's how come the Patrol don't get 'em."

"The *coyote* will be one among the group, *ese*. No way to tell him apart from the others."

Whicher writes it down.

"Central American." Carrasco says. "They'd be more likely to give up a guide. A *coyote* out in the brush, if he thought it looked like he was about to get caught..."

Whicher stares at the edge of the desk. "He might shoot the people he's trafficking?"

"I've known a few that would."

The marshal turns the idea over. Maybe it'd explain the Hispanics. But not the two Americans—not Williams and Creagan.

Carrasco leans back, eyes shining. "Belly of the beast..."

The marshal lifts the hat from his knee.

"It means, it's dark down here."

"The border?"

The agent nods. "Black as pitch, *ese*. Only set on getting darker."

᛭

Waves of heat roll across the lot at the sheriff's department. Beyond it, the flats stretch to the river, Piedras Negras a dirty haze. A coal town, it sits over the border, dwarfing Eagle Pass on the opposite bank. Full of *maquilas*, factories, import-export. Whicher thinks of thousands gathered living, working, one eye over their shoulder. On the fast flowing river. *El norte*, beyond.

He makes for his truck—parked at the far edge of the lot.

Beside it is a half-ton GMC pickup. In the driver's seat, Jim Gale.

Whicher checks step, pulls the keys from his pocket.

Gale swings down from the truck.

"Something I can do for you?"

"Saw you parked," Gale says. "I figured I'd wait."

"You wanted to see me?"

"I want to see Creagan's apartment. The apartment across town."

Whicher thinks of Scruggs—pissed, calling from Laredo.

"I know you've been there, your boss done told me."

He can't keep refusing.

"You know where it's at?"

Gale's face is clouded.

Whicher opens the door to his truck. "You know? Or you want to follow me down?"

⋏

Inside the Chevy, he starts the motor, cranks the A/C to max. He drops it into drive, pulls around, heading out on the highway.

He feels a lick of adrenaline. Steers with one hand, flipping open the glove box. Jim Gale's number is in there, the name and number on the scrap of paper. He searches for the apartment key. Snaps the glove box closed.

At the intersection with the four-lane he makes a right, heading downtown, glancing in the rear-view.

Gale's sitting behind—the black pickup filling up his mirror.

Whicher lights a smoke. Picks his way through the traffic. Tells himself to stay calm, take things slow.

He steers along the highway, sees the turn lane up ahead.

He hits the blinker, waits for a gap. Then guns the Chevy up the dusty road.

At the end, at the intersection, he eyes the shade trees where Dane Vogel had been parked.

The twin porches at the house are deserted. He parks at the curb, Jim Gale pulling up behind.

The two men step out. They walk from their trucks, cross the bare dirt yard to the door.

"You can head out," Gale says.

Whicher takes the key from his pocket. He opens up, careful. "I'll wait."

"Anybody been in? Anybody carry out a thorough search?"

"It's not the scene of any crime."

The two men step inside the apartment.

"You're the only one been in here?" Gale takes out a pair of latex gloves. He pulls them on. "You didn't find anything—according to Marshal Scruggs."

"I was checking Creagan wasn't killed here. That's all."

The big marshal opens drawers, cupboards, he lingers in the area around the phone, eyes roving every surface.

Whicher stares into the little kitchen, fine layer of dust on the side, sink dry as a bone.

Gale searches a low shelf. "The way he was found—chained to a freight car? I seen that before."

Whicher turns to look at him.

"Way of moving a body," Gale says. "Low risk way."

Outside in the lane a garbage truck rumbles by the house, two Hispanics in filthy coveralls hanging off the back. A shot glass rattles on the draining rack. The truck rolls down the street. Silence heavy in its wake.

"You put a body on a freight car," Gale says, "you can move it up country—you know the network."

"How about if it falls off?"

"If it traveled far enough, it don't matter. Real hard to identify when it don't tally with any local report."

"You think Creagan was killed someplace else?" Whicher thinks of Sheriff Owens standing by the corpse on the rail line. Mexico, he'd said. He'd pointed the finger, straight out, reckoned it was over the border.

Gale stands watching, feet planted—like a bar room brawler. He cocks his head to one side. "I want to see Harris."

Chapter 11

Carrizo Springs, TX.

At the Dimmit County courthouse, Whicher dumps the Chevy beneath the palms at the sidewalk. He checks the rear-view, Gale's not behind, he's dropped him coming through the town.

He crosses the square, enters the courthouse.

Benita Alvarenga's by the counter with a female clerk.

He waves her to one side of the lobby.

She steps over, frown line creasing her brow.

"I got somebody with me," he says. "Marshal Gale, from Eagle Pass."

Her eyebrows arch.

"Don't mention the auto yard, Creagan's yard."

"What's that supposed to mean?"

"I want to check it out first, just don't mention it..."

The main door opens. Gale steps through.

He raises his hat to the ladies. "Where's Harris?" he says to Whicher. "Upstairs in the cells?"

"I'll take you on up..."

Alvarenga steps forward. "No—you can't do that." She crosses to the counter, whips up a two-sheet form. "He made bail."

"Harris made bail?"

"We got him into court," she says. "He was arraigned, we had no option. The judge said a charge of hunting out of season was too minor to keep him in here."

Whicher steps to the counter. "How long's he been gone?" He stares at the release form.

"A little over an hour."

Gale turns around toward the main door.

"Wait," Whicher says. "Are you going after him?"

The big man stops. "I came here to see the son of a bitch. Last night, I wanted to see him. So far, you're doing a pretty fine job screwing that up for me." He heads out, no backward look.

⋏

In the corridor by the office, Whicher smokes a cigarette, rear door open onto the square. Harris would likely take to the back country, Lake Amistad, not any of the river camps—who knew where else the guy might have? He could disappear in the brush, but how long would he last?

The marshal sticks his head in the door to the office. "We need everything we can get on Todd Williams and Randell Creagan."

Deputy Alvarenga looks up from behind the desk.

"Creagan's out of east Texas—nobody seems to know a damn thing about him."

"I checked out Williams for a record," Alvarenga says. "He didn't have one."

"We need somebody that knew him, there has to be something..." From his jacket pocket, he pulls out a list of auto plates.

"What's that?"

"License plates of all the vehicles I could see inside of Creagan's yard." He hands it to her.

"There's a girl, Gina," she says, thinking. "Works over in the county clerk's office..."

He looks at her.

"I think she lived not far from Catarina one time. I could talk with her, she might know something on the Williams family? You want me to see if she's in?"

Whicher nods. "I need to call Brady Iverson, the guy that rented out that little crash pad to Creagan. We have a number?"

"In the file."

She steps from the office, brushing against him. He stares after her. Then sits at the desk, snatching up the phone, flipping through the file to the number for Iverson.

He punches it in on the keys.

It's ringing, he puts the cigarette to his mouth.

"Iverson Realty."

"Mister Iverson—Deputy Marshal Whicher. We met the day before last. About Randell Creagan—the apartment he was renting from you."

"What can I do for you, marshal?"

"I went out there again, to the apartment, this morning. Took another look around. Didn't seem like the guy ever used it."

"I wouldn't rightly know. He paid the rent regular," Iverson says. "I let him be."

"The place next door, you own that too?"

"Yessir. It's another rental unit. It's been empty a couple of months."

"There's no neighbor, nobody I could talk with?"

"I don't guess."

The marshal takes a pull at the cigarette. "Did you rent a garage property to Creagan? Out near the train line—South Monroe Street?"

"No, sir."

"You didn't?"

"All of my property's residential, I don't do commercial."

Whicher rolls a pen across the desk. "You said he was paid up on the rent? How'd he pay it, cash, a check?"

"He paid cash."

"Always?"

"Except the first time. I take a check for the deposit. When somebody first takes a place."

"You cash it?"

"Yessir."

"Which bank, you remember?"

"Not right off the top of my head. I guess I could take a look on back through my records, see if I could find out?"

"It could help." The marshal thinks of hanging up.

"I can tell you Creagan did rent something else off of me..."

Whicher straightens.

"Parcel of land," Iverson says, "a hunting concession. I have a few parcels, here and there."

"Where would that be?"

"About halfway between Eagle Pass and Carrizo Springs. Off of 277."

"You have an address?"

"There's no address as such," Iverson says. "It's just some land out in the brush. I can give you directions..."

"Can you fax them over to Dimmit County Sheriff? The courthouse, in Carrizo Springs?"

"Yessir."

Whicher makes a note at the desk.

"You have any idea why somebody went and killed Mister Creagan, marshal?"

"We're working on it," Whicher says.

Benita Alvarenga arrives at the doorway of the office.

"I'll be looking out for that fax, Mister Iverson. And let me know about that bank account, if you can find it." He hangs up.

Deputy Alvarenga waves a small yellow square of paper. "Lindy Page," she says. "Girlfriend of Todd Williams. Former girlfriend, works at a diner up in Crystal City. Just up the road from here."

Whicher takes the note.

"I got a work number, plus a home number."

He reads it.

"Todd was going steady with her for a while. According to Gina."

Two-thirty in the afternoon, she'd most likely be at her job if she was working in a diner. Crystal City was maybe twelve miles north.

"There's a message for you," Alvarenga says. "At reception, from Marshal Scruggs."

Whicher clamps the cigarette to his mouth.

"The desk clerk took it—your line was busy."

"I was talking with Iverson."

"Scruggs is asking for you to meet him, out near Laredo. Something to do with Merrill Johnson?"

"Don't tell me Johnson's dead, too?"

She shakes her head. "I think it's about paying the guy a visit."

"I better call."

"You want me to get a hold of Lindy Page? Arrange a meet?"

"Not yet. Let me talk with Scruggs first." The marshal reaches for the phone.

"I could take a run at those license plates? Put them in the system, see what takes." She picks the list from the desk.

"Brady Iverson's going to fax up directions to a hunting concession," Whicher says. "Some land Creagan was renting off him. Can you make sure we get it?"

"I'll make sure."

*

Webb County, north of Laredo, TX.

Beneath a stand of cottonwood and black willow, Whicher waits with Scruggs—the trucks parked off road by a thicket of mesquite. Beyond the shade of the willow, a sun-scorched ranch road stretches out over empty scrub. Nothing moving, not even the wind. The mass of air above the land is super-heated, charged with light.

Whicher feels a trickle of sweat run down his back.

Scruggs stares out at the ranch road, eyes of flint.

Laredo court hadn't called his testimony—he'd be back again next morning.

"Creagan's yard in Eagle Pass could be a pretty good lead," Whicher says.

"If you saw evidence, you could have gone in—on the 'plain view' rule."

"He had a bunch of vehicles in there. Deputy Alvarenga's running a check."

"If it's in plain sight, you don't need a warrant."

"Creagan might have been killed there."

Scruggs adjusts his hat. "We get done here, I'll talk with Sheriff Owens. See about opening the place up."

Whicher scans the deserted ranch road. "I spoke with Miguel Carrasco at INS. Some of the vehicles in that yard could've been used transporting people. Moving wets north."

"What did Carrasco say?"

"He hadn't heard about it."

A muscle works in the side of Scruggs's face.

"We have a couple more threads might get us some go-forward," Whicher says. "Former girlfriend of Todd Williams. Plus some land Creagan rented off of Brady Iverson. I wouldn't mind taking a look."

"Yesterday you arrested Jug Line Harris. Today he walks. I got Jim Gale hollerin', account of the way you're doing things..."

A sound carries in the air, the noise of a motor approaching.

Both men turn to stare at the bend in the road. A rig and horse transporter is coming into view, glaring white against the tan grass and scrub. It's oversize for the ranch road, tires on the edge of the track, a cloud of dust in its wake.

It draws level, passes.

"That it?"

"According to Vic Delossantos," Scruggs says. "Border Patrol say that thing should be carrying Merrill Johnson's latest equine acquisition."

"You think he'll admit to knowing Randell Creagan?"

Scruggs's eyes are on the horse transporter. "I'd guess not."

"We going after it?"

"You drive. I'll ride with you."

Whicher crosses to the Chevy, opens up.

Scruggs jumps in the passenger seat. They pull out onto the ranch road from the shade of the mesquite.

"Vic Delossantos," Whicher says. "He knows about this how?"

"APHIS vet. They had all the paperwork a day or so back. Veterinarian service put it through Border Patrol at the port of entry."

"Merrill Johnson buy a lot of horses—out of Mexico?"

"Patrol say he does more selling than buying."

Whicher thinks about it. "He sells horses over there?"

"Man's a customs broker, freight forwarder. Reckons to deal in a lot of things. Delossantos says APHIS know him from shipping live US horses out for slaughter."

"That's part of what he does?"

"A dirty little part of it, yeah."

Whicher throws his boss a look.

"You know what a puntilla is?"

"A point?"

"Killing knife," Scruggs says. "Stabbing blade. How they do it out there. Real cheap. Real nasty."

Whicher steers around a curve in the road—the land opening out onto a series of paddocks, white-painted fences. Ahead is a ranch house, a group of barns. There's stabling, a bunch of horse boxes. The rig and transport is pulling up in a yard at the front of the house.

A dark-haired man is watching them. He's dressed in a city suit, despite the heat.

The marshal takes him in—he's in his forties, compact, groomed, a thick mustache. Wearing metal rimmed eye-glasses.

"Block the rig," says Scruggs.

"You want me to block it in?"

"Make it tough for him to get out."

Whicher picks a spot behind the transporter. Parks at an angle.

The man in the suit's already striding toward them—moving fast, staring.

Whicher shuts off the motor. The two marshals step out.

"Can I help you gentlemen?"

Scruggs takes a pace. "US Marshals Service."

The man's expression shifts like sunlight on water. "We're taking delivery of a new mare, here."

"That's alright," Scruggs says. "Y'all go ahead. Mister Johnson, is it? Merrill M. Johnson?"

The man gives a curt nod.

A stable hand walks from a barn—yard brush in his hand.

Johnson glances at the horse transporter. "Did you want to talk with me?"

"Yes sir."

"Couldn't you have called ahead?" He turns to the stables, shouts at the hand. "*Ramon.* Get on over here, can't you?"

"I just have a couple of questions."

Merrill Johnson screws his head around.

The rig driver steps down from the cab.

"I'm running a homicide investigation," Scruggs says. "Into the death of a man name of Randell Creagan..."

Whicher stares directly at Johnson's face.

"Do you know him?" Scruggs says.

Inside the transporter, the horse stamps, clattering the sides.

The hand and driver step to a door in the trailer unit—opening up, fastening back the door on a rope.

"Creagan..." Johnson says. "A truck driver?"

"He was."

"He used to work for me."

"Randell Creagan used to work for you?"

"Three, four years back, I guess it was. I'm in the freight business, I work with a lot of people—they work with me." Johnson takes a pace toward the trailer, the hand stepping inside. "Ease her on out, Ramon, quick as you can." He turns back to Scruggs. "I must say that comes as quite a shock."

"Did you know Creagan well?"

"Not well, no."

The driver puts out a short ramp from the box to the ground.

"How would you describe your relationship?"

Johnson looks at him. "He worked for me. Driving trucks, delivering loads. I'm in supply chain management."

"That it?"

"Anything that needs moving, I figure out how to do it. We're like the stagecoach operators of old."

"Stage coaches," Scruggs says. "That where you get your interest in horses?"

The driver fixes pieces of board to the sides of the ramp, twin uprights—a gangway. Ramon leads out the horse, firm grip at the halter. She's sleek and black, maybe fifteen hands. A white star beneath her forelock.

Whicher steps in as the mare passes down the ramp. He peers into the transporter unit. "Quite a size, in there..." He breathes the heavy scent. The interior's divided into stalls, padded at flank-height, restraining ropes at the sides. It's roomy, light—there's ventilation from the roof. "All this, just for one horse?"

"That's a valuable animal," Johnson says. "Broodmare. In need of careful handling." He turns to Scruggs. "How exactly can I be of help to you gentlemen?"

"We're kind of short of people to talk with," Scruggs says. "It looks like Creagan went a little off the rails since he quit the freight business. We've been trying to pick him up last couple days. Laredo court issued a warrant over a non-appearance."

"He was charged with something?"

"Handling stolen vehicles. Nobody seems to know much about him. But your name came up."

"I can't understand why it would," Johnson says. "I hardly knew him. Like I said, it's been a good while since he worked for me."

Whicher watches the driver and hand walk the mare to a fenced paddock. "I take a look around in those barns?" he says. "Long as we're out here."

Johnson stares through the steel rimmed glasses. "Did you come here to search my property? Do you have a warrant?"

"No, sir." Scruggs says, folding his arms.

In the paddock, the hand turns the mare loose.

Merrill Johnson looks to Scruggs. "In my business, a fellow gets used to following certain procedures. I expect to see the right paperwork."

Whicher's already walking to a new-built timber frame barn. The yard's swept clean, there's not a thing out of place, tack well ordered, brushes hanging from a wall. There's fresh straw. But no horses.

He turns back to Johnson. "You know a feller by the name of Jug Line Harris?"

"Why?" Johnson says. "Something happened to him?"

Whicher throws a look.

Johnson frowns. "Just an expression."

"You know him?"

"He some kind of a fisherman? With a name like that."

"I guess. I guess he likes to hunt and fish."

"I do some fishing, maybe I've come across him, I can't say. He doesn't sound real familiar. But I get to meet a lot of people, my line of work."

"Where were you four nights ago, sir?"

Johnson looks at him.

"Were you here?"

"I'm not sure I like the direction you're taking, marshal. Neither your tone."

"I'm not taking any direction, Mister Johnson. It's just a simple question."

Scruggs steps forward, brittle smile at the edge of his mouth. "No, that's alright." He catches the younger marshal's eye. "We were just leaving."

Whicher lifts the Resistol—settles it back in place.

Scruggs is walking to the Chevy.

Whicher follows, striding around back of the horse transporter.

"Let's roll," Scruggs says. He's not smiling.

⋏

Beneath the black willow, Whicher stops the Chevy.

Scruggs slides out. He stands at the edge of the dusty ranch road. "Too much, too soon," he says, finally. "You need to slow it on down."

The younger marshal gazes out the windshield, saying nothing.

"A man like Johnson—we got to do things right. We turn up, no warrant, no probable cause, no evidence. We start questioning, making accusations, we'll get our ass kicked."

Whicher glances at his boss.

"Johnson can afford a good attorney. We screw up, they'll throw us out of court, day one. You need to go home trooper," Scruggs says. He grabs the door to swing it shut. "Go on home. Get some rest."

Chapter 12

Laredo, TX.

Too empty. The apartment had been too empty. He'd taken a shower, changed—grabbed something to eat. He'd checked the answer machine, nothing from Benita Alvarenga—a single message from Vic Delossantos at Laredo Border Patrol.

Delossantos had said to call. He said he had news of Alfonso Saldana, from out of Brownsville.

Whicher called Border Patrol, they'd told him Delossantos was out working a shift—he held while they found out where.

After, he sat out in the yard with the glass doors open. Smoked a cigarette in the kitchen, TV on.

He'd read his notes. Stared at the four walls of the apartment. Then locked up, headed out, riding Clarke Boulevard and 35 to Convent Avenue.

It's gone six in the evening as he pulls into the truck lot at the side of the Rio Grande in downtown Laredo.

Delossantos is by a group of stock trailers and cattle trucks.

He's in rough-duty uniform, fatigue shirt tight against his heavy frame. With him is a sandy haired young woman in jeans and a dark blue polo shirt.

The marshal makes his way across the hot asphalt.

Inside the trailers he sees horses moving, shifting through the open-slat sides. The whites of their eyes show—they dart away again into darkness.

The young woman in the polo shirt carries a clipboard securing reams of paper. Underneath an arm she has a bunch of carbon-backed forms.

Delossantos spots him, a look of surprise in his face. "You got my message?"

"I got it."

"What're you doing down here, man?" Delossantos steps from the cattle trucks, grinning. "You don't have a girlfriend or nothing?"

The woman with the clipboard glances over.

"Border Patrol called from Brownsville," Delossantos says.

"About Saldana, right. I wanted to hear."

"Aguilar, it was. The guy at the port of entry? The day we went out there, Agent Aguilar, you remember?"

Whicher pictures the man; shaved head, the hi-top boots. He thinks of the family in the pickup—the couple with the little girl.

"Brownsville Patrol took another look into the whole thing," Delossantos says. "The arrest log, the deportation."

"They took another look?"

"The county medical examiner's office want to know, for their record."

"They find something?"

"Maybe. It turns out, Saldana claimed to have a son that died. At the time of the arrest."

Whicher eyes him.

"He claimed his son's death was being looked at by the university but they wouldn't talk to him. That's what he was doing up there."

The marshal gazes out across the river at the Mexican flag hanging slack above the tree line in Nuevo Laredo. Three times Saldana went there; three times in and out of campus trying to speak with someone, trying to ask about his son. They didn't like the look, the way he was dressed. Maybe his English hadn't been so good.

"You think it changes anything?" Delossantos says.

"I don't know."

The Border Patrol agent shoves his hands in his pockets. "How you get along, anyhow, this afternoon? With Merrill Johnson? You go on out there?"

"Yeah," he says. "We went up. To that ranch."

Delossantos nods. He stares at the cattle truck. "This bunch of horses is one of Johnson's shipments."

The marshal watches the animals, nervous-looking, agitated, some barely moving. "What are they—for slaughter?"

The woman in the polo shirt steps over. "Afraid so."

"This is Hannah Scott," Delossantos says. "From Animal and Plant Health Inspection Service."

She writes on a form, slim hands moving quick, cross-referencing some kind of certificate.

"Hannah's a vet. She gave us the tip about that brood-mare. I told Hannah, anything to do with Merrill Johnson, she could let me know."

"Does Johnson put a lot of horses through here?" Whicher says.

"Enough." She looks at him, skin of her face freckled, the features petite.

"That horse transporter seemed pretty big just for moving one mare."

"Anything comes in like that," Delossantos says, "we search it inside and out."

"Easy way to give a bunch of folk a ride."

"In a horse transporter?" the vet says. "It would be."

Delossantos shakes his head. "Man, anybody hitches a ride, they're going to scatter at the border."

Whicher stares at the cattle trucks, smell drifting on the over-heated air.

Hannah Scott checks-off more permits.

"Lot of paperwork," the marshal says.

The vet shrugs. "We need certificates. Live horses, they need inspection not more than thirty days prior to export. The vehicles have to have been cleaned, disinfected..."

"Just to ship 'em out and kill 'em?"

"Any sign of infectious disease or parasites, we can't let them go."

Whicher glances across the lot to the next two trailers, all filled with horses.

"Same shipment," she says.

"All organized through Merrill Johnson?"

"Yep. And the same destination."

"You mind if I ask you something?"

She looks up from the papers on the clipboard.

"You know much about rabies? The situation, how it is in the area?"

"I know it's on the rise."

"The sheriff in Dimmit County reckons they had twelve cases so far this year. Something like a hundred across the whole of south Texas."

"Canine rabies is a problem along the border," she says.

Vic Delossantos studies Whicher. "Why you want to know that?"

"The shooting in Dimmit, the victims were moved, on account of it. Before a justice of the peace could give permission."

The vet chews her pen. "You fight crime, we fight the war against disease..."

"Does Merrill Johnson come up regular on your radar?"

"I guess. He's a prime contact for any deal involving horses."

"It's his main business?"

"Along this sector," Delossantos says, "rail freight would account for the bulk of it."

"But road loads come in to it?"

"Man has a lot of irons in the fire."

"Wonder how he keeps from getting burned?"

⚹

In the dim-lit bar a block north from the river, Whicher sits alone at the long counter. The place is filled with office girls, suits out of downtown, drunk cowboys in tooled boots. A bunch of Hispanic construction workers sit around a table sharing pitchers of beer, they're covered head to foot in cement dust; their skin whitened, hands like leather around their mugs.

He sweeps the room—more working men, truck drivers, guys out of the meat packing plant. Merrill Johnson and his horse farm was another world. Two hours upcountry, a different universe.

The long-neck on the counter reflects neon and brass. Hannah Scott would still be at the river, her and Delossantos, certifying horses for slaughter.

The news from Brownsville could be something. He stares at his reflection in the bar-room mirror—big guy in a suit and hat. Busted nose. An air of something nobody wanted a piece of.

He swivels on the stool. At the edge of the group of construction workers, one man sits vacant rocking back in a chair, staring into space. Whicher takes a swallow of beer. Thinks of Eric Kessler on the porch at Eagle Pass.

He reaches in his jacket. Feels the hard edge of a business card. Slips it out.

If Saldana had a child that died in the hospital, there'd be a record of the mother.

He stares at the card.

University Campus, Brownsville. Professor Joyce Kinley.

Two numbers are printed on it—one the university, the other a private number. He leans into the bar, catches the eye of a girl working. "Y'all have a phone?"

She points to the far end of the counter. "Out by the restroom, honey."

He takes the long-neck and the business card. Walks the length of the bar.

In the lobby he places the beer on top of a wall-mount call box. He stares down the corridor to a glass door leading out to the street. A guy walks by him, clothes covered in cement dust, boots leaving a mark on the floor.

Whicher eyes the white-gray powder. He feeds quarters into the slot. Punches the number on the card.

The ring tone is soft, muted, expensive-sounding. He pictures her out somewhere, some campus gathering, dinner. He thinks of hanging up.

"Joyce Kinley..."

"Professor Kinley?"

There's a pause on the line.

"This is Marshal Whicher, we met a couple days back. Regarding an arrest on campus."

"Yes. Marshal. What can I do for you?"

He runs his hand down the side of the bottle. "Something came up," he says. "You don't mind my calling?"

"I don't mind."

"We have some more information since the last time we spoke. Some of the particulars on the arrest."

"I see."

"It may or may not be relevant. There was something I thought you ought to know, that you might want to know..."

The professor's silent.

"One of the cases you're handling was actually the child of this guy Saldana. At least that's what he claimed," Whicher says. "I can't imagine why a man might lie about a thing like that."

No response.

"I guess he never married the mother. The name wasn't going to be Saldana."

"I'm truly sorry if we got that wrong..."

"No, no," Whicher says. "It was just..."

Neither of them speaks for a long moment.

Outside on the street, cars and trucks rumble past, evening light from the southern sky streams in through the dirty glass pane in the door.

"How come they couldn't survive?"

She clears her throat. "Was it a girl or a boy?"

"A boy."

"The little boy was born without a brain. Without a functioning brain. Both the other infants were girls. Presenting differently."

"What happened to the mother?"

"The mother."

"Can you tell me her name?"

"I can't give you that kind of information."

"I could call the hospital..."

"The mother was a migrant woman, non-US. If you want a name, you'll have to make it official, marshal."

They'd have to make it official. They'd have to be investigating Saldana's death.

"I'm sorry," Professor Kinley says. "That's just the way it is. Was there anything else?"

Whicher chews on his lip. "The field of toxicology, ma'am—is it a field you've studied extensively?"

"Excuse me?"

"I mean, outside of infant mortality?"

"I'm not sure I follow?"

"I wanted to ask about returning service people. From the Gulf."

"Oh. You mind if I ask why?"

"Some of the troops are thought to have suffered exposure to toxic chemicals, pollutants?"

"Is this something personal to you?"

He snatches up the bottle, takes a sip.

"I can tell you that some problems have been noted. Among a small but statistically significant percentage of the people stationed overseas."

"There is something?"

"No hard evidence, nothing like that. But there's a pattern of illness. Is this in some way connected with the death of that man?"

Whicher leans against the wall. Unsure what to say. "I have a buddy. He got sick."

"I'm sorry to hear that."

Whicher stares down the dim corridor out into the street. "I'm sorry for taking up your time, ma'am."

"I'm sorry too," she says. "Sorry for all of it."

CHAPTER 13

Maverick County, TX.

Across the flat expanse of brush, heat's already stacking into a colorless sky. It's early morning, buzzards wheeling in the distance, the highway deserted as Whicher drives his truck west.

First stop of the day had been Carrizo Springs, the county courthouse. He'd picked up the faxed directions from Brady Iverson; a map, crudely sketched up in pen.

He studies the land butting up to the edge of the highway—short brown grass, the dirt thin, hard as cement. The land's fenced. Flat, dry, grazed out. Why lease a hunting concession in a place like this?

A caliche track runs south into the brush—Whicher slows, turns the truck onto it, big tires lifting up a cloud of fine white dust.

He picks the hand-drawn map off the seat. Holds it in one hand as he steers.

Creagan was killed someplace, chained to a freight car—till his body fell off. According to Jim Gale, it was a way of moving a corpse—low risk, no chance getting caught with it, no evidence left behind in any vehicle. If you knew where the loads stopped, Whicher guessed you might retrieve it.

He stares through the windshield at a group of tracks leading off the caliche road. The sketch arrows a trail ranging west; Whicher picks it out, steering into featureless scrub.

A hundred yards on is a group of low buildings—crude shelters, board shacks painted red and yellow. An iron windmill turns slow, pumping ground water. The marshal lifts off the gas, slowing to a roll.

At the edge of the track he sees a carved wooden figure set on top of a pile of stones. He brakes the truck to a stop. The figure is a praying woman. At the foot of the stones are candles, all burned out.

In the shade of a yellow shack, a Hispanic woman sits, arms working, grinding something.

He steps from the truck. Straightens the Resistol.

She's grinding maize, making up a pile of corn tortillas.

"Morning. I'm with US Marshals Service."

Her face is sunburned, clothes worn thin.

"Looking for a hunting concession? Man named Randell Creagan?"

She shakes her head.

Whicher glances around the property, a water tank—a mule standing by a clump of mesquite. In a wired-off run, chickens peck the bare earth. There's no vehicle, but tire marks. Stains of oil and gasoline. "You live out here?"

Her arm moves steady, grinding the corn. "*Sí.*"

"What's the story on the statue?" He jerks his head toward the track.

Her eyes slide away.

"It some kind of a shrine?"

In the dirt yard, tin flowers turn in the wind. Rusted, abandoned years ago. All except for one—still bright with turquoise paint. Turquoise, like the bead from the girl at the ranch.

He touches his hat brim to the woman. Steps back to the truck, climbs in, feels the cold air of the cab.

Brady Iverson's sketch shows the hunting lease somewhere up ahead. He drops the transmission into drive.

Along the worsening track he scans the brush for signs—evidence of people on foot. A bunch of *mojados* coming through at night, they'd be safe from the regular patrols. The border must be twenty miles, the highway running parallel—on foot, it'd make a good route.

Behind a dense bank of agarita he sees a dirt spur leading off the track.

He slows, swings the Chevy into a half-acre piece of cleared ground in the scrub—three sagging trailers in its center, up on blocks.

He parks. Climbs out.

All around is a litter of debris, old clothing, rags, abandoned shoes. The trailers are bleak-looking. Beneath them, scores of crumpled water bottles blown in on the wind.

He squats. In the earth are wheel marks, two or three different dimensions of tire and tread.

He draws the Glock from its holster. Listens. Walks to the trailers—footprints everywhere.

At the nearest trailer, he mounts a cinder block step. He pulls at the door. It opens.

Inside, flies are buzzing, the heat intense. A bunch of thin, dirty mattresses are strewn around the floor. He stoops to a discarded shirt—like the shirt of the *campesino* laying dead across the wall of the Channing Ranch.

He'd have to check the distance, he guesses it between twenty and thirty miles through the brush.

At the end of the trailer is a pile of ripped T-shirts, covered in dirt and dust and a fine red powder.

He thinks of climbing the steel ladder welded to the side of a hopper car—climbing up to look inside, white gray dust, some kind of mineral. That, and a fine red powder that left a stain.

He picks out one of the T-shirts, rubs the stained collar against the back of his hand.

It marks his skin. It leaves a red mark, just the same.

⋏

Carrizo Springs, TX.

In Dimmit County at the courthouse, Marshal Reuben Scruggs is already waiting. He sits behind the office desk, grunting answers into the phone.

Whicher enters the room.

Scruggs nods, one hand running up and down his tie, phone clamped at his neck.

Whicher steps out in the corridor, looking for Benita Alvarenga.

Scruggs finishes up the call. "That was scene of crime up to Eagle Pass. They got 'emselves into Creagan's auto yard."

"They find anything?"

"They're saying nothing out of place for a vehicle yard. The man was shot with hollow-point rounds—there'd be a bunch of blood, at least."

"Anything else?"

"Police department are going to trace all the vehicles in the yard—that's pretty much it." Scruggs pushes the phone up the desk, clearing space. "Where you get to, anyhow?" He fixes the younger marshal with a look.

"That hunting concession," Whicher says. "The land Creagan was leasing?"

"You find it?"

"He had a bunch of trailers out there."

"What kind of trailers?"

"Single-wides. Up on blocks. It looked to me like some kind of laying-up spot."

Scruggs leans back from the desk. "Makes you say that?"

"They had a pile of mats on the floor, old clothes, general garbage—just about everything you'd expect to see if people were stopping, breaking up a journey."

"You think he could've been killed there?"

"No sign."

The older marshal grimaces. "We don't find where, we got the Devil's own time saying who. We don't even know when."

"I'd like to know was Creagan still alive the night Todd Williams was killed? With the *mojados* at the ranch."

Scruggs pushes himself up out of the chair, smoothing down the black suit. "Supposed to be a doctor showing up around now, autopsy doctor."

"A coroner?"

"County don't run to a coroner, they have a doctor appointed in place. What's on the back of your hand?"

Whicher rubs at the mark. "Some kind of dye."

Scruggs looks at him.

"Off the clothes at the trailers—the same stuff was all over the hopper cars in Laredo, the night I went looking for Johnson."

"That a fact?"

"You think chemicals could be among the shipments Merrill Johnson handles? Trains could be a connection, those illegal crossers could have traveled up from the south."

"What if they did? Mexican's been riding up on freight trains since forever."

"But if we could narrow it down—specific trains, loads, specific lines."

"You think Merrill Johnson will be at the heart of it?"

"First time I went looking for him in Laredo, I nearly got my head took off by a guy with a wrench."

Scruggs studies on the thought.

"Jim Gale reckoned whoever chained Creagan to a rail car, knew about freight."

"You're quoting Jim Gale?"

Whicher feels heat rise in his face.

"Williams and them wets were found in the brush," Scruggs says. "Miles from any rail line." He adjusts the set of his hat. "Let's go take a walk upstairs, find the sheriff. I want to see if the doc made it in."

Whicher follows his boss along the back corridor toward the central lobby. He spits on a finger, tries to rub the mark from the back of his hand.

"You see any of that on the bodies out at the ranch?" Scruggs says. "Red marking."

Whicher shakes his head. "The autopsy could've picked something up, you think they tested for toxicology? Chemicals could be something, there's a possible link to the runner, Saldana—guy had a stillborn son, something linked to pollutants..."

Scruggs blows the air from his cheeks.

"He was arrested in Brownsville trying to find out what happened with his kid..."

"Cousin, you're reaching."

They cross the back of the lobby, climb the set of stairs to the next floor.

The scent of the sheriff's cigar is already in the air. Stationed outside his office door is a uniformed deputy, short guy with a horseshoe mustache.

The deputy looks at his watch. "Going to be couple of minutes."

"The autopsy doctor get in?"

"Doctor Schulz, yessir. They're in there now."

Scruggs turns for the opposite end of the corridor, Whicher follows all the way down to the holding cells.

They stand by a row of locked doors. Steel plate painted white, every bolt welded.

"I had some time this morning," Scruggs says, "I made a couple calls." He lowers his voice. "I called Laredo Police Department, Detective Simms."

"The detective that put together the auto theft case on Creagan?"

Scruggs nods. "Simms reckons before LPD ever caught up with him, FBI already suspected the man of running cars into Mexico. Running them over the border, returning in clean cars. With illegal aliens, on false papers. LPD didn't like it. Feds dicking 'em around. After I got done with Simms, I called up my buddy at Houston FBI. Gerry Nugent."

"He confirm any of that?"

Scruggs stares back down the corridor, eyes unfocused. "In twenty years of law enforcement, I never had the impression anybody was less than straight with me. But it was flat out denied."

Whicher looks at him.

"I never felt like anybody tried to brush me off, or sell me a bullshit line." Scruggs runs a thumb over the skin beneath his chin. "Until today."

CHAPTER 14

Doctor Elaine Schulz stands in front of the desk in the sheriff's office, leather briefcase laid open. She's late-thirties, blonde, the lean body of a runner beneath a navy two-piece. A collection of forms and files is propped against the lid of her case.

Cole Barnhart sits on a corner of the big, oak desk.

Deputy Benita Alvarenga's side-on to a long table lining the opposite wall, pen in hand, notepad open.

The sheriff adjusts the palm straw cowboy hat, pale eyelashes blinking slowly. "Might as well get started with this. I've asked Deputy Alvarenga, as liaison, to take notes." He looks at her. "For the record, Marshals Scruggs and Whicher are present. In addition, Doctor Elaine Schulz, responsible for the autopsies."

"Which autopsies?" says Scruggs.

"All of 'em," the sheriff answers. "Todd Williams, Randell Creagan. Plus the Hispanic victims at the ranch."

Scruggs sits forward, face tight. "Creagan was discovered in Maverick County. That's a change to procedure right there, sheriff."

"Maverick County cleared it with us," Barnhart says.

"A different doctor attended the body out at the rail track..."

Elaine Schulz cuts in, "That was Doctor Evans," she says, "I have all of the field notes from the scene."

"Elaine has the full confidence of both this and Sheriff Owens's department," Barnhart says. "Neither county's big enough to run to a permanent medical examiner."

Scruggs sits back. Folds his arms across his chest.

Doctor Schulz picks up a typed report, streaks of color in the skin at her throat. "All of the autopsies have been completed," she says. She skims the lines in the report. "The Hispanics recovered at the Channing Ranch had no identification on their persons. None is likely to be forthcoming."

"We still have no ID?" Scruggs says. "None whatever?"

The sheriff shakes his head. "I done told you the first day—they weren't carrying ID. They could be from anyplace. Nobody reported them missing. Even if they did, we'd never hear about it."

Doctor Schulz reads on. "Given the risk of contamination, the known risk of rabies at that locale, the bodies were removed as an emergency precaution—compliant with the public health guidelines currently in place..." She glances at Sheriff Barnhart.

"I stand by it." He hutches his shoulders.

"The victims at the Channing Ranch had all been shot multiple times," the doctor says. "Nine millimeter, soft-nosed rounds. A semi-automatic pistol. All the same gun."

"How about Randell Creagan?" Scruggs says.

"Different gun," the doctor answers. "Forty caliber Smith and Wesson."

"Everybody at the Channing Ranch is killed with the same gun," Scruggs says. "Except for Alfonso Saldana."

The doctor looks at him. She checks her notes. "Saldana—is the fatality taken by Webb County?"

"Yes, ma'am. Presumed part of the same group."

"He was shot with a rifle?"

Whicher answers; "High velocity full-metal-jackets. From distance."

Scruggs raises a finger. "I put in a call to Laredo Coroner's Office. On Saldana. They didn't get any of the lead—not even a bullet fragment. They can tell he was shot to death, the number of times he was hit. But nothing else."

Sheriff Barnhart gazes down at Scruggs. "Do you know yet where Creagan was killed?"

"Not yet."

Benita Alvarenga reads from her notes. "The prelim from Eagle Pass crime scene was faxed down—concerning the auto yard. It's a straight negative. For the record."

Whicher looks at Sheriff Barnhart. "I found Creagan's hunting concession this morning. He had a bunch of trailers on it. No sign of a struggle there either."

"We need a time of death on Randell Creagan," Scruggs says to the doctor.

"T.O.D. is going to be in a window five to six hours around the time of the other deaths," she says. "We have to take care, temperatures here, rates of decomposition can be significantly higher..."

"On a corpse outdoors," Scruggs says, "we know."

"Ten hours decomposition might take place over five."

Scruggs scowls.

"There's still a few test results to come back. We can get it narrowed down."

Sheriff Barnhart crosses one boot over the other. "Deputy Alvarenga says you're looking at a couple fellers in particular—Merrill Johnson and that guy Harris. Feller you arrested on the hunting charge."

"Right," says Scruggs.

"That done made bail..."

"Right again."

"Are you considering the pair of 'em for your killers?"

Scruggs shakes his head. "There a possible connection with trafficking illegal aliens. Some evidence for that, so far nothing more."

Through the sheriff's open window, the wind carries the sound of a truck horn on the main drag. Whicher thinks of Creagan, turns to Doctor Schulz. "Ma'am, the group of Hispanics at the Channing Ranch—did any toxicology test take place?"

"Tox reports can take a week or more," she says. "They're expensive and we know they weren't poisoned. We know how they died."

"Could you run tests?"

The sheriff looks at him sharp. "What's on your mind?"

"There's a chance the victims could have traveled north by train. With freight loads."

"What's that have to do with toxicology?"

Deputy Alvarenga's watching from the side table, eyes still.

"Some of the loads could have been bulk chemicals."

"This is just an idea," Scruggs says, voice testy.

"If they traveled on loads Johnson brokered, there might be evidence of that."

Sheriff Barnhart leans in. "Meaning what? This guy Johnson gets them up country, to the border. That what you're saying?"

"They could cross the river on their own," Whicher says. "Hook up with hunting types that know the terrain. The US side, the man's a freight forwarder. All the rail traffic, he knows it, the road loads, the truck drivers."

Doctor Schulz puts down the report. She folds her arms over her chest.

"Could we still run tests for toxicology?" Whicher looks at Sheriff Barnhart, avoiding Scruggs.

"Son," the sheriff says. "I'd think that might not be real easy. We done buried the bunch of 'em yesterday..."

Chapter 15

Thirty minutes later, on US 83, Whicher leaves the highway north of Carrizo Springs, turning down the Crystal City exit.

The place is stretched out either side of a four-lane strip—typical small town Texas, dirt yards, palms, ranch style housing.

Todd Williams was the sole victim from the ranch remaining unburied, his mother broke, no way of paying for a funeral. So far, Williams was practically an unknown—twenty-something, a backwoods kid, minimal education, prospects zero. Only thing he had going was his skill at hunting and fishing. So far as the toxicology went, Todd wouldn't have ridden any freight train—the doctor could test, he'd come up zero.

Benita Alvarenga had tracked down Lindy Page. A former girlfriend of Todd's, if they'd been close there was a chance to get something on him. She'd called the manager at the diner Lindy worked at, arranged for Whicher to stop by.

He can see the eatery ahead at the side of the road—a Mexican grill, tin roofed with a stone-built chimney.

Three vehicles are out back—it's late afternoon, slack time. Whicher pulls in, parks. He steps from the Chevy onto the baking concrete lot, tar joins melting in the heat.

Inside the restaurant, the dining room's dark, A/C running, ceiling fans sweeping the air. A few people sit at tables, they shift to look at the big man entering. Suit and tie and a hat, all business.

A middle-aged Hispanic in a white shirt steps from the counter. "*Señor*," he says.

"United States Marshals Service. I'm here to see Lindy Page."

The man looks at him.

"Sheriff's department put in a call. Arranging for me to see her."

The man nods.

"Are you the manager?"

"Carlos Perales," he says, "I'm the owner."

"Does Lindy Page work here?"

"She works here, but she left, *señor*. She already left with a cop." Perales spreads his palms.

"What kind of a cop?"

"A guy in a suit."

"When was this?"

"Fifteen minutes."

"The guy show a badge? He show ID?" The ceiling fan turns cooled air. Whicher feels a line of sweat beneath the hat band.

"She was expecting police, *señor*. I told her take off, take the rest of the afternoon."

The marshal glances at Perales.

"They sent someone—and didn't tell you?" the man says.

He could ask what the guy looked like, asking would sound strange. "No problem," he says. "Thanks for your time."

Whicher walks out of the restaurant, stares down the street at the side of the main strip.

Meeting Lindy Page was routine. Talk with her, get whatever background. Instead of that, she's gone.

He opens up the Chevy, climbs in, sparks a cigarette. Starts the truck, rolls it off the lot.

He drives slow, searching left and right in the little streets. *How could somebody get there ahead?*

Marshals Service was investigating the death of Todd Williams. Their case, their deal, their leads. No other agency involved. Except for Dimmit County Sheriff. He smokes the cigarette, cruising slow.

Traffic's light. Farm workers in pickup trucks—junk sedans, kids hanging out the window.

Ahead on the road, he sees a sign for Zavala County Sheriff. He hits the blinker, turns in, heads over to a single-story brick building—the law enforcement center.

Maybe it's just a crossed wire. He could check no local cop wanted to see her?

He pulls up, stares at a payphone on the side of the brick building. Something tells him not to go inside.

He could call Deputy Alvarenga, in Carrizo Springs. See if she had a home number?

If he called, he'd have to tell her why.

Perales. The restaurant owner ought to know.

He climbs out of the Chevy. Taps his pocket down for change.

⋏

Ten minutes later he steers onto a cement driveway fronting a run down, one-floor property, the east side of town. A battered mail box on a post reads—*Page*.

In the driveway is a ten year old Chrysler Town and Country. Beneath the branches of a Mexican white oak, a bunch of molded concrete deer graze motionless in the yard.

A woman is at the window. Heavy-face, dark hair running to gray. She pulls back the drapes, staring at Whicher, the truck on her drive.

He climbs out.

The front door's opening.

He walks around the station wagon, the woman steps out.

She's middle-aged, fifty pounds overweight. On her crumpled T-shirt is a butterfly motif. "What do you want?"

"US Marshals Service," Whicher says. "I telephoned, there was no answer."

She stands in the door frame, out of breath. From inside the house a TV's blaring.

"I'm looking to talk with Ms Lindy Page."

"Lindy?"

"She your daughter, ma'am?"

"What did she do?"

The marshal steps toward the house. "She didn't do anything. It's about a former boyfriend."

The woman's face hardens. "Todd Williams," she says. "That son of a bitch."

"Is Lindy here? Is she in the house?"

"No. And she don't know squat about his ass." She glares at Whicher. "What do you want with her?"

"Just some background. Did you know Todd was shot?"

"Whatever he done, it all ain't nothing to do with her."

"You have any idea where Lindy's at?"

"She'll be working."

The marshal feels a tick in the pit of his stomach. "She's not there."

The woman rolls her eyes. "I'm not her God damn keeper." She folds her arms across the butterfly motif. "There's a roadhouse out on 83. The Silver Dollar. She'll go there."

"Anything else? Friends?"

"She supposed to be someplace?"

Whicher doesn't answer.

"She has a friend—Shanon. Out on West Nueces. Shanon Summers."

"You have the house number?"

"It's right the other side of town. Red house, out near the highway."

"Shanon Summers."

"Don't ask me to pretend none," the woman says. "I heard about it, I ain't sorry."

"You didn't care for Mister Williams?"

Her laugh is bitter. "I done told Lindy something would happen."

"Did you know him?"

"Met him two times, once was enough. I said his ass wasn't nothing but trouble. Lookit how it turns out."

"If Lindy comes by," Whicher says, "you be sure and tell her I called."

He turns, walks back to the truck.

"If you want to know about Todd Williams—it's Zach Tutton you be needing to ask."

"Say again?"

"Tutton. Zachary God damn Tutton. Lives out the other side of Comanche Lake. Him and his old man got a farm."

"What's this have to do with Todd?"

"Lindy went out there with Shanon, they used to hang around there, the bunch on 'em. Zach Tutton and Todd was friends."

Whicher climbs in the truck.

"Comanche Lake," she calls out. "Go on and ask out there. You leave Lindy be..."

Whicher pulls in by a red clapboard house on West Nueces Street. He lifts the radio transmitter off the dash hook. Hits the call key.

He waits while the dispatcher at Dimmit County tries to find his boss at the courthouse. Lights a Marlboro, cracks the window. Listening to the static hiss.

"Scruggs. Go ahead."

"I ran into a problem," Whicher says. "Lindy Page. She wasn't there."

"I thought you'd be done with that?"

The marshal stares across an evergreen hedge grown into mesh-wire fencing. "No sir. I'm still out looking for her. The manager at the grill told me Lindy left—with a cop."

"A cop?"

"That's what the man said."

In the yard of the house, the grass is thin, a few shrubs sit by a five hundred gallon propane tank.

"I took a ride around," Whicher says, "looking. Called in at her mother's. Lindy wasn't there."

Scruggs is quiet on the end of the line.

"I could check with Zavala County Sheriff? Somebody there might be talking to her?"

"She probably just ran out," Scruggs says. "Happens a lot, unreliable types. She's most likely slacking off work using you for an excuse."

"You think?"

"I say leave it. I have to head out, anyhow."

"You're headed out?"

"Customs office in Eagle Pass. Thought I'd see if I can't dig out something on this guy Merrill Johnson."

"I thought you weren't buying Johnson?"

"I ain't. I called up Customs, anyhow. They have a bunch of records on him, shipment transactions, types of business. Now that I talked with 'em, I want to know."

A side door swings open at the house. A girl steps out, blond, pale. Wearing a green and white sundress. She moves into the yard.

Whicher sits up in the driver seat, looking across the hedge.

The girl reaches for something behind the propane tank. A wheelchair. She catches hold of it, rolls it backward, turning, pushing it toward the house.

Scruggs's voice crackles on the line. "There ain't a bunch we can do about Lindy Page not showing. She's not accused of any crime."

"Alright, sir. I guess you're right."

"I'll go check out the customs record on Johnson, see what they got. I'll meet you back here tomorrow, in Carrizo Springs." Scruggs clicks out the call.

In the yard, the girl positions the wheelchair close to the door. She brushes dust from it. Finally she turns, sees the Chevy outside her house, Whicher sitting inside.

He puts out the cigarette, steps down from the truck. Sets straight his hat. "Shanon Summers?"

She's the right age, early-twenties. Low-key pretty.

"I'm a US Marshal. Looking for Lindy Page." He takes the badge from his jacket. "It's about Todd Williams, Lindy's mom said she might be here."

She walks to the pipe steel garden gate.

"You know about him?"

"I know he's dead."

She opens the latch, steps out on the sidewalk looking at Whicher, eyes wide-set in her face. Pale eyes. Watercolor blue.

"Is Lindy here, miss?"

She shifts her weight on one foot. "There's just my dad and me. He's not real mobile. I take care of him."

"Lindy's mother mentioned a bar, a roadhouse. The Silver Dollar? Out on 83."

"She'll be working at the grill."

"I tried it," he says. "She's not there."

"Oh." She holds her elbows, uncertain.

Whicher glances at the wheelchair in the yard. "I ask you something?"

She looks at him.

"How'd Lindy take it? Todd's death."

"She was upset, if that's what you mean."

"Did you know Todd?"

She shakes her head. "Not really."

"How about a guy named Zach Tutton?"

A hunk of blond hair falls forward onto her face. "I know Zach."

Whicher thinks of hitting the highway—heading out, checking the roadhouse. "You think Zach Tutton would be a guy to ask—for background on Todd?"

"Maybe."

"They were friends? Could Lindy be out there?"

"With Zach?" She takes a step back. "No."

"It's some farm, right? Near a lake. Comanche Lake?"

"It's right out in the brush."

The marshal nods. "Think you could show me?"

Chapter 16

"This here track run all the way to the river?" A low sun sits above the mesquite as Whicher steers along the grit road. He looks at Shanon Summers in the passenger seat. She doesn't answer.

Set back from the track is a cluster of old-growth trees, Texas live oak, sugarberry. He sees an opening in the mesquite. "That the place?"

She nods.

The marshal slows the truck, steering into a small clearing.

A rutted gravel path leads beyond the trees.

Whicher cracks the driver window. Above the truck noise, dogs are barking somewhere. He steers by a thicket. Across the scrub is a group of wood slat barns.

To one side of the barns is a house built of river stone. Three dogs are running out, German Shepherds, teeth bared.

The farm's deserted, weeds grown high, no vehicles, no stock, no grazing animal.

"Kind of place is this?"

"I don't know," Shanon says. "The family had it a long time."

They reach the group of barns, dogs snarling, jumping around the truck.

Whicher parks by up the house.

"There's just Zach and his old man," Shanon says. "We'd come out late, after the bars closed. Listen to music."

Inside the house no lights show, despite the dusk.

"What's Zach do?"

"I don't know, they just kind of live here."

Whicher cuts the motor. "I guess I'm going in. If you want to stay here, it's okay."

"I'll come."

He opens the driver's side, dogs circling. "Walk steady, don't let 'em see you're scared."

The dogs fan out, growling. Whicher knocks at a battered door. He tries it, it's unlocked.

The door opens onto a mud room, a mess of boots, garbage. Jackets hung from wood pegs. They step inside.

A second door opens into a kitchen. There's a gnarled-looking table, dirty refrigerator. Every surface covered in junk, old papers, piles of rag.

"*US Marshal*," Whicher calls out. "*Anybody home?*"

No answer.

"What made Todd Williams friends with Zach, you think? They hunt, fish? There's a lake close to here, that right, Comanche Lake?"

She nods. "Todd was in high school a while, they met then."

"Only a while?"

"He was kicked out a lot, I think he moved one place then another."

Whicher steps into the worn-down kitchen, smell of mold and grease thick in the air. "What y'all talk about?"

"I don't know."

"You don't know?"

"Movies. Stuff. Getting away from here..."

Outside in the yard, the dogs are still barking, hollow-sounding.

Whicher steps through the kitchen into a front room. "Anybody home?"

Through the grime on the windows, he sees the scrub grown right up.

There's a noise—a door slamming. He steps back into the kitchen.

In the mud room, a man in a plaid shirt is toting a shotgun, face tight. "What the hell y'all doing in my house?"

Beneath the John Deere cap, his eyes dart from Whicher to Shanon in the sundress.

"I'm a US Marshal."

The man's raw-boned, cords tight in his neck. He steps in the kitchen. Skin at his throat reddened. "I want to see a God damn badge..."

The marshal lifts a hand, slips out his ID, holds it open.

"The hell y'all mean a-coming in here? This all is private property..."

"Looking for the owner. The door was unlocked, no answer when I called."

The man lowers the barrel of the twelve-gauge. "What do you want?"

Whicher takes him in; around sixty, skinny, the hard dry look of an outdoor man. "You have a son—Zach? Like to talk to him."

The noise of the dogs is broken up now, a ragged burst then silence.

"He was friendly with a young man name of Todd Williams, that right?"

Tutton's jaw clamps shut at the name.

"Todd Williams was murdered four days back. Did you know that? My office is investigating." Whicher glances around the squalid kitchen. "Is your son here, Mister Tutton?"

The old man cuts a look at Shanon. He doesn't answer.

"A homicide inquiry, people are expected to cooperate."

Tutton's hands move on the shotgun. "I don't like a bunch of folk bustin' in on my property."

"I can get a warrant, come back. I'm only looking to ask a couple questions. You want me to get a warrant, I'll do it. Take the place apart, if I've a mind to..."

The old man whips around on his heel, disappearing into the mud room. He bawls at the dogs; *"Shut the hell up."*

Out the kitchen window, Whicher sees Tutton stomping up the yard.

Shanon steps by him. "I'm not staying in here..."

Whicher follows her outside.

Tutton's striding by a barn, shotgun in hand, the dogs running in his wake.

"I'll take a look around," Whicher calls, "if you don't object..."

The old man steps out of sight around the back of the property.

Beyond the barns are live oak and cottonwoods, their leaves moving above the scrub. Something in the branches catches at Whicher's eye—low sun shining on strips of wire hung out in lengths. He's seen something like them before. He walks ahead, staring. *Improvised antennae.* Wires strung high in date palms—he's seen it before out in the desert, in the Gulf. Antennae for radio.

He turns back, walks to Shanon at the open door of a barn.

He steps inside, onto fresh straw, finds a stand-pipe, cranks it open. Water runs out. He cups a handful, smells it. It's clean. "When you came out here, you and Lindy and Todd, where y'all hang out? Back there in the house?"

"No," she says. "There's a little barn, Zach has his stuff."

"What stuff?"

"I can show you."

They walk up through the yard to a wooden shack. Shanon steps inside.

There's a mess of old couches, a table, empty beer bottles, cigarette papers. Along one wall is a stereo. Hi-Fi—expensive-looking.

"This it?"

"We just listened to music, drank some beer. No big deal." She stands in the center of the room, sweeps back a lock of blond hair.

Whicher steps over the stained rug, studying the music system. There's a deck, an equalizer, valve-driven amps, a limiter. A stack of speakers good as anything he's seen.

At the far right of the speakers a drape hangs from a wooden rail. The marshal pulls it back. A door's set into a rough frame. "What's this?"

"I didn't know that all was there..."

Whicher tries the handle. It opens.

CHAPTER 17

Zachary Tutton sits with his back to the door, unaware of people entering the room. His hair is long, mid-brown, greasy. He's wearing a pair of closed-ear headphones, leaning forward in an operator's chair.

In front of Zach are rows of amplification units—rackmount tuners, strips of dials and switches.

Whicher studies the young man—thin shoulders, curving back, a dirty, long-sleeve top. The jeans have a sheen of grime. But the sneakers are new-looking, fresh from a box.

The air in the room is hot. Fans whirring on amps, receivers, transformers. It's like the comms unit of a mobile ops post.

Shanon Summers steps a pace into Whicher's sightline—eyes bugged, seeing it all for the first time.

Zach senses movement, spins around, pushes back sharp in his chair. He rips off the headphones, "Shit, man..."

"US Marshal," Whicher says.

Zach stares at Shanon, eyes startled, skin taut across his cheeks. "What're y'all doing here?"

"Looking for Lindy Page," Whicher says.

"Lindy?"

"It's about her boyfriend, Todd."

Zach clutches the arms of the chair.

"I was up to Crystal City, couldn't find her," Whicher says. "Somebody mentioned your name. Miss Summers here helped me find my way over."

"I didn't think you'd mind," she says.

"Lindy's not here..."

"You have any idea where she's at?" the marshal says.

"No." Zach looks at Shanon. "She'd know better'n me."

"It's you I'm asking."

He puts a foot on the ground. "I don't hardly know her even..."

"But you do know Todd. You know—about what happened?"

"I heard he was shot."

"What else you hear?"

He stares at his knees. "Well, nothing."

"He was found with a bunch of wetbacks—out in the brush. You ever hear he might have been involved with something like that?"

No reaction.

"You need to think real careful," Whicher says.

"He was working as a guide, the huntin' camps. Is what he told me..."

Shanon rubs the back of her bare arm. "That's what he told Lindy."

Whicher studies Zach—thin, lank, awkward in his own skin. Not hard to picture him friends with a guy like Williams. "You see much of Todd lately?"

Zach scratches at his hair.

"When was the last time?"

"Couple weeks."

The marshal stares at the equipment, glowing in the darkened room. "What's all this gear, radio? You got a license?"

"I'm qualified, got my papers, an' all."

"What else you do?"

Zach looks at him.

"You have a job?"

"I help out."

"Doing what? I don't see any animals, crops..."

"It's rented out—all the land."

"That's how you make a living?"

"There's a bunch of it," Zach says. "From here, on out to the river."

The marshal scans the gear. "Who you talk to with that stuff?"

"All kinds of people."

"Folk here?"

"Yeah."

"In other countries?"

"It depends on the signal."

"How about Mexico?"

The young man shifts in his seat.

Whicher looks at him. "I saw that bunch of wires in the trees yonder. How come you don't have a regular mast?"

Zach loosens the headphones at his neck. "Pop won't have one, land this flat. There's a risk of lightning, anything up high." He looks at Whicher, needle starting to creep in. "Are you here to search the place? You got a warrant or somethin'?"

"Maybe time I got one," Whicher says. "Now that I know the way, I guess I can come on back."

The headlight beam of the Chevy falls like a rolling wash on the deserted county road. Whicher steers through the dark, windows open. Smoking on a Marlboro Red.

The land's empty under a moonless sky—he thinks of people, silent people walking through the night, one behind another; spirits from a shadow world.

Ahead is Crystal City, lights winking over the high scrub.

He searches for the turn, for the road to skirt the edge of town south.

Shanon Summers watches from the passenger seat.

He takes a hit on the cigarette. "Pretty quiet?"

He blows out a stream of smoke, asks himself when he's going to quit. The Gulf, he had an excuse, everybody smoked. Year down the line, things ought to be different.

"I was thinking on Lindy," Shanon says.

"I'll get you home. Head down 83, stop by that road-house. Maybe she went out there, after all."

"You want me to come?"

"It's on the highway, The Silver Dollar? I reckon I could find it."

Beyond the cemetery the turn is coming up. He slows the truck, steers off the county road.

"I guess I don't really understand any of this," Shanon says. "Todd getting killed an' all."

Whicher flicks ash out the window, warm air buffeting through the cab. "Were they close? Lindy and him?"

"Not really. They pretty much broke up."

"They broke up?"

Shanon stares out the window at a warehouse—stacks of empty palette crates caught in the headlight beam. "Around here," she says, "a lot of things don't amount to much. People hook up. It works out, it don't."

At either side of the lane lights show from houses. They're coming into a run down subdivision.

"The thing I don't get?" she says. "People crossing the border is nothing here, nothing at all. It's every night of the week." She wraps her arms around the thin fabric of the sundress.

"Seven people don't get killed."

They drive the blocks of the subdivision. Big tires whining in the night air.

"I didn't know it was that many," Shanon says.

Whicher grinds the stub of the cigarette. "You need to keep that to yourself. I don't know how much of that all went public..."

At the corner of the last block is a sign for West Nueces Street. He turns out onto the dead-end lane.

Either side of the road is deserted, cars and trucks in their owners' yards. Except for one. Fifty yards down. A lone sedan.

Whicher pulls up by the hedge at the side of the red clapboard house. "There be somebody home?" Light from the street catches the frame of the wheelchair by the house. "Your old man be alright?"

"He's okay."

"What happened to him?"

"He got in a car wreck."

Whicher rests his hands on top of the steering wheel. "I'm sorry to hear that." He looks over at her. "'Preciate you helping out."

"I don't mind."

"One last thing," he says. "Did Lindy have somebody else?"

She gazes at the lit-up dials in the dash.

"She's not on trial," he says.

Shanon gives a little snort. "You don't know folk round here."

He stares out the windshield at the empty lane.

"You want to go somewhere?" she says quickly. "After..."

He turns to her.

"After you get done?"

He looks at her in the passenger seat of his truck. Fingers tracing the green and white pattern down her dress.

"Probably not a good idea."

"Oh."

She tilts her head.

"Me being a cop."

"That all you are?"

He smiles. "Maybe not all."

She looks off into the dark along the sidewalk.

"You could do a lot better than me," he says.

"You think, around here?" She opens the passenger door, steps out.

He sets the Resistol forward.

"You know," she says, "you scared me a little. When you put it like that—seven people getting killed."

"Miles from here," he says. "Out in the brush."

"Well." She swings the door shut. "Goodnight."

Whicher nods, drops the truck into drive.

He steers from the curbside down the empty subdivision, takes another smoke out of the pack. He lights up, rubs a hand across his jaw, settles at the wheel.

In his rear-view a set of headlights snap on.

He screws his head around, checks—it's the sedan from the street, nothing else is moving.

At the end of the block he makes a right, heading south.

Thirty seconds later, the sedan lights are pulling out from the junction—turning out behind him.

He stamps on the brakes, locks the wheels.

In the rear-view he sees the headlights dive.

The sedan's stationary.

"Jesus Christ," he mutters. A snatch of tire smoke curls in the open window.

He clamps the cigarette in his mouth, cranks the steering, floors the gas—whipping the Chevy round till it's facing the opposite direction.

The headlights on the sedan glare at him along the street.

He shifts his foot on the throttle, the motor picks up under the hood.

The sedan pulls out, front wheels spinning.

Whicher feels his breath stop—the car barrels toward him on a straight collision course.

He yanks the steering, braced for the hit.

The sedan mounts the curb, a blur of metal speeds by—inches from him, over the yard of a house.

Whicher freezes the image—a Buick Le Sabre, windows dark, male driver in a suit. He turns the Chevy in a circle, ditches the smoke.

The tail lights on the Buick disappear up a side road.

He hits the gas, heart hammering in his chest. At the turn, he follows the Buick—it flicks right into another side street, fast, tight, in control.

Whicher floors it out, gripping the wheel, tearing along the road to the next turn. The road's narrow, scarcely lit. No Buick. He keeps his foot in, speed climbing.

Ahead is a blind bend—he snaps the steering, pinning the truck in a drift.

Out of the turn, the lane's full dark, no lights, no sign of the Buick. He feels his gut twist, slows at an intersection, staring down each side road in turn.

Moments pass, thirty seconds, a minute. No sign.

He comes off the gas, listening through the driver window.

Nothing but the beat of cicadas in the night air. Low rumble of the highway in the distance.

CHAPTER 18

Thirty minutes driving around Crystal City—no sign of a Buick LeSabre.

A full thirty minutes, working the grid streets, the town practically deserted.

Somebody'd known. They'd known he'd be there. They'd waited outside Shanon Summers's house, followed him when he left—no chance he could've missed it.

He'd left Crystal City.

Five minutes out of town he found the bar on US 83, The Silver Dollar. Inside, three women about the right age. But none of them were Lindy Page.

He sat out in the lot, smoking, watching the highway from the truck.

He could go home to Laredo. An hour and a half, he could be there.

But he wouldn't sleep. He'd think of the Buick, driving flat out, missing by inches. He thinks it over, thinks of Zach Tutton with all his comms gear in that shack. Zach

Tutton knew; he knew or he would've guessed—Shanon needed a ride home.

Across the lot, on the wall of the roadhouse is a payphone.

Whicher slides out, walks over, feeds in quarters, dials Maverick County Sheriff.

A duty officer picks up.

"Deputy Marshal Whicher—is Miguel Carrasco still in the building?"

There's a pause on the line. "INS closed up an hour ago. I can leave a message in his office?"

"Can you tell him I want to see him? I'll call again, tomorrow."

"Alright, marshal."

Whicher replaces the receiver.

In the desert sky, he sees the lights of Eagle Pass, forty miles away. Beyond it, Piedras Negras.

He thinks of Randell Creagan, killed, chained to a freight car.

Somewhere in one of those two cities.

⋏

Eric Kessler's on the porch of the house in Eagle Pass. He's slouched in a plastic chair, head on his chest as Whicher pulls up.

At the neighboring houses, Hispanic families are cooking out, talking, gathered in groups. Whicher parks, shuts off the motor. Steps down from the truck. In the yard is a Mercury Cougar, as well as the Trans Am.

Eric rouses himself. He pushes back his chair, stands, unsteady. "That you? What you doing down there?"

The marshal walks to the porch, climbs the wooden steps.

Eric's beard is longer, the table stacked with bottles. He picks one up—holds it out.

Whicher takes it. "I was in town."

Eric flops back in his seat. "Yeah, man. Good to see you..."

Whicher eases into a chair, pops the cap, takes a pull at the beer. He stares out from the raised porch—across the river, lights of Piedras Negras on the other side.

He reaches in his pocket for the pack of Marlboros. Flips them onto the table. "You want one?"

"No, man."

Whicher lights up. Music drifts from the neighborhood houses. Eric watches him in the light-spill.

"How you doing?" the marshal says.

"Same as ever. Pretty much like shit."

A car rolls along the street—four Hispanics in a cut down Camaro.

Neither man speaks for a minute.

"I was down in Brownsville," Whicher says.

Eric shifts his weight in the seat, denim shirt creased like it's off the floor.

"My boss sent me down to research something. About a guy I saw getting shot."

In the half-shadow, his friend's face is gaunt, cheeks sunken.

"It turns out this guy had a record. A little piece on file. He was arrested trespassing in a research facility, down in Brownsville."

Eric makes a face.

"He had a son born. A son that died, at birth." Whicher pulls himself straighter in the chair. "I talked with a professor down there she told me about a spate of births with serious defects, fatal defects. They're working in toxicity, that's their research field. I called her up again yesterday, asked her did she know anything about guys coming back from the Gulf?"

Eric's mouth clamps shut.

"I didn't mention any names, I just asked what she heard. Anything about people coming back, problems and such. She said enough cases have been seen for it to be noticed."

His friend reaches for the pack of Marlboros. He lights a cigarette with a kitchen match.

"No hard evidence. But a pattern of illness."

Eric leans forward, shoulders bunched beneath the crumpled shirt. He stares at the floor, holds his hands between his knees. For a long time, he barely moves.

He sits staring down, smoke curling up into his face. "Nobody ever said that..."

Along the street, a Hispanic family cooks out on a griddle at the side of a house. Kids fooling, laughing, catching a softball. Whicher rolls the beer around the bottle. "They have now."

Behind Eric, the front door opens—a shaft of light arcs from the house.

Karen Kessler steps out.

She's dressed in a business suit, streaked blonde hair pulled tight off her face. She takes a pace forward, face made-up, a little stark—just as hard as Whicher remembers it.

Her red lips part at the sight of him. "Hello, John."

He stands.

She steps to him, leaning forward, kissing his cheek, a beat too long. Up close her scent is heavy. A rich perfume.

She steps back. "Look at you."

"Long time."

"Isn't it?"

"You like the hat?"

"Not really."

Eric slumps at the table, cigarette in his mouth.

"I was working nearby," Whicher says. "Thought of swinging in. Eric was out here..."

"Oh, he's always out here."

"I should've called."

"There's no need."

Whicher runs an eye up and down her suit. "Still in realty?"

She nods.

"How's business?"

"I'm working double shifts to make half the sales." She cuts a look at Eric. "There's really not much of a choice."

"Day and night," Eric says. "Ain't that right, honey?"

Karen breathes a constricted little sigh.

"Maybe I ought to come by another time..."

"No," she says, "don't do that. Stay. Talk about the old days." She touches Whicher on the sleeve. "Remind him who he used to be." She turns, walks down the porch steps to the Cougar in the yard. "I have to head out, show a property to a client..."

Eric tips himself back in the chair.

Karen opens up the car, gets in, fires it up.

"I guess things have been pretty rough on her..." Whicher says.

Karen guns the car off the yard, headed into downtown.

At the neighboring houses, people watch as she drives past.

"Kind of late for a viewing," Whicher says.

Eric stares at him. "You think you could make a couple calls for me? Old times sake."

"You want me to call the professor—down in Brownsville?"

Eric shakes his head. "No, man," he says. "That's not it."

CHAPTER 19

Eagle Pass, TX.

In the parking lot of the Maverick County Sheriff's Department, Whicher finishes the last of a carry-out cup of coffee. He snaps on the lid, tosses it on the floor by the wrapper off a breakfast biscuit.

Sleeping on Eric's couch had been the best option, after they got done drinking. It was that or find a motel. Heading out had seemed a good way of getting busted by the Highway Patrol—or ending up in a bar ditch.

Karen came back late. He thinks of Eric asking him to check on her, like a PI. He told him no, left the house early, before anyone was awake.

From a side pocket in the driver door Whicher takes out a road atlas.

He flips to a page where he can see the position of the Tutton farm. Traces a line with his finger—cross country to Randell Creagan's trailers—on down to the Channing Ranch.

All three locations are walking distance from the border. He closes the map, straightens his tie. Steps out of the truck.

It's not yet nine, already the lot's half full. He fits the Resistol in place.

Entering reception he sees Hector Medrano.

"I need to see Miguel Carrasco. I left a message, last night."

Medrano looks among the notes on the counter.

"Is he here?"

"In his office..."

"I know the way." Whicher strides toward the corridor, not waiting.

Carrasco's door is open, the INS agent seated at his desk.

He looks up. "I got the note, *ese*."

"I come in?"

The man checks his watch.

"This won't take long." Whicher enters the small room.

Carrasco folds his arms across his chest.

"Who do we know in Piedras Negras?" Whicher says. "In law enforcement."

The INS man only stares, eyes black as coal.

"Tell you what I'm thinking, maybe you can give me a name? I got two US citizens murdered—plus five non-US."

"You're not investigating them..."

"I can't exclude them, they're part of it. You told me they were likely other-than-Mexican."

Carrasco points to a chair on the other side of the desk. The marshal sits. "You told me OTM, Central American. Different ball game, the stakes way high. I got somebody I'm looking at, a customs broker, connected with freight. They must know something across the border. Somebody in Piedras Negras must have a line on the people involved."

"Things are different over there, *ese*."

"They won't co-operate?"

"You mean the ones that aren't on the take?"

"People don't get shot, that's what you said. They hit trouble, they stick together with the *coyote*. If they're kicked out, they try again." Whicher leans back. Pushes a notepad over the desk.

Carrasco shakes his head. "Alvares." He writes the name on the notepad. "Alejandro Alvares."

"The guy have a number?"

The INS agent adds a number after the name. "He's in police intelligence."

"I mention you?"

"You can mention me."

The marshal takes back the notepad, staring at it a moment. "One more thing. Who was responsible for the zone around the Channing Ranch the night of the sweep?"

"Apart from you, *ese*?" Carrasco stands, reaches for a box file from a shelf on the wall.

He takes down the file, opens it up, flicks through the pages.

"Somebody might have seen something," Whicher says.

"We can't cover every inch, *ese*." The INS agent flips another page in the box file. "Raul Talamantes from Border Patrol," he says. "Deputy Hagen, from Dimmit County Sheriff. You. Your boss, Marshal Scruggs, at the eastern end. Plus Marshal Gale. Jim Gale."

"*He* was there?"

"He was a late draft, no particular section..."

"But he was out there?"

Carrasco nods. "He was backup, moving around in case of trouble. He could move quick—be wherever he needed to be..."

Crystal City, TX.

In Crystal City, the station wagon's gone, the beat up Town and Country. Whicher sits in the driveway thinking of Jim Gale.

He opens up, steps from the truck, walks to the front door. Molded concrete deer still motionless beneath the white oak in the yard.

He knocks hard. Hears a noise inside. Someone approaching. The door opens.

A young woman stands in the doorway, a twenty-year younger version of her mother. Hair dark. Rounded face. Just waiting for something to piss her off.

"Lindy Page?"

She looks him up and down. The suit and hat.

"Deputy Marshal Whicher."

Her face is clouded, small mouth closed.

"You and me were supposed to meet up yesterday afternoon."

She shakes her head.

"Dimmit County Sheriff's Department arranged it. How come you weren't there?"

"I don't have to talk to you."

He looks at her. "You know what this is about?"

Her eyes slide off him. "Todd." She stares out over the empty dirt yard. "I spoke with you people," she says. "I already did this."

"You spoke? With who?"

She presses her lips together.

Whicher reaches in his jacket, takes out the pack of cigarettes. He holds it out to her.

"I don't smoke."

He lights one up. *Earlier and earlier this is getting.*

Lindy holds herself in the doorway. Sweatshirt tight.

"Yesterday," Whicher says, "I turned up at that restaurant, your boss told me you done left. With a cop. If you did, you need to let me know who it was."

She shakes her head. "I don't know anything about what happened to Todd."

Whicher takes a pull at the cigarette.

"I talked yesterday," Lindy says. "I already said everything I know. They told me not to talk to anybody else. That's what they flat-out told me..."

"You don't talk to me I can arrest you. Take you in to the jail, till you do."

"There's reasons," she says, her voice shaky.

The marshal smokes the cigarette. Looks at Lindy, scared.

"You need to leave me alone," she says. "You go talk with whoever you God damn want. But leave me alone, you hear?"

He stares in her face.

She steps back. Slams the door closed.

⋏

Carrizo Springs, TX.

Reuben Scruggs's blue and white Ford Ranger is parked up in the courthouse square. Whicher leaves his Chevy at the curb.

He hurries inside the courthouse, passing through the lobby down the corridor to the back office.

Scruggs is seated at the desk with a ream of paperwork.

"You seen a pile like this here lately?"

Whicher takes off his hat, drops it on top of the metal file cabinet.

"Cargo manifests," Scruggs says. "Import export. Certification courtesy of US Customs, last night."

In the corridor is the sound of quick footsteps. Deputy Alvarenga appears in the doorway, citrus scent sweeping in the room. "Sheriff Barnhart wanted you to know Elaine Schulz is coming back in this afternoon."

Scruggs arches an eyebrow. "The autopsy doctor?"

"The sheriff took a call from Marshal Lassiter. He wants an update. Sheriff's asking if you could be present?"

"Is Quint Lassiter coming down here?"

"That's what he said." Alvarenga reaches into the front pocket of her uniform shirt. She takes out a square of paper, unfolds it. "Also, Brady Iverson called this morning, the real estate guy. He found Randell Creagan's bank account in his statement." She holds it out. "Southern Surety Bank. In Eagle Pass."

Whicher takes the paper from her, reads the details.

She waits in the door a moment.

Whicher catches her studying him—without the hat. "Can we get in and take a look?" he says.

"I can call the bank, find out?"

She backs out into the corridor.

Scruggs sits staring at the cluttered desk. "Lassiter..." he says.

Whicher thinks of the western district marshal turning up in Laredo, the night after the murders.

"It's his district," Scruggs grunts. "But the sheriff asked us, I believe. Not like we went looking."

"You think he wanted this, the investigation?"

Scruggs stares at the stack of papers on the desk.

Whicher reads a couple of the topmost sheets on the pile. "These are deals tied to Merrill Johnson?"

Scruggs nods. "Everything the guy brokered, the last two years. Man does a lot of freight with Jalisco and Mexico City. According to customs."

"Rail freight?"

"A lot of it's rail. Those are the manifests."

Whicher picks up a sheet. "Jalisco—that's a long way south."

Scruggs doesn't respond.

"If the autopsy doctor is coming in again, we could press for a time of death on Creagan?"

Scruggs nods. "We still need the place of death."

"If she can gives us the time, we could lean on Merrill Johnson. See if he can account for his whereabouts? He admitted knowing him."

Scruggs pulls at the collar of his shirt. "I talked with Vic Delossantos about Johnson. The idea of him helping Creagan make his little road trips. Bribing the right officials, that kind of thing. Vic's going to ask around at Border Patrol; they already have their eye on him."

"How about money changing hands between them?" Whicher gestures at the square of paper left by Benita Alvarenga. "Bank accounts?"

"I doubt they'd use accounts."

"We'd only need a couple definite links."

Scruggs shakes his head. "If Lassiter's coming down this afternoon, we need to show this thing has some clear direction."

Whicher steps to the file cabinet. "I think Jug Line Harris could give us something." He takes out Alvarenga's list. There's a contact number for Harris—a booking line for hunting trips up at the lake. He writes the number in his notepad.

Scruggs frowns. Leaning back in the chair.

"I did some searching around Crystal City last night," Whicher says. "Looking for Lindy Page."

"I thought she skated on you?"

"Her mother gave me the name of a friend—Shanon Summers. Told me go check a kid named Zach Tutton."

"These are people connected with Todd Williams? With Lindy Page?"

Whicher nods. "Zach Tutton lives out on a farm west of Crystal City, out in the brush."

"You talk with him?"

"He was out in a barn with a bunch of short wave radio gear."

Scruggs looks at him.

"Claimed he hadn't seen Todd in a couple weeks. Thought he was working the hunting concessions along the river. As a guide."

"You believe him?"

"Matter of fact, no. I didn't."

The older marshal makes a face.

"That radio shack could be something—some kind of comms room, a way of talking to *coyotes*. Different groups were out crossing that night. Zach Tutton could have been talking to them, helping 'em through."

Scruggs is silent, thinking it over.

"There's something else..."

His boss looks up.

"After I got done with Tutton, I had to drop the girl, Shanon Summers, back at her house. Somebody was waiting there. They came after me when I left."

Scruggs pinches his nose between a finger and thumb.

"They drove right at me. Then took off."

"You get an ID?"

"Buick LeSabre. I didn't get the plate."

Scruggs stands. He looks at Whicher a long moment, saying nothing. "We have to present something for Sheriff Barnhart and Quint Lassiter."

"Let me bring in Harris again."

Scruggs shakes his head.

"Zach Tutton. We could lean on him?"

"What about Lindy Page?"

"I went back this morning. Saw her. She refused to talk."

Scruggs's face colors up. "Go get in your truck, drive on back there. She talks. You arrest her if she won't. For obstructing my inquiry."

Whicher reaches for his hat. "You want to try for Harris?"

Scruggs glares at the floor. "I'll have the son of a bitch brought in."

"Deputy Alvarenga has the number, she knows where it is..."

"I'll call up Gale."

Whicher stops mid-stride.

"Go ahead, get the hell out of here," his boss snaps. "I'll have Jim Gale bring him in."

CHAPTER 20

Zavala County, TX.

Whicher hits the turn for Crystal City, powering the truck along the four-lane. He makes a left at the intersection with the main drag, scorched palms stretched out either side of the road.

At the next intersection, he sees a sign for Zavala County Sheriff.

The stop light's against him. He brakes. Stares along the side road at the brick law enforcement center.

He makes a right on red—parks, steps out, strides to the wall-mount payphone.

Taking the notepad from his jacket, he feeds quarters into the slot. He dials the number for Jug Line Harris—he could tell him to drive to Carrizo Springs; just bring himself in, ask for Scruggs or Benita Alvarenga.

The phone rings over and over. No answer.

Whicher slams it down, rattled.

What the hell was he doing?

Back at the truck he turns around, drives to the end of the street. He swings onto the main drag. Floors it out.

Up the road, he sees the restaurant, the Mexican grill.

He pulls in to the lot, takes a breath.

From a pocket in the door he finds a pair of cuffs. He steps out, crosses to the restaurant.

Lindy's setting tables. She looks up, shrinks at the sight of him. "I got nothing to say to you..."

The owner, Perales, moves out from the bar.

Whicher holds up a hand to him. "Two times I've come for you, Lindy."

"Leave me alone."

"You need to come with me, now."

"Hey," Perales says, "she hasn't done nothing, man."

The marshal doesn't look at him.

"I'm working," she says.

Whicher reaches for the cuffs. "This is a multiple homicide investigation."

She steps back. "I didn't have a thing to do with any of this..."

Perales moves closer. "Come on, man, her boyfriend was killed. Give her a break..."

Whicher gives the man a final look of warning. "Lindy Page," he says. "I'm arresting you for obstructing a law officer in the line of duty. Put your hands out in front of you..."

Carrizo Springs, TX.

On the upper floor of the Dimmit County courthouse, Whicher waits outside the holding cells. Deputy Benita Alvarenga approaches along the corridor.

"I'm going in and talk with Lindy," he says. "I'm just letting her cool down a piece."

"You read her her rights?"

He nods.

Under one arm Alvarenga's holding a document wallet. "You might want to see this." She slips it out. "It's from the Southern Surety Bank in Eagle Pass."

"That account? Randell Creagan?"

"I asked if we could take a look. They faxed a written agreement."

"They said yes?"

"Marshal Scruggs has gone to get a warrant, he wants full access."

Whicher thinks of Scruggs getting paperwork in front of a judge—he must be feeling the heat.

Deputy Alvarenga gestures at the cell door. "You think a female officer might do some good?"

"Be my guest."

She takes a set of keys from her duty belt.

Inside the cell, Lindy's sitting on a fold-out cot. Blank look on her putty-like features.

"Lindy. My name is Deputy Benita Alvarenga. I'm the officer you spoke with yesterday."

Lindy looks up. Mole eyes blinking in the light.

"We spoke about you meeting with the marshal here. He's going to ask you a few questions. I'm going to sit in."

"You do whatever the hell y'all want to." Lindy turns away to stare at the floor.

Whicher steps in the cell, leaning back against the wall. Arresting waitresses not among the reasons he joined the service. "This thing's about gone far enough," he says.

She twists her head an inch.

"You don't need to be here," he says. "I don't want you here."

She presses her small mouth shut.

"Why don't you just tell us what happened?" Alvarenga says. "Nobody's accusing you of anything."

"I already told him." She glares at Whicher. "I cain't. You people need to listen what I'm tellin' you..."

"You claim you spoke with a law officer," Whicher says. "You need to tell me who it was."

She puts both hands to her face.

"Lindy," he says. "We're trying to find out about Todd getting killed."

She rocks back and forth.

"Who killed him, and why."

She shoots up from the side of the cot. "I'm glad that little prick is dead. You think I give a God damn about his ass?"

Alvarenga looks at her.

"He was nothing but a mistake. You never made a mistake?"

"We think Todd was trafficking aliens," Whicher says. "Did you know about that?"

She crashes back down to the cot, puts her head in her hands.

"You've got to be smarter than this," Alvarenga says.

"If somebody approached you," Whicher says, "if a trafficker threatened you, we can protect you. We run the witness protection program..."

Lindy looks up, eyes shining. "I got nothing more to say to you people."

"It's not playing out like that, Lindy. You think this is a game?"

"Y'all don't even know what this is, you got no idea. I said all I got to. I want a God damn lawyer."

"Marshal," says Alvarenga. "I think we need to step outside."

⅄

At the take-out window of the roadside cantina down the block, Benita Alvarenga buys quesadillas. The store owner heats flour tortillas on a griddle, melting grated cheese. He spoons red salsa, peppers, guacamole.

Alvarenga faces Whicher. "Are we keeping Lindy? Are you going to charge her?"

"Scruggs wants her."

"Marshal Scruggs wants a lot of things today."

The vendor wraps the quesadillas, handing them over in paper napkins.

Alvarenga pays the man, passing one wrapped tortilla to Whicher. "She gets a lawyer. She interviews on record."

"We need her under pressure," Whicher says.

"We need rules of custody applied."

The marshal follows her to a bench, sits down at her side. He takes a bite, suddenly hungry. "You believe any of what Lindy has to say?"

"Tell you the truth—I think she's enjoying it. For once in her life, she's the center of attention. How often you figure that happens to a Lindy Page?"

The salsa, cheese and peppers are hot in Whicher's mouth. "Nobody seems to miss Todd Williams..."

Alvarenga chews slowly. "Except his mother."

"I talked with two of Todd's friends, Zach Tutton and Shanon Summers. Neither one of 'em was busted up. You think we're missing something? People that knew him better."

"I don't see he had a bunch of friends."

"Neither him, nor Randell Creagan."

"That bother you?"

He takes another bite. Thinks about it. "I don't know."

"We know Todd Williams had a job in Chicago," she says. "Plus he worked with Creagan, at that auto yard."

Whicher leans back into the bench. "Creagan drove trucks, ran hot cars. And trafficked people."

"You don't have to like them," she says. "Just catch whoever killed them."

Back in the courthouse, Benita Alvarenga picks up a pile of cargo manifests from the desk in the office. "What exactly is all this?" She pulls out a chair.

He eyes the stack of paperwork. "US Customs records."

"What're you looking for?"

He shrugs. "Bulk chemicals, maybe. Loads recorded coming in by rail."

"When Marshal Scruggs gets back, I have to speak to him about holding Lindy. Meantime, we could go through these. You want to give it a shot?"

He nods, sits on the side of the desk. "Keep an eye out for horse imports. Or imports by road."

She looks up.

"Merrill Johnson's into horses. A lot of horse transports are crossing the border."

"They'd never get people through that way."

"Maybe Creagan's name will come up," Whicher says. "The guy was a truck driver, Johnson knew him from that."

She shuffles the papers. "How far back are we going to look?"

He stares at the forms, eyes already blurring.

For ten minutes they work in silence—scanning each sheet, placing it in order on a separate pile.

Alvarenga glances up. "You really think Lindy's scared?"

"Something ain't right."

The deputy pauses. She takes another look at the sheet in her hand. Places it on the floor by her foot.

"What?" Whicher says.

Alvarenga's already staring at the next sheet. "Chemical and mineral. This one and the one on the floor."

"I take a look?"

She hands him both. "There's a third here," she says.

He reads through the listed information. A deal brokered through Merrill Johnson—the name prominent. Clearing US Customs at Eagle Pass. Exporting address given as a company in Jalisco, Mexico—maybe seven hundred miles south.

The manifest lists titanium oxide, plus assorted mineral pigments. For use in the construction industry. The marshal checks the other forms—all three the same, spaced at intervals a couple of weeks apart.

Titanium oxide was white, so far as he could remember. He could check. Mineral pigments—there'd most likely be a red. "There someplace we can make copies?"

"Xerox machine off reception—down the hall."

Whicher steps in the corridor, walking fast to the central lobby.

In a wall recess he sees a printer-copier.

He thinks of bulk chemicals—the most likely way to bring them up would be in hopper cars, sheeted over. There'd be space inside, space for people to get in. They wouldn't fill them, they'd never keep 'em on weight.

A sixty mile-an-hour train, running seven hundred miles—they'd be breathing dust, getting it on their clothes, their skin—eleven, twelve hours straight.

He opens the cover on the Xerox machine. Feeds in the sheets.

The main lobby doors open. Silhouetted in light from the square is the giant figure of Sheriff Cole Barnhart—palm straw hat tipped back on his head.

Beside him is Marshal Scruggs.

The copies arrive at the base of the machine, Whicher picks them out of the tray.

He steps out from the recess.

"I got the warrant," Scruggs calls over. "For Creagan's account in Eagle Pass."

Sheriff Barnhart breezes by toward the stairs.

"I want this executed, right now," Scruggs says, "before Marshal Lassiter shows up."

Whicher takes the signed paper.

"Look for large sums, any pattern of transaction that stands out for a low-life like Creagan. Go over the records with one of the clerks," Scruggs says. "And get a print-out." He looks at Whicher. "You get a hold of Lindy Page?"

"Upstairs. Arrested."

His eyebrows arch. "She talking now?"

"Asking for a lawyer."

Scruggs scowls.

"Deputy Alvarenga found something from customs," Whicher says. He holds up the Xeroxed sheets. "Records of chemical shipments by rail..."

"Head on up to Eagle Pass." Scruggs reaches in his jacket, pulls out an envelope. "By the way—I meant to give you this."

Whicher looks at it.

"It's a list of workers from the Laredo switching yard. Everybody rostered—the night you got jumped."

"I already got the names."

"This is the official list. I spoke with the boss of the yard, when I was kicking my heels waiting on Laredo court. I told him to get it done, else I'd come at him for lax security. Bring along Border Patrol."

Whicher takes it.

"You're so fired up about trains an' all, maybe it'll turn out something."

CHAPTER 21

Eagle Pass, TX.

The Eagle Pass bank is close to the river, not far from Eric Kessler's place. The top floor room is bare, featureless white walls, gray carpet—all attention focused on a row of computer screens.

A senior clerk waits at a desk to one side. Whicher scans the entries on the Creagan account.

Transactions are sporadic. A few hundred here, couple of thousand there—checks paid in, cash deposits. Creagan takes money out from time to time—small amounts, the kind a guy takes to the store.

There's nothing that stands out. No large sums, nothing that looks like it could be connected with Merrill Johnson. The balance on the account is less than three thousand dollars.

Whicher turns to the clerk. "We print off a bunch of this? Without violating the fourth?"

"I don't suppose the account holder will be complaining about an expectation to privacy."

"Considering he's dead," Whicher says.

"How far back do you want to run? I can check when the account was opened?"

Whicher pushes back the chair, making space for the clerk. He watches the screen switch to a list showing accounts opened, beginning with the most recent.

The clerk types *Creagan* into a search field. Another list comes up—checking accounts beginning the same fiscal quarter.

"February, last year," the clerk says.

He clicks onto the Creagan account. The screen shows a list of transactions, beginning with the opening balance.

"There's really not much here, I can print this whole thing it probably won't run to more than fifteen to twenty pages."

Whicher nods. "I'd be obliged."

The clerk hits a key. "Print room's downstairs, I'll go get it for you." He hits another key, the screen returns to the list of checking accounts. He steps out.

Whicher gazes around the room, thankful not to spend his days there. His eye comes to rest on the computer monitor.

Half way down the list for the February quarter is a name he recognizes. He sits forward. *Kessler, K.*

He reads the line over on the screen.

Karen Kessler. It's in Karen's name only. No Eric. It's not a joint-account.

He sits, immobile a moment. Then glances at the door, pushing it closed with a boot.

He clicks onto the account. Transactions listed are mainly sums of money paid in. Three to four hundred at a time. There are outgoing transactions, one regular every month since the account was opened. He looks at the name of the payee. An insurance company, *Moreland Life*.

Sixteen payments. Every month since the previous February.

He finds the close command, clicks it. The screen returns to the prior display.

He pushes back the chair from the monitor. Stands, looks out the window across the river.

The city of Piedras Negras stretches out before him. City of black stones.

⋏

Carrizo Springs, TX.

It's close to five o' clock as Whicher returns to the court-house square, afternoon light harsh. Wind is picking up, sweeping dust through the town. He thinks of Karen Kessler. Working double-shifts, selling realty. While her husband drank himself senseless.

Palm fronds bend and turn in the wind, shadows dancing on the Chevy hood.

Did Eric know about the account?

Whicher looks at Sheriff Barnhart's office, the window open. No sign of the man himself.

Marshal Lassiter was due in. Whicher picks a large envelope from the passenger seat, steps from the truck, locks it. Around the square he checks for San Antonio plates, any sign Lassiter's arrived.

He enters the courthouse, clips down the corridor to the rear of the building. Benita Alvarenga's in the office.

He dumps the envelope. "Print out of Creagan's account," he says. "Southern Surety Bank."

She reaches over.

"I didn't check every detail, but so far there's nothing ties him to Johnson nor anybody else."

"Let me look."

"Is Lassiter here yet?"

She nods. "With the sheriff. And Marshal Scruggs."

"Did Scruggs talk to Lindy?"

"He and I attempted to question her. She's claiming the fifth amendment, she needs a lawyer if she's going to keep this up."

The phone rings.

Deputy Alvarenga answers it. She lets the print-out from the bank rest in her lap. Listens a moment. Then replaces the receiver. "Looks like we're wanted," she says. "Upstairs."

Sheriff Barnhart is in his customary position at the window, cigar in hand. Marshal Lassiter sits wide-legged in a Tattersall shirt, fine gray Cattleman hat on the desk.

"We know where Todd Williams was killed," Scruggs says. "We know how, we know when."

Doctor Elaine Schulz reads from the autopsy summary. "Cranial gunshot. Soft-nosed, nine millimeter round. Fired at close range."

"The problem with Williams is finding sufficient background," Scruggs says.

"I thought this guy was local?" Lassiter cups an elbow, one hand at his tan face.

"Local, but pretty much a loner," says Scruggs. "Marshal Whicher here's spoken with the mother. We have a girlfriend in for questioning..."

Lassiter looks at the younger marshal. "This the bird that don't sing, army?" He shoots a grin.

"She's giving us the run around," Scruggs says. "Looks like somebody might've gotten to her. A trafficker, maybe." He glances at Benita Alvarenga.

The deputy nods.

Sheriff Barnhart blinks slowly, beneath the palm straw hat.

"We know for sure Todd Williams was a hunting guide—expert on the local terrain. Working *coyote* would be a fit..."

Whicher raises a hand. "There's the friend—Zach Tutton, guy I tracked down yesterday at the farm."

Sheriff Barnhart looks at Scruggs. "This the place up in Zavala County?"

"Yes, sir."

The sheriff taps his ash out the open window.

Scruggs checks his notes. "Coming to Randell Creagan, we got the opposite situation—we got a bunch of background, we still don't have place of death."

"We know he was killed with a different weapon," Doctor Schulz says. "Forty caliber Smith & Wesson."

"Creagan was found thirty-six hours after Williams," Scruggs says, looking at Doctor Schulz. "But time of death would be a step forward."

The doctor crosses her arms on her chest. "I'd put TOD almost certainly the night Todd Williams was murdered. Early next day at the latest."

"If we're questioning people for their whereabouts," Whicher says, "that night's legit for both murders? Potentially?"

"Something on your mind, army?" Lassiter says.

"Merrill M. Johnson."

"He's a customs broker," Scruggs says. "Admits to knowing Creagan. Laredo Border Patrol know the pair of them."

"Sheriff said you had another suspect, name of Boyd Harris?"

"Jug Line Harris. Known-associate of Creagan and Williams. Hunting, fishing type."

"Y'all interview him?" Lassiter says.

"Marshal Whicher arrested him on a misdemeanor," Sheriff Barnhart says. "He made bail. Didn't say squat."

"I left a message for Jim Gale to pick him up," Scruggs says.

Lassiter leans his head on one side, eyes coming to rest on Benita Alvarenga's shirt front. "I'll tell you, Jim's kind of ticked off. Getting stepped over an' all." He runs a hand through his silvered hair. "What're you thinking on this guy Harris?"

"One of the non-US victims was killed with a hunting rifle," Whicher says.

"This the thing you saw with that night scope an' all?"

"I think Harris knows something about it."

"Think he might've been the shooter?"

"I questioned him over rifles, he was evasive."

Lassiter nods. "Webb County Coroner have the body in Laredo?"

Doctor Schulz cuts in, "I spoke with the Coroner's Office—they have nothing at all for ballistics."

"Then we're not about to get a damn thing to tie him in," Lassiter says.

"We could take another look out there?" Whicher says. "Search for evidence."

Sheriff Barnhart sits forward at the window. "Y'all have Todd Williams, Randell Creagan and maybe Jug Line Harris as *coyotes?*"

"They have the background," Scruggs says.

"This Creagan feller's a known car thief and fence?"

"FBI were looking at him," Scruggs says. "Somebody in the bureau thinks he was running stolen cars across the border. Returning with aliens on false papers."

"Somebody?"

"They're not saying."

"Where does Merrill Johnson fit with this?" Lassiter says.

"Trains," Whicher says. "Johnson could be bringing up illegals; the likes of Williams and Creagan and Harris getting them over the border. Through the brush."

Lassiter looks at him. "You have evidence for that, army?"

Deputy Alvarenga lifts up a folder. "Johnson has a lot of transactions with US Customs."

"The guy's in freight."

"There's something else," Whicher says. "I talked with INS in Eagle Pass—Miguel Carrasco. He thinks the Hispanic victims were likely Central American. Not Mexican."

The room's silent. Whicher aware of Benita Alvarenga looking at him.

"There was no ID on any of those victims," Sheriff Barnhart says. "Proving that is going to be impossible."

"Johnson could have been bringing up people from way south in Mexico," Whicher says. "Laredo rail yard and Eagle Pass both handle imports of bulk chemicals..."

"We have some of the manifests from US Customs here," Deputy Alvarenga says. "Three with Merrill Johnson as broker."

Sheriff Barnhart plugs the stub of cigar into his mouth.

"I found evidence of chemical residue on discarded clothing at a hunting concession leased by Randell Creagan. A bunch of trailers out in the brush."

Doctor Schulz frowns. "There were no traces of any chemicals on the Hispanic victims."

"Illegal crossers change clothes," Alvarenga says. "Soon as they get on US soil. Border Patrol go for people that look a mess. They all know that."

"If we could show the Hispanic victims traveled up from the south," Whicher says, "if they traveled on freight trains, shipments brokered by Johnson, we'd have a heck of a lever."

"I told you," Doctor Schulz said. "There was no evidence for that."

"We weren't looking for it."

She gives him a cold-eyed stare.

"Say those people traveled in freight loads twelve hours straight. They would've breathed dust that entire time."

"I'm not sure exactly where you're going with this," the doctor says.

"Toxicology would show it—if their lungs bore any trace of chemicals from a shipment." Whicher points at the folder Deputy Alvarenga's holding.

"These people are already in the ground," Sheriff Barnhart says.

The doctor's face is tight. "Are you asking that an exhumation take place?"

Scruggs steps in. "No. We're not asking for anything of the sort."

"Seriously?" she says. "A disinterment?"

Scruggs cuts an angry glance in Whicher's direction.

"Damn if I want to be digging up folk we just buried," the sheriff says.

Marshal Lassiter picks at a snap on the cuff of his shirt. "It's your county," he says to the sheriff. "But I'll tell you one thing. I reckon army might just have something there. A bunch of people getting shot up? Dammit, Central American sounds about right."

"Y'all want me signing for a disinterment?" the sheriff says.

"It's your call," Lassiter says. "If it was mine, I figure that's what I'd be looking to do."

Chapter 22

The room feels warm, too close, full of trapped-in air. Whicher leans forward at the desk in the downstairs office. He takes off his jacket, swings it onto the back of the chair. Notices the envelope sticking out from a pocket.

It's the list from Scruggs—from the boss at the Laredo switching yard.

He thinks of Johnson. The chances of the sheriff disinterring the bodies were close to zero. He takes out the list, leans back in the chair. Scans the names, all of them meaningless. It's longer than the original list, set out with shift patterns, times, number codes he doesn't recognize. Payroll numbers, maybe.

A name stands out.

Jose Talamantes. Same family name as Agent Raul Talamantes at Carrizo Springs Border Patrol.

He turns to the file cabinet. Finds the number for INS, Eagle Pass, picks up the phone. He dials, checks his watch—six-thirty. The phone's ringing, nobody answers.

He sifts through his notes, finds the name of the Mexican police guy, the name and number Carrasco gave him. *Alvares—Alejandro Alvares.*

The phone's still ringing. Nobody there. Whicher replaces the receiver.

In the corridor is the sound of footsteps. He stands, looks out the door.

Benita Alvarenga is approaching. "They're done upstairs."

"What's going on?"

"Sheriff says we can keep Lindy Page on hindering an inquest. Class B misdemeanor."

He stands in the door frame. "She call a lawyer?"

"Doesn't have one, can't afford one. The court can appoint tomorrow."

"They talk about exhuming the Hispanic victims?"

"Doctor Schulz is against it. Sheriff wants to talk to the county attorney. Lassiter's stirring it up."

Whicher bites his lip. "He said he'd do it, if it was up to him. How about Scruggs?"

"I think he would. They're unidentified, unlawfully killed. The law says we have to find out." She meets his eye, doesn't say more.

"They done with us?"

She nods. "Scruggs has to be in court in Laredo tomorrow. They said we can go. Pick it up again in the morning."

⅄

A burnished disc of sun hangs above the feeder road into Eagle Pass. Whicher steers down the loop, skirting town to the east.

Dust is blowing over deserted lots, commercial units, car dealers—he slows as the road narrows, traffic starting to build.

He counts off the blocks, reading names off the street panels. People out in doorways, hanging on the sidewalks, around upturned crates piled with bottles and cans.

Eric would be waiting downtown. *The Southern Surety Bank.* What to tell him? That his wife had a bank account, she could be paying insurance, any number of things. And yet it wouldn't lie down.

He thinks of the date; February, a year back—they'd both been overseas. The ground war just starting in Iraq. He reaches the street, pulls to the curb by a block-unit, cement rendered, blacked out windows. He shuts off the motor, locks the truck. Heads for the door.

Inside is a dim room, A/C cranking out cold air. Eric's sitting at a bar counter, long hair pushed back off his face.

He's clean-shaved, wearing a laundered work shirt. Fatigue pants, hi-top boots.

He swivels on the stool. "Hey, man. What you drinking?" He signals the barkeep.

Whicher takes out a fresh pack of Marlboro Reds. "Lone Star." He slips out two. Lights them both.

The bartender brings a frosted bottle.

"They got a terrace up on the roof," Eric says. "You rather sit out?" He lays a bill on the counter. Slides off the stool.

Whicher takes the bottle, follows to a side door at the end of the room.

Outside is a worn steel staircase. They climb to a rooftop terrace, walls topped with scrolls of pre-cast cement.

They grab a table, sit facing out over the river.

At the corner of the terrace, a group of Hispanics sit drinking beneath a faded parasol.

Eric clinks the bottle against Whicher's. "Come on, you going to sink that? Having one of my better days."

"It work like that?"

Eric takes a pull on the cigarette, more light in his eye. "I don't know how it works."

Out across town, the noise of traffic drifts. Cars wait in line on the international bridge.

People are streaming back to Piedras Negras, day workers headed home. The marshal sips his beer, stares at the flat horizon over the city. Sky flecked with cloud. An amber light.

"What you looking at, man?"

Whicher shrugs. "The river. The border. The country, the whole thing."

"Come again?"

"Another life."

"You ever go over?" Eric looks at him. "To Piedras Negras."

A screech of train brakes is on the evening wind, mournful, sharp.

"You want to?"

Whicher looks at his friend.

"I could take you over. If that's what you want?"

Chapter 23

Piedras Negras. Coahuila, Mexico.

One phone call. A ten minute walk downtown on East Garrison. The port of entry, cars lined up under a rusting hangar roof. Everywhere, posted signs warn against the carrying of guns—the Glock is locked up, back in Whicher's Chevy.

On foot across the bridge—out over wasteground, the river down below.

Through the Mexican checkpoint—on into the big square. *Gran Plazo—la zona centro.*

Piedras Negras.

Tall palms stretch in an uneven row behind a dirty concrete gallery of tourist booths.

In one half of the drab square is a street market. Rows of stalls, bright fabrics. Hats and sunglasses in the evening light.

A Mexican in a cotton suit watches from a food stand. Already waiting.

Whicher walks on into the square with Eric, trying to shake the discomfort. Last time he'd crossed a line anyplace with Eric he'd been an armored cavalry scout. Nineteen-delta. Thirty men under his command. In M3 Bradleys. With co-ax and chain guns.

The man watching from the food stand is seated at a little counter, eating from a bowl, spoon in hand.

Whicher approaches. *"Señor Alvares?"*

The man stays the spoon. "You are the marshal?"

Whicher nods.

"You want something to eat?"Alvares gestures at the empty stool beside him.

Eric pulls a pack of cigarettes from his work shirt. "Why don't I take a look around a piece?"

Whicher sits beside the man at the stall. He watches Eric move into the market, stopping to look at the wares.

"Miguel Carrasco is a friend of yours?" Alvares says.

"Work friend."

Alvares nods.

"Six nights back, he ran a sweep operation picking up illegal immigrants. For INS and Border Patrol."

Alvares peers out into the evening gloom, watching Eric in the square.

"Did you know about the sweep? Five people trying to cross were killed."

Alvares dips his spoon into the bowl.

"Two women," Whicher says, "three men. All of them young." He searches the Mexican's face. "Along with five dead crossers, there was a *coyote*. An American *coyote*."

"You like spicy soup?" Alvares says. "Why don't you have some?"

"Miguel Carrasco says you work for police intelligence."

"You know, it's very good *menudo*." Alvares lifts another spoonful of the hot soup to his mouth.

"I got a couple names." Whicher leans forward. He lowers his voice. "Merrill M. Johnson. And Randell Creagan."

At the far side of the square a young woman approaches Eric from beneath a tree in a trash-strewn park. She's wearing a cropped skirt, blouse top open to the navel. Eric takes a cigarette from the pack in his shirt. He gives it to her. Looking without looking. She lingers a moment. Steps away.

"Creagan?" Alvares repeats.

"Randell Creagan."

The Mexican officer shakes his head.

"How about Johnson?"

The man nods.

"You know him?"

A moment passes, Alvares considering the question. "He's known." He shrugs his shoulders. "There are many *maquilas*—factories, along the border, señor. Twin plants. Assembly plants. Many *nortenos* involved. *Supervisores. Gerentes.*"

"You know him as a transport man? Freight man?"

"Why do you want to know this?"

Whicher shifts on the stool. "We know the guy does a lot of business—cross-border. I want to know about him here."

"*La zona*," Alvares says. "*La zona de tolerancia.* You know? Girls. Prostitutes."

"That's where he goes?"

"That's where all the *nortenos* go, s*eñor.*" He takes another spoonful from the bowl. "You are investigating these deaths?"

"I think some of the victims came from far in the south. Maybe riding trains."

"People come from all over, they don't need trains, s*eñor.*"

"People don't get shot up."

Lights are coming on across the half deserted square—in bars and cantinas.

"I have a question for you, s*eñor.* Your people have intelligence. Why don't you talk to them?" He finishes the *menudo* in silence. Puts the empty bowl and spoon down on the counter.

Alvares stands. He pushes money to the stall-holder.

Whicher follows the man a little way into the square.

They stand beneath the window of a hacienda; voices carrying from inside, smell of cooking in the air.

"A lot of people were caught in the sweep that night," Whicher says. "They were taken to the jail in Eagle Pass. From there, they VR'ed. They must have been recorded?"

Alvares gives a disbelieving look.

"They must have stayed places here, had rooms, stayed on floors. They had to eat, sleep, get organized. They must've had help..."

"They will be gone." Alvares points across the river. "Gone into your country. You have any money?"

The marshal looks at him.

"Try your luck in *la zona*."

Eric Kessler's watching, starting to walk from the market, toward the hacienda.

"If you're looking for Merrill Johnson, you're in the wrong place." Alvares points up the road stretching west from the side of the square. "Look in *la zona*. *Viajero*."

"*Viajero?*"

"It's a bar. The kind of place everybody goes. People from the country, the young ones, that's where they end up. If two girls were killed," Alvares says, "they could have come from there." He stares across the square, light almost gone from the sky, street lights flicking on.

"I mention your name?"

"No," he says, "you mention nothing, s*eñor*." His eyes meet Whicher's for the first time. "We never met."

⅄

The cab ride is two miles of dirt road out along the river. To either side, shacks, chain-link fences threaded with hub caps and rags.

The road twists and turns through dark scrub, passes factories—the *maquilas,* guarded by dogs.

The driver says nothing. He steers the battered LTD, radio blasting, wrecked cars abandoned left and right.

Finally, he slows at a compound out on its own—set apart in the empty brush.

Cement block walls surround a clutch of buildings, a dozen strong. The rough wall of the compound is painted a lurid pink.

The cab turns from the dirt road, through a gateway in the wall.

The *taxista* pulls up close to a small police office—like a bus station stall. A single light shows in its window.

Opposite are strip clubs, bars, a bunch of dingy one-floor cribs.

Whicher steps from the cab, pays the driver, Eric sliding out.

A uniform cop steps from the police stall. He watches, smoking on a small cigar, no expression on his face.

Eric's already headed toward a bar displaying a neon heart—*Viajero,* a sign reads on the wall.

Whicher follows. The tail lights of the cab disappear on the dirt lane.

The door of the bar is guarded by a gangbanger—security, thick-necked. Covered in jail-house art.

Inside, music's booming, the room dark, a bunch of women plus a handful of men. The men are mostly middle-aged, Caucasian—truck drivers, factory foremen, slouched over, drinking. In one corner is a group of college kids.

The girls are good-looking, in their twenties. Half-dressed, still getting ready for the night. They're drinking shots, smoking, fooling among themselves—hardly glancing as two more *nortenos* walk in.

A waiter steps from behind a counter. He's carrying two beers, plus glasses on a wooden tray. Canned Tecate. He gestures to a table. Standing, till he makes eye contact.

The marshal shakes his head. He points to the bar counter, strolling toward the scuffed-looking length of timber, climbing up on a stool.

The waiter takes the canned beer from the tray, he starts to pour. "*Lo que quieras.* You want something, you tell me. Romero." He points at his chest.

"Romero, got it." Eric winks at the guy.

Whicher pulls out a twenty dollar bill.

The waiter takes it, stepping back behind the counter, disappearing through a rear door.

Eric takes a slug at the beer. "Lot of Americans. I quit coming, since I married Karen."

Whicher surveys the room—a stage in back, heavy black drapes, a piece of scaffold bar rigged with lights. "I thought only losers came." He looks at Eric. "And fat old men with money."

"Guys working in the factories, where else they going to go? Ain't just the low-life."

Whicher shrugs.

"You name it, man," Eric says. "*La zona* caters to all walks. Businessmen. Politicians. Cops, judges."

The marshal looks at him. "You know that for a fact?"

"Way it is. *La vida,* life on the border."

Whicher stares out across the room.

A lone man at a table gets to his feet, unsteady, a girl at his side. She links arms with him, walks him out.

"So what's the deal?" Eric says. "Feel like making something happen?"

"Maybe."

Eric takes a slug at the beer. "Scout Troop all over again." He wipes his mouth.

"How's that?"

"In front of the forward line. You're not supposed to be here, are you? Officially."

Whicher doesn't answer.

"Don't tell me it don't remind you," Eric says.

"Does it make you feel like doing it again?"

Eric takes out a couple of cigarettes. Flips one at Whicher. "The army?"

"You seem better today."

"Like I told you, man. I'm up and down."

Whicher lights the cigarette. Thinks of Merrill Johnson, imagining him in the place—the neat suit, trimmed mustache, self-satisfied air. How to ask about him, without it standing out?

"Let's grab a table," Eric says.

Whicher takes his beer and a tin ashtray from the counter.

They cross the room, pick out a table between the bar and the door.

Two guys eye them—both heavy, in T-shirts and leather vests. They're unshaved, wired on something, like they haven't slept in a while. Drinking tequila, arms resting on a scarred up table.

A girl walks over, hips swaying to the music. Her eyes are feral—a wild cat, quick and watchful. She reaches the table, pulls out a chair close to Whicher.

She sits, leaning in, wrapping one arm around the other. "*¿Que tal?*" she says.

"Good. I'm doing good. *Estoy bien.* You speak English?"

"*Si.* I speak."

Eric grins at the girl from across the table. "What's your name, honey?"

"Tierra." She twists her body in his direction. "*Un trago.* Buy me a drink?"

Whicher turns toward the bar—the waiter already approaching.

"Cuervo," the girl says.

The waiter looks to Whicher.

"No. We're good."

"You like here?" the girl says. "You look for someone?"

"Yeah. I'm looking."

"No problem."

"No problem?"

"We can go somewhere, maybe."

He looks her over. *Tierra.* Pale skin, ebony hair. Her features are fine beneath the make up. He guesses she's around twenty.

She leans forward at the table, weight on one arm, her slim shoulder pushed sideways. "You like Mexican girls?"

Whicher nods, barely listening. An image flickers in his mind.

"Everybody likes Mexican girls," Eric says.

She gives a wide-mouthed smile.

The marshal stares at the smooth skin—taut at the top of the girl's arm. He thinks of a tattoo, a bird in flight. The dead girl at the ranch. "I'm looking for somebody in particular."

She cocks her head.

"Like you. But not as pretty."

The girl frowns.

"She has a bird. On her shoulder. A tattoo. A tattoo like a bird."

"Why you look for another *chica?*"

The marshal thinks, quick. "I told her I'd come back..."

She looks at Whicher through narrowed eyes.

The waiter brings the glass of tequila. He sets it on the table. Tierra snatches it up.

Another girl approaches, older, late-twenties—a scarf of red velvet tied in her short cut hair. *"Buenos noches, caballeros."*

Tierra inclines her head as the girl pulls out a chair by Eric.

"Speak English?" Eric says.

"Un poco."

"What's your name?"

"Lucila."

Tierra speaks to the girl in a rapid burst of Spanish—words flowing, Whicher can't understand.

Lucila sits very still a moment. Something in her face is troubled. She fires back a question, words and phrases too fast for the marshal to follow.

"Lucila..." he tries to catch her attention. "Do you know a girl—like Tierra? With a tattoo..." He points to the girl's bare shoulder.

Lucila's face is clouded. And then she meets his stare. "*Quizás.*"

"Maybe?"

The waiter approaches again from the counter.

Eric looks at Lucila. "Tequila, honey?"

She nods.

"Tequila, and two more beers," he tells the waiter.

Whicher offers his pack of cigarettes. Both girls take one. He tries again with Lucila. "You know a girl like her?"

"She left, *señor,*" Tierra says, flicking hair from her eye.

He nods, still looking at Lucila. "Left when? How long?"

"*Una semana.*"

A week ago.

"She's a friend?" Whicher says.

"*Sí.*"

"What's her name?"

A thought passes behind the woman's eyes. She shakes her head.

The waiter returns with two more canned Tecates, plus a bottle of Cuervo.

At the door to the bar, the uniform cop walks in. He glances at each of the tables, cigar butt in his mouth. Gaze resting longest on Whicher's table.

"Can you tell me the girl's name?" the marshal asks again.

"Why do you want to know?" Lucila says.

He lowers his voice. "I was going to meet with her. She was going to meet me—across the border."

Lucila's eyes are wide now. She takes a drink of tequila. "You are a *coyote*?"

He shakes his head. "Can you meet me somewhere?"

She takes a fast hit from the cigarette.

"Not here," Whicher says. "Can you meet me someplace else..."

Chapter 24

Two hours later. A fine rain falls on the run-down square at the top end of town.

Whicher sits with Eric Kessler beneath the awning of a street-side bar. Sipping more beer, smoking a pack of Delicados, the last of the Marlboro Reds gone.

Cars and trucks pass along the street, tires loud against the wet road.

People are moving on the sidewalk, the town filling up with the late hour.

Eric lifts the glass to his mouth.

Whicher studies his friend, bleary eyed now—drinking all day, deep into the night. Wind rucks up the side of the awning, water dripping from its frayed edge.

"Damn, I like Mexico," Eric says. "Get on a toot. Cheap chow, cheap booze. They finally kick my ass out of the army, maybe I'll come live here." He grins at himself.

Pulls a cigarette from the pack. Lights it, breathes the heavy smoke. "Damn it, maybe I will."

"How come you're living in Eagle Pass still?"

"It's where I grew up."

"Since your folks left..."

"The family left, so what?"

"Corpus Christi, you don't think you might like it?"

"The Texas Riviera."

"You don't think Karen might?"

Eric stares at the burning end of the Delicado.

Neither man speaks for a minute. More cars roll by out of the rain.

A trans-border bus out of San Antonio stops to let people off in the square.

"Reckon Karen will be wondering where you're at?"

Eric snorts a laugh. He looks at Whicher. "You really can't help me out any with her? With Karen, an' all."

He shakes his head. "I'd think it's none of my business."

"Thought you were an investigator?"

"You need a PI." Whicher sips the beer, thinks of heading back for the port of entry, the bridge. Everything would still be waiting in the morning—showing up beat, hungover wouldn't likely help.

"Why you need to talk with this girl, Lucila?" Eric says.

"She might give us a name. One of the victims."

"Y'all don't know their names?"

"Four went in the ground, we don't know who they were."

Eric looks at him.

"Law says we have to know," Whicher says.

"No shit."

"Nobody reported them missing, we got no ID. If I could find something..."

Eric runs a hand over his face. He stares at the cloth on the little table. "I saw a backhoe push bodies in a pit one time. Out in Iraq. Open grave. Ever see a thing like that?"

The marshal nods.

They sit in silence—mood descending. Rain swirling in the wind.

"I ain't saying I wished it was us. Our guys."

"I know that." Whicher cuts his friend a look.

"But a man's still a man."

A group of teenagers hustle down the sidewalk, pausing a moment to stare in the bar. They move on.

A taxi cab rolls in view.

It drives slow up the side of the square. Pulls in, rear door opening.

A woman steps from the back. She's wearing a light coat, short dress.

Whicher pushes back his chair, steps out in the street.

The woman pays the driver, turns toward the bar.

Whicher stands looking, Resistol tilted against the rain.

She hurries up the sidewalk, one hand at the short hair framing her face. She reaches the bar, nods. "Inside," she says. "Let's go inside."

Eric's upright, suddenly alert.

"You want to cover the door?" Whicher says.

"I got your back."

The marshal grabs his beer, grabs the pack of un-tipped Delicados. He follows Lucila to the rear of the bar. She draws out a chair from a table right in back. Whicher sits where he can see the door.

A waitress appears. Lucila and the girl exchange kisses. She sits, takes the cigarette the marshal's offering.

"Didn't think you'd come," he says.

She lights the cigarette from a candle in a bottle.

"I waited. I think you know the girl I was talking about."

Her eyes are hooded.

"I have something I ought to tell you," he says. "I think maybe something happened to her."

Lucila's face is hard in the candlelight.

"I'm trying to find out."

The waitress brings coffee and a glass of brandy. Lucila takes it. The marshal waits for the waitress to step away.

"I'm a cop," he says, beneath his breath.

She stares at him, alarm in her face.

"Over the border," he says. "The US side."

She doesn't answer. She sits rigid in her chair.

"You don't have to talk to me," he says, voice quiet. "You're not in any trouble. But you said she left around a week ago? Did she leave to cross the border?"

The woman lifts the cup of coffee. Takes a sip, eyes quick with thought.

"Did she leave for the US?"

Lucila nods.

"Alright," Whicher says. He lifts his hand an inch above the table. "It's okay," he tells her.

No response.

"Did you hear from her since she left?"

She sets the cup down. "No." Thoughts are passing quickly, one after another behind her eyes.

"You haven't spoken with her?"

"*Teléfono.* She was going to call."

Whicher leans in. "She was going to call, but didn't?"

Lucila nods.

"The girl I'm looking for," Whicher says. "I think she came from the south of the country. Far south, maybe from Central America."

Lucila's eyes are still. "She came from Sabinas."

"Sabinas?"

"Is not far."

"You're sure?"

"Is what she told to me. Not far. You drive, less than two hours."

Whicher feels his gut sink. "Tell me her name?"

"Carmela Ramirez."

He takes out the pad, notes it down. "When she set out, did she leave with a group?"

"*No lo se.*"

"You don't know?"

"I don't think," Lucila says.

"She was traveling alone?"

"There was another girl. Sara. Sara Pacheco."

"From here?"

"From *la zona*."

The marshal writes the name on the pad, puts it away. "Did you hear from Sara since they left?"

Lucila's eyes drop. "*Nada, nada*."

"Do you know where Carmela was going—after she crossed? Do you know what she was going to do, who she might have been meeting over the border?"

Lucila's eyes drill into him from across the table.

"Was she meeting someone?"

"*Sí*," she says, barely a whisper.

The marshal turns the pen in his hand. "Can you tell me?"

"She never told me a name."

"She must have told you something?"

Lucila searches the room, arms clutching her sides. "*Tira*," she says. "She was meeting a cop."

⅄

The air outside is cool, wet. Eric Kessler sits at the street-side table, nursing the last of his beer. Rain is blowing on the wind, drifting beneath the bar's awning. He doesn't seem to notice, his face is set, eyes focused on something, staring straight out across the square.

Whicher puts a hand on his shoulder.

Eric nods, not looking up.

"What's going on?"

"I'm thinking somebody's watching."

The marshal follows Eric's gaze out into the rainy air—around the square there's a steady stream of cars and trucks, foot traffic. Nothing that sticks out.

"Same car's been by three times." Eric tilts his head toward the corner of the square. "Twice it's come in that side, one time, over on the left. It stops a minute each time."

Whicher glances at Eric—sees the man he was a year back in the Gulf—sharp-eyed, picking out hostiles. "You ready to leave?" He traps a twenty on the table.

They step out from the awning into a fine mist of rain.

"See anybody?" the marshal says.

"Hard to say."

Eric takes a step toward the river.

Whicher puts a hand on his arm, stopping him. He looks toward the opposite side of the square.

"Bridge is that way, man."

"Let's head the other way," Whicher says.

Eric grins under the street light.

They turn around, walk to the far side of the square, groups of young men drinking, workers headed home, plenty enough people to mix with.

A pitted road leads away from the river. "Head a couple blocks, we'll switch direction," Whicher says. "Nothing happens, we can head back."

They move fast down the street off the square.

Half a block in, Eric stares at a car parked along the road. "That's it," he says.

"The car?"

By a closed-up store is a narrow street. Whicher cuts into it, Eric following.

Twenty yards along the sidewalk is a service alley, the marshal points—they back up into it.

"What happened with the girl?" Eric says.

They wait thirty seconds. Nothing comes by.

"I got a name—couple of possible IDs for two of the victims."

At the street end of the alley, a car cruises past—a Grand Marquis, dark blue, silver rims.

The marshal looks at his friend.

Eric nods. "That's the one."

⋏

Fifteen minutes later. More traffic fills up the narrow roads. At the back of the street market, close to the bridge, Whicher watches from the dark.

The market's empty, the stall-holders all gone.

Eric Kessler's moving up the left-hand edge of the *Gran Plazo,* scouting the flank.

Whicher looks in the direction he's headed—tarps on the stalls block his line of sight.

Eric's stopped. He's signaling.

Whicher moves in shadow, along the dark rows.

He reaches Eric at the concrete edge of a line of closed-up tourist booths.

"The car's out there," Eric says. He jerks a thumb in the direction of the bridge.

The marshal takes off his hat. "Let me get a look." He inches around the side of the wet concrete.

A stream of cars are rolling out of the port of entry from the US side. He can see the dark blue sedan. Two men up front, one in the rear. He feels his stomach turn. "They keep it parked there, they got the bridge."

"We could wait 'em out," Eric says, "see if they leave?"

"I don't like..."

"How about we head someplace. Get out of the way, grab a motel? Couple hours, they might give it up."

"Who the hell are they?"

"You got no idea?"

The marshal stares out into the rain. "Del Rio. We could cross there..."

"Del Rio's sixty miles, man."

"I can't have any piece of this..."

"You're a cop."

"Not here."

In the rear of the Grand Marquis, the man on the back seat turns sideways—profile to the window. He's Hispanic, hair in ringlets. The street light catches something at his ear—something gold. Whicher feels an image snap into his mind, then fade.

Cars from the bridge stream toward him, he cuts behind the booth, trying to hold the picture in his memory—a blur of light and movement in the rain.

Chapter 25

Dimmit County, TX.

The highway is empty. Truck windows rolled. Whicher drives the Chevy by a high-fence pasture outside Carrizo Springs. Sun behind the bull mesquite.

Del Rio—an hour and more it had taken. Through dark country, nothing moving on the wet roads. *Taxista*, silent, chewing on a match.

They'd crossed the bridge at Del Rio. No interest either side, US or Mexican. On home soil, a second cab ride all the way back to Eagle Pass. Eric strangely energized, limbs snapping, eyes full of light.

The marshal thinks again of the Grand Marquis blocking off the bridge approach. In the pocket of his suit he feels for the notepad, pictures the names written there, the names of two women.

Carmela Ramirez. Sara Pacheco.

He steers the Chevy down a spur for town. Red-eyed, fatigued from a night in the truck. Eric had offered him the couch, he told him no. He drives by a brick church—thin spire cutting the air. Thinks of Lucila. The young woman in the bar.

Lucila reckoned Carmela Ramirez from Sabinas—barely an hour from the border. Last thing she knew of her, she was leaving to cross to the US. To meet with a cop.

He slows at a stop light in the center of Carrizo Springs. Hits the blinker, makes the turn for the court-house square.

It's early, plenty of spaces. He parks up, puts on his hat.

Somebody followed them last night. He turns it over in his mind as he locks the truck.

He crosses the square, reaches the entrance of the courthouse. In the lobby, a female officer regards him. Hispanic, black-rimmed eye glasses. He hasn't seen her before.

"Can I help you?"

"Working the Williams-Creagan homicide. For US Marshals Service." He takes out his badge. "I need to see the custody officer, ma'am."

"On the upper floor, marshal."

"I go up?"

"You know your way?"

He nods, crosses the lobby, moving to the set of stairs in back.

He climbs to the next floor, finds a uniformed officer—the short deputy with the horseshoe mustache. "I need to talk to Lindy Page."

The man checks a clipboard.

"She's down at the end," Whicher says. "Last cell."

"No can do, marshal." The officer shakes his head. "Lindy Page got out last night. Late last night."

"Who released her?"

"Releasing officer signed as Deputy Benita Alvarenga..."

In the back office Whicher sits at the desk. He takes out the notepad from his jacket. *No Lindy Page.*

He finds the number for Miguel Carrasco in Eagle Pass—he can call INS about the girls.

He keys the number in—it starts to ring.

INS could call the Mexican side—police, federal law enforcement, either of the names might get a hit.

There's a clicking sound, the call switching to answer machine. The marshal clears his throat.

"This is Whicher, over in Carrizo Springs. Do me a favor, have somebody check out two names for me— Carmela Ramirez—and Sara Pacheco." He pauses. "Both women are missing. Last known working out of *la zona* in Piedras Negras. Could be the female victims I got at the ranch."

He puts down the phone. Shoots his jacket sleeve.

Carrasco would want to know where he got that.

He turns to the file cabinet, pulls out a folder. The phone starts to ring.

He picks up; "Carrasco? That was fast..."

"It's Scruggs. You're in early. You get home last night?"

Whicher eyes the empty office. "I stayed with a friend. In Eagle Pass."

"I need you to meet with me this afternoon. East of Guerro," Scruggs says. "A horse fair out there. Out in Jim Hogg county."

"A horse fair?"

"I got a call last night from Border Patrol. Merrill Johnson's going to be out there. You have a pen?"

Scruggs reels off an address south of Laredo, Whicher notes it all down.

"I have to head out for court," Scruggs says, "I'll tell you about it this afternoon. Before you come out, be sure and talk with Lindy Page. Just soon as she gets a lawyer."

Whicher stands. "Lindy got released."

"She done what?"

"I just found out. I just got here, custody officer told me Deputy Alvarenga released her last night."

"Sheriff said he was going to keep her."

"That's what I thought."

"You talk to Alvarenga?"

"No, sir. She's not here."

Scruggs is silent at the end of the line. "I want to know what the hell that's about."

The younger marshal nods.

"Damn wheels are starting to shake on this, we're not even rolling..."

Whicher stares at the wall.

"Last night," Scruggs says, "Quint Lassiter told me Jim Gale's been called out to LA."

"LA?"

"Lassiter didn't want it coming out in the meeting, front of the sheriff an' all. But looks like some of the folk drafted for the riots might have gotten a little trigger happy."

"Law enforcement folk?"

"I'm just getting this off of Lassiter. He said Gale was stationed down in South Central, it's a Latino area. A bunch were killed."

Whicher thinks of the coverage. "Is Gale accused of something?"

"I don't know."

Whicher sits heavy on the side of the desk.

"What I do know is, he cain't pick up Jug Line Harris."

"You want me to go get him?"

"I put out a stop order—Highway Patrol or any PD spots him, they're going to notify Dimmit County Sheriff."

"Alright, sir."

"I got to head for court, but meet me out in Jim Hogg this afternoon. Around three. Guerro, check the map, there'll be signs..."

⋏

Whicher stands in the center of the office, phone hanging from his hand.

Gale in LA. *A shooting charge.*

He runs a hand across his face. No clear idea what to do.

He puts the phone back down on its cradle.

No Lindy Page, no Jug Line Harris. No Benita Alvarenga.

Think of something—think of one sure thing.

The first night.

First thing he'd seen with his own two eyes—staring down a night scope, a man running, shot down from a pickup in the brush.

Start all the way back. Start over.

Start from there.

Chapter 26

Webb County, TX.

The stock tank in the clearing is filled with muddy water—
sun reflecting on the galvanized sides. Flies circle overhead. The sails of an iron windmill turn in the baking air,
gearbox creaking, pumping groundwater. A trickle runs
from the discharge pipe.

Mojados drank it. They'd see windmills, find a tank. But
it was cattle water, not fit for human consumption.

Whicher stares at the hoof-beaten dirt, beyond it a
stand of plateau live oak and paloverde.

On the gnarled fence posts smooth wires run out into
the brush.

There's no mark on the ground where Alfonso Saldana
bled to death.

He steps across the hard earth, clutching the map from
the Chevy.

Saldana had been running for the river—south and west.

The truck had come from the north, from the direction of the Channing Ranch. Whicher re-checks it against the map.

He tries to visualize the distance, the range at the time the last shots were fired. Six hundred meters? He stares across the low scrub, picking out a clump of Spanish bayonet—a rough estimate of the firing position.

Saldana was hit multiple times. Full-metal-jacket, no bullet frags, no lead in the body.

Nobody had searched the ground. Nobody was investigating his death.

He scans the tangle of wild scrub. A jacketed round could strike a man, pass clean through—the energy would take it on who knew how far? The lead could sit at the foot of a clump of brush till the end of time, nobody seeing it.

Brass. Shell casings. They'd be at the firing position, ejected from the rifle. They might have ejected in the truck cab, some could have flown out on the ground.

If not brass there could be tire marks, ground sign where the vehicle flattened the brush.

He crosses to his Chevy. Checks the bearing to the clump of Spanish bayonet. Tosses the map inside the cab.

He picks a way forward into whitebrush mesquite and granjero. Steps slow, trying to keep his suit pants from snagging on thorns and spines. Away from the clearing, just yards into the brush, the temperature's rising—no breeze, no breath of air. Radiated waves of heat swarm his senses. He feels the reaction on his skin.

He thinks of the Gulf. Of sitting in hot vehicles, breathing shallow—trying not to let the lack of air get to him.

Pushing on, he twists through brush and thorn, mindful of the sun, correcting each deviation of his track.

How could anybody stand it? Days walking, avoiding the Patrol. They'd see a stock tank, drink the water, get sick fast. They'd be vomiting, messing themselves in hundred degree heat.

He feels his core temperature climbing. Stops, lets his breathing steady. A sensation hits him—a heightened feeling. He studies the withered clumps of vegetation.

He moves off again, wiping sweat from his eyes, the ground dipping and rising, heat roiling, trapped above the earth.

Making serious mileage would be suicide. Anybody crossing would take shelter, the middle of the day. He thinks of the Channing Ranch—big stone walls, some of the roof intact. Chances of discovery would be low, the land known for carrying rabies.

His mouth is dry, sweat running. Again, he feels the sensation—awareness heightened. He scrambles up a gravel bank to a low ridge. The clump of Spanish bayonet is ahead.

He studies the ground, blowing now. No tracks or signs from any vehicle.

The land to the north is open; a pickup truck could get through. Turning to the south he sees the iron windmill in a heat haze—the stand of plateau oak, the top of his Chevy. Somewhere along the ridge, the shooter had taken aim.

Whicher estimates his own position on the night. Roughly due east, in the truck.

He thinks of Agent Talamantes. Raul Talamantes had the sector, according to Carrasco. Jim Gale roving—moving as he pleased.

He turns away, searches the ridge for any sign—a tire mark, a brass case glinting from the ground.

He stops. Straightens. Turns full circle, slow.

Again the sensation. But nobody's in sight. The Gulf, it might be some kid. Here, there should be no-one.

A fresh bloom of sweat pricks his skin. An animal, it could be. A wild dog—plenty carried rabies.

He reaches for the Glock, takes it out. Chambers a round, senses sharp, the heat forgotten.

Across the brush, he sees a rough route to the windmill, a different route. Vegetation taller but less dense. He starts down the gravel bank into mesquite and Mexican olive. Dust rising, the grips of the Glock wet with sweat.

He quickens the pace, instinct overriding reason. The primeval feeling of being stalked.

Something moves in the edge of his vision. He stops by a guayacan tree.

Something's close. He steadies his breathing.

The brush is silent. Above the mesquite the sails of the iron windmill turn.

He moves forward, trigger finger on the Glock.

Seconds stretch out. He picks his way to the clearing, shirt soaked.

The truck's just yards off. He heads toward it, wrenches open the door. The heat in the cab is like a furnace. He starts it up, cranks every dial on the A/C. Puts away the gun. Sits a moment in the blown air. Wondering at his own reactions. Spooked.

A line of scrub guajillo marks the route out through the high brush.

He sticks the truck in drive, steers to a bend in the primitive track.

Clearing the turn, he sees a truck parked side-on.

A 250 Dodge Ram. Blocking the way out.

Either side of the truck two Hispanics are standing, arms outstretched.

Their hands are wrapped around pistols. Black muzzles trained at his windshield.

Chapter 27

Whicher brakes to a standstill. Neither of the two Hispanics move.

They're dressed in sport shirts, the man on the left in pale blue, second man in white. The square-looking pistols in their hands are semi-autos. The man in blue moves first.

Whicher's hands are on the steering wheel, he thinks of going for the Glock.

The blue-shirted man's already at the driver window.

The man in white walks forward, reaches the passenger door. He opens it. Steps up into the cab.

"I'm a US Marshal," Whicher says, adrenaline coursing. "*Policia...*"

He glances at the man beside the driver window, compact SIG between his hands.

The man in the white shirt reaches over, takes the Glock from Whicher's holster. Sweat's running down the side of his face. He sits. Closes the door. "Drive," he says.

The man at the window moves off, walking fast to the Dodge Ram, climbing in.

"Go by him. Go on in front."

The Dodge Ram reverses into the brush, opening the way.

Whicher steadies his breathing, thinks of flooring out the gas. He steers through the gap, the Dodge Ram already turning in behind, dirt billowing beneath its wheels.

The man in the white shirt holds the pistol steady.

Whicher glances sideways, catches his eye.

It's unblinking.

⅄

Fifteen minutes later. Headed roughly north-east. The mesquite opens out, Whicher stares through the windshield at a building above the line of scrub. He's seen it before. It's built from faded brick, abandoned-looking, tall palms rising above it.

Beyond, he can see the edge of a highway. He checks the rear-view, the Dodge Ram is right behind.

The man in the passenger seat points to a spot in back of the building. "Over there."

Whicher slows. He pulls up at a wall of sun-bleached brick.

The day he'd called on Reba Williams, he'd passed the place, with Benita Alvarenga. *Ghost hotel.* That's what she'd called it. Left to hunters and drunks.

The man in white pushes open the door, slides out. He stands looking in at Whicher—pointing the marshal's own Glock.

The Dodge Ram pulls alongside.

"Get out, now."

The man in blue climbs from the truck, SIG in hand.

Whicher cuts the motor, steps from the Chevy.

"Inside," the white shirted man says.

Whicher steps to a rotting service door. The two Hispanics behind.

Ahead is a corridor, paint peeling, plaster crumbling, the ceiling half down.

"Go ahead, move..."

The floor's littered with empty beer cans. Cigarette butts, peeling linoleum.

Whicher walks in, reaches a set of narrow stairs—bare boards broken.

"Up the stairs. Go ahead."

Whicher feels a push in the back. He climbs, legs heavy, mind racing. If they're traffickers, he's running out of time.

At the top of the stairs is an ante-room—stripped out, the windows smashed. A set of double doors bars the way to the next room.

The white shirted man opens it. "Through there," he says.

The marshal pushes the door wide.

On the other side, a big Hispanic is standing in a derelict room. Arms folded on his chest, head tilted as he stares at Whicher. Curled hair. Gold hoops in his ears.

Whicher sees the image of a Grand Marquis. *Piedras Negras*. The bridge. He waits for the man to speak. A second image flashes in his mind—a Chevy Caprice, garnet red, parked beneath trees. In Eagle Pass. Outside Randell Creagan's apartment.

The man unfolds his arms, steps by him, out of the door.

Whicher stares down the full length of the room—a ruined space, thirty yards long, bright light glaring from broken windows.

Graffiti. Broken glass. Ripped up floor. At the far end, in shadow, he can make out a man.

Staring out the window. Blond-haired. Suited. Dane Vogel.

人

Neither man speaks.

For the longest time the only sound is the wind outside, blowing in the mesquite.

Whicher thinks back to the first morning after the shootings, six days back. Looking to serve out a bench warrant. The big Caprice parked under the trees.

Vogel finally turns from the window.

The marshal starts to walk down the room.

"Those floorboards are pretty weak there, in the center," the FBI man says.

Whicher feels his hand close in a fist.

"Slow down..."

"Slow down?" Whicher stops. He stares around the empty space.

"Last night, you were in Piedras Negras," Vogel says.

The marshal feels a prickling sense of danger.

"Strange place to be?"

Whicher reaches for the pack of Marlboros in his shirt pocket. Takes one. Lights it.

"Were you working?"

The marshal draws the smoke down.

"Against the law for you to do that." Vogel studies him. "You've been going a lot of places. Last night, Piedras Negras. The night before, a farm—west of Crystal City." He leans against the graffitied wall.

Whicher thinks of driving back from the Tutton place—dropping Shanon Summers. The Buick Le Sabre coming after him.

A bird appears in the broken window, blur of wings—digging, ripping at the rotten frame. It lands. Stares with glass bead eyes.

Vogel whips a hand toward it, it flies from the sill. "What were you doing just now?" he says. "Out there in the scrub?"

"Searching a murder scene."

"What murder?"

"Alfonso Saldana."

"You're not investigating him."

The marshal feels the tightness in his chest.

For a minute neither man speaks.

Out beyond the hotel, heat warps the horizon. A truck moves along an empty stretch of highway.

"How come you're alone?" Vogel says. "No Marshal Scruggs?"

"He's testifying in court."

"Pretty convenient." Vogel stares directly at the marshal.

"I thought to look for lead," Whicher says. "For bullets. I was there on the night, I was going through it one more time."

"You were there?"

"I went looking for casings—up on the ridge..."

"You know where the shooter was?"

"I saw him."

"You saw him—but didn't stop him?"

Whicher smokes the cigarette, the burning tip glowing white. *You saw him. But didn't stop him.*

The FBI man touches a slim finger to his temple. "Border Patrol had charge of that sector on the night, that right? Agent Talamantes."

"That's right."

"Why were *you* there?"

The heat inside the room presses—stale air trapped beneath the peeling roof.

"Retrieving evidence," Vogel says. "Or getting rid of it?"

The marshal shakes his head.

"You're part of a homicide investigation," Vogel says. "A lot of things don't look consistent with that." He steps from the window. Studies the shine on his city shoes.

"You want to tell me what in the name of hell you're talking about?"

"Maybe I'm going to take a chance," Vogel says.

Whicher throws down the cigarette. He stands on it.

"You're new. If I'm wrong, it won't change anything."

Whicher grinds glass and grit beneath his boot.

"The department I work for is running an investigation." Vogel's voice is flat, hard. "Into US Marshals Service."

Whicher looks at him. "Say again?"

"I think you heard me."

⋏

"Am I under arrest?" Whicher takes in the man in the dark suit. Out of place, urban, impatient.

Vogel's face is tanned, hair almost white blond.

"If I'm not under arrest, then I'm free to go..."

"That wouldn't be smart."

Whicher takes off the Resistol. He runs a finger round the inside of the hat band—it's wet with sweat.

Vogel takes a pace forward. "What were you doing in Piedras Negras? We know you talked with a bunch of hookers from *la zona*. You and that army junkie pal."

Whicher fits the hat back in place. Suppressing a lick of anger.

Vogel grins. "Let's just hear it."

"I was searching for ID."

"What ID?"

"Four Hispanic victims. From the Channing Ranch."

"You're not investigating their deaths."

"Dimmit County buried them," Whicher says. "They were unidentified. I want them disinterred."

Vogel's mouth twists.

"I want them re-examined. There could be evidence linking to people we're investigating." Whicher's gaze blurs on the graffiti at the back wall, mind turning. An FBI investigation into US Marshals Service was federal on federal—neither side presiding over the other.

"I want to know what you've been doing."

Whicher stares at the FBI man.

Gale—Jim Gale, he must be part of it. Was it Gale? He was in LA—were they moving in while he was gone? They had Creagan's place under surveillance, they must know Creagan and Gale were connected.

"I said..."

"I heard what you said."

Vogel folds his arms over the dark suit.

A hot wind flickers at the broken window.

"I can indict already, make it stick," Vogel says. "If you were in Piedras Negras on fed business last night, you were breaking the law, you'll be out of the service, minimum."

Whicher presses his tongue against the sharp edge of his teeth. "Maybe I was there drinking beer with a buddy. Looking to get laid."

"Think that'll sound more convincing?" Vogel looks at him. "Maybe you're hooked in already. Traffickers use enforcers..."

"They do what?"

"*La zona's* a hub, maybe you went out to shut somebody up?" He steps from Whicher to the center of the room. With the toe of one shoe he rolls an empty beer can to the edge of a hole in the floor. "Right side or the wrong side? Which are you?"

"I'm a lawman."

"Then hear this. You keep your mouth shut, cooperate with this investigation. You go about your business. Talk to no-one. Not to Scruggs, not to anybody. I'm taking a chance. I wanted to look you dead in the eye."

"That's not all you want."

"You open your fuckin' mouth..." Vogel tips the can into the void. "Your world is going to fall through the floor."

The can rattles onto the ground below.

The FBI man walks down the room. "Believe it," he says. He pauses, turning at the door. "You're going to be seeing me..."

CHAPTER 28

Jim Hogg County, TX.

The horses in the ring turn and wheel, hooves stamping in the grass. By a cedar rail fence Marshal Reuben Scruggs waits, watching the riders from beneath the broad brim of his hat.

Whicher dodges the crowd milling through a late-spring afternoon, eating ice cream and chili dogs, drinking beer from plastic cups.

The sound of diesel generators fills the air, smell of hot sugar drifting.

In the main show ring, riders with English saddles jump painted fences. Tannoy system cutting in and out.

Whicher thinks of Dane Vogel. Of taking back his gun and his truck at the hotel.

Scruggs turns, spots him, pushes past the people at the rail.

"You took your time..."

Whicher says nothing.

Scruggs leads the younger marshal away from the main show ring.

The fair's spread out—acres of tented stalls, trailer units, vehicles parked in rows around the site.

"Johnson's here," Scruggs says. He holds out an arm, stopping by a stall filled with tooled leather and custom stirrups. Beyond it, a group of trucks and trailers make up a smaller ring.

In a roped-off space, horses graze. Stable hands are gathered, dressed in Western shirts and hats.

Whicher scans the weathered faces.

Scruggs looks from one group to another. "The man was just in here, dammit..."

They move off through the crowd of people—along the arc running by the main ring.

"I made a bunch of calls," Scruggs says. "Between times, hanging around in court. Border Patrol. INS. Plus I spoke with FBI..."

Whicher cuts his boss a look.

They pass a kids' shooting gallery, ducks swimming a mechanical tide. Shots crack out, singles and bursts.

Scruggs stops. He peers into Whicher's face. "What's the matter with you?"

"Nothing. I'm alright."

The older marshal frowns. He points to the side of a beer tent. A gap leads to another ring of trucks. "Try there."

They step into a corridor of trampled glass.

"I've been pressing Gerry Nugent," Scruggs says. "From Houston FBI. Pushing him for information. It's looking like somebody in FBI was working Creagan over."

"What does that mean?"

"Trying to turn him. Get him to turn informer." Scruggs walks to the edge of the clearing—more horses corralled, men; mostly Hispanic—nobody that looks like Merrill Johnson. "For what it's worth, I'm not sure how long he's known..."

"Somebody wanted Randell Creagan to inform on Merrill Johnson?"

"Not the Houston FBI office."

"They tell you who?"

Scruggs shakes his head. "I wasn't about to get that."

Whicher stares at the tractor-trailers lining the little grass ring.

Scruggs looks at him. "What do you see?"

The younger marshal doesn't answer.

"Apart from horses?" Scruggs says.

Whicher shrugs. "People."

"What else?"

"I don't know. Tents. Trucks, cars."

"Transportation. There must be a couple hundred trucks and horse transporters here. We know Creagan was a truck driver. Merrill Johnson admitted knowing him as such."

Whicher looks at his boss.

"Laredo Border Patrol think Johnson's been running non-doc illegals up country. The likes of San Antonio, Dallas, Houston. Chicago, even. Reckon somebody in FBI was thinking the same."

"Nobody at Border Patrol said a thing like that to me."

"You're new," Scruggs says. "And these ain't allegations, they're by way of suspicion. They got no proof. But FBI could have been looking for that, with Creagan."

"Randell Creagan gives up Johnson? In return for what?"

Scruggs gestures with his chin to head back to the main ring. "They likely had federal charges they could bring. Creagan was dealing stolen cars, maybe running them across the border. They could have offered him a deal."

Whicher thinks about it.

"There's a couple thousand folk here, how many cops you see?" Scruggs adjusts the black Stetson. "Few hours from now, all of these eighteen-wheelers will be rolling out—plenty places on board."

"You mean for folks in need of a ride?" Whicher says. "You think Johnson could be working that angle?"

"Border Patrol have a source at APHIS," Scruggs says. "A vet. They know when he has horses coming up."

"Hannah Scott," Whicher says, "I met her."

"That's how we know the man's here."

The younger marshal stares at the mud stained tires on a horse trailer unit. "Chicago? You said Chicago just now?"

"That's one of the places he ships to."

Todd Williams worked there one time. Reba Williams told him that. *The only time he ever left Texas.* Only regular job he ever had.

Merrill M. Johnson is standing at a gun dealer's stall. Racks of hunting rifles, pistols, knives. Accessories and ammunition.

He has a rifle scope sight in his hands. He lifts his metal-rimmed eye glasses—places them on top of his head. He puts the scope to his eye, draws a line on a group of cottonwoods at the far side of the fair.

Whicher studies him—dark hair, neatly-groomed mustache. Dressed in a fine suit. Sage green country-check.

His fingers work the lens adjuster on the scope, tight grin at the side of his mouth.

The younger marshal steps forward, Scruggs moving at his side.

Johnson takes the scope from his eye, replaces the glasses.

Whicher leans in to the stall, sifting through boxes of ammunition.

He picks out a box of .270 Winchester. Full-metal-jacket. Turns to Johnson.

A flicker of recognition is in the man's face.

"These any good?" Whicher says. "Shooting up stuff?"

Scruggs steps in the man's sight line.

"You're the marshal…"

Whicher turns the box of FMJs in his hand, making a show of reading the label. "You like to hunt?"

"What?"

"Shoot things."

Johnson looks at him. "I hunt. I fish…"

"Nice-looking scope." Whicher holds out a hand. "I take a look?"

Johnson's face is sour. He passes over the scope, turns to Scruggs. "What're you doing here? Are you looking for me?"

"Yessir."

Whicher waves a hand at the stall owner; heavy guy with a beard. "All of this here registered with FFA?"

"Yes, sir. Sales is all registered."

"If I wanted to take a look at your records—that be a problem?"

"No, sir. ATF get a copy of the receipts."

Whicher puts down the scope.

"What's this all about?" Johnson says.

Scruggs tilts his hat forward. "Three days back, we last spoke, you told me you knew a feller name of Randell Creagan."

Johnson looks at him.

"Been hearing you knew him maybe better than you made out."

He stiffens. "I didn't make something out."

Scruggs runs an eye across the racks of guns.

"You asked me did I know him, I told you I did."

The older marshal nods. "Maybe I mistook you," he says. "First impressions, know how it is."

Neither man speaks for a moment.

"Anyhow," Scruggs continues. "Last couple days I been looking at a bunch of paperwork, with your name on it."

"My name?"

"Trying to get a few things straightened out."

"Are you going to tell me what this is about?"

"US Customs records. Cargo manifests."

"You mean my work?"

"You do business all over the country, according to the records. Rail and road. Import, export with Mexico. If a feller wanted to ship a thing, y'all could get it about anyplace. That about right?"

Johnson adjusts his eyeglasses.

"I'm asking, is all."

The man nods.

"You organize a lot of freight to Chicago?"

"I run a freight forwarding business," Johnson says. "Chicago's a major hub for rail and road."

"Randell Creagan used to drive some of them runs?"

Johnson steps away from the gun stall. "He may have."

"To Chicago?"

"I'd have to check. But so what if he did?" Johnson takes another step from the stall. "Look, you mind if we make this conversation a little more discreet? I know a lot of folk here."

Whicher steps into his space. "What kind of folk?"

"All kinds."

"Seems like a place a lot of deals might get done," Whicher says. "Cash deals. Undocumented."

"It's a horse fair—what do you expect?"

"Same go for people?"

"People?"

Whicher changes tack; "Ever do any hunting out at the river?"

"I said I hunt."

"How about south of Carrizo Springs? Out at the Rio Grande. Ever hunt in any of the camps?"

"What the hell does that have to do with anything?"

Scruggs clears his throat. "This time last week where were you Mister Johnson? Seven days ago. Specifically overnight."

The man's eyes are guarded.

"Were you traveling, were you on the road? Were you home—where were you?"

"Am I being questioned here?"

Scruggs doesn't answer. He lifts up his hat, smooths the hair at the back of his head.

"Frankly, I'm not obliged to say anything."

Whicher steps another pace closer to Johnson.

"I'll ask you again," Scruggs says. "Where were you this time last week?"

"I'm not obliged to answer that. I'm not real inclined talking with y'all."

"If you obstruct my investigation, I'll just as soon take you in." Scruggs turns to Whicher. "You have your cuffs?"

"Hold your damn horses," Johnson says.

"Where were you overnight? Seven nights back. I need an answer."

"I can't remember." Johnson thrusts out his hand. "I can check. If that's what you want? I keep a diary, appointments, suchlike. I'll need to head back to my vehicle."

Scruggs looks at Whicher. "Go with him."

Half way back around the main show ring is a holding area for livestock and horses. Generators run loud, cables coiled like nests of serpents. The smell of hay is heavy in the air.

"You didn't answer my question back there," Whicher says. "About the hunting camps. The river, up by Carrizo Springs."

Johnson strides toward a parking area, full of semis and horse trailers. "I've hunted lots of places."

"You know a guide by the name of Harris? Jug Line Harris?"

The man doesn't answer.

"How about Todd Williams, you know him? Williams was a hunting guide, he's one of the murder victims we're investigating."

"I don't know, marshal. Maybe I've met him, maybe not. I know a lot of people, it's my job..."

"You like to hang out in Mexico?"

Johnson shakes his head. "What? What the hell are you talking about now?"

"Piedras Negras."

"I'm a customs broker—understand? That means I work the border."

"How about *la zona*?"

Johnson stops at the rear of a polished horse transporter. "The night you're talking about, I'll tell you where I was at, if I can find it. But that's it." He holds up a hand to the marshal. "I'll get my business diary from the cab. Anything else, you'll have to talk to my lawyer—I don't give a God damn if your boss arrests me or not."

Whicher stares at him.

"You got that?" Johnson ducks behind the trailer unit.

Whicher stands at the edge of the stock clearing, high-sided vehicles all around.

Snatches of words drift from the Tannoy, late sun slanting through the gaps between trucks.

He lights a cigarette, stares at the side of a trailer. Johnson could shut up shop, try to stall it out. But Scruggs would work him. He takes a drag, blows out a thick stream of blue-tinged smoke.

His stomach drops like a stone.

He throws down the cigarette, runs behind the horse transporter, reaches the cab steps—pulls himself up.

The door's locked. The cab empty.

He jumps down, head snapping left and right.

Trucks and trailers are parked one behind another in a sweeping curve. He whips the Glock from its holster.

He races from the trailers, through the stock clearing, jumping the rope.

Fastest route out would be around the show ring—lost in the crowd. He hustles into the main circle, straining to pick out Johnson's green suit.

A dark haired man is moving quickly—fifty, sixty yards ahead. Whicher tries to sprint—a sound starting up around him, a woman's voice calling out.

He runs on, rows of stalls to the left, the ring to his right.

Music's pumping, riderless horses turn at the edge of his vision. From behind, he hears a shout.

He stares at the dark-haired man—almost out of sight. Sees movement left, between a row of tents—a figure dressed in tan shirt and pants.

A sheriff's deputy. Gun between his hands.

"Drop your weapon..."

"US Marshal..."

"Hold it right there—drop your weapon..."

Whicher stops, stares into the crowd.

"Drop your weapon—do it now..."

CHAPTER 29

In the empty diner at the side of the county road, Scruggs faces opposite Whicher in a booth.

"I still say we should have somebody try to stop him."

"We don't know what vehicle he's driving," Scruggs says. "And we ain't ready to make an arrest."

"Why come looking for him here?"

"To pressure the son of a bitch," Scruggs says. "Besides, there was a chance he'd be running wets."

"Out of the fair?"

Scruggs nods. "Something in him sure as hell cracked."

Neither man speaks for a minute. Outside on the county road, every other vehicle is a pickup pulling horses.

Scruggs taps a pen against a bunch of papers. "Let's talk about Randell Creagan," he says. "And this boy, Todd Williams."

Whicher leans back in the booth.

"Despite what Border Patrol and maybe FBI are saying—we got nothing to show Creagan's anything more than a car-thief and fence out of east Texas. And maybe a snitch."

"Johnson was hooked up with him."

Scruggs looks out the diner window. "We got no evidence. If Jim Gale was right about Creagan getting tied on a freight train, maybe that nails Johnson in harder."

"You ever hear of that style of killing?"

The older marshal thinks it over. "No," he finally says.

Whicher rubs at his chin.

"How about Todd Williams?" Scruggs says.

"Lindy Page was the best lead. You want, I could call Carrizo Springs?"

Scruggs swivels in the booth. "See if they have a phone."

Whicher slides out, crosses the diner, walks to the end of the counter. By a bunch of menu cards there's a boxy-looking pay phone. He picks up the receiver, feeds quarters into the slot.

Reception at Carrizo Springs courthouse answers.

He waits while they bounce the call around.

He lights up a Marlboro, thinking on Dane Vogel. If Vogel could pull a stunt like that in the hotel on a US Marshal, he'd be more than capable of scaring the likes of Lindy Page.

Last thing Vogel had told him was; *talk to nobody*. Had the same gone for Lindy?

A female voice comes on the line; he recognizes Benita Alvarenga.

"It's Whicher." He glances at his boss. "I'm with Scruggs, out in Jim Hogg County."

"There was a call while you were out. Miguel Carrasco. At INS."

Whicher takes a hit off the smoke.

"He said two names you gave him—two Mexican females—they're both confirmed. Wait," she says, "can you hold?"

He stands straight, takes another drag, pushing the phone close to his ear.

Behind the counter a woman appears, drying her hands on an apron.

"Carmela Ramirez," Alvarenga says. "And Sara Pacheco. Police in Piedras Negras confirm they're both prostitutes, known to work in *la zona*."

The woman behind the counter looks at Whicher. He shakes his head.

"Where did you get that?" Alvarenga says. "Carrasco's message said you think it might be the two female victims from the Channing Ranch."

"Listen," he says, "I'm with Scruggs, he wants to know what happened with Lindy Page?"

He hears her breath of frustration.

"You let her go?"

"She changed her story. She said she didn't talk with any cop."

"Say again?"

"Yesterday, after you left, I went and talked with her in her cell. She said she didn't mean to lie. She was meeting someone, a new boyfriend—she didn't want anyone to know."

"You believe that?"

"Honestly? No, I don't."

Whicher stares out at the road. "Why'd you let her walk?"

"I talked with the sheriff. He told me to turn her out."

"Yesterday he said keep her till she sees a lawyer. On hindering an inquest."

"That was yesterday."

The marshal smokes the cigarette. Glances over at Scruggs.

"Lindy said she didn't want folk knowing—on account of how recent Todd was killed. I think she's lying, but what choice did I have? The sheriff wanted her out."

"She better not skip town. Or end up dead."

Neither of them speak for a moment.

"I have to go," Whicher says.

"Don't blame me."

Alvarenga hangs up the phone.

Whicher mashes out the stub of cigarette. He crosses to the booth. "Lindy Page changed her story."

"She done what?"

"She was meeting some new boyfriend, not a cop. Said she didn't want anyone to know. Sheriff Barnhart kicked her loose."

Scruggs sits back, lays his hands together on the pile of papers. "By long forbearing is a prince persuaded..." He sits a minute, black hat set forward on his head.

"Sir?"

"*Proverbs 25:15.* On patience. Not my strongest suit."

"You want me to go pick her up again?"

The older marshal shakes his head. He gathers up the papers, sticking them into a worn tote. "Come on," he says. He leaves money for the tab.

They slide out from the booth, head out into the parking lot.

A stream of vehicles is passing now, jacked-up trucks, horse boxes, families in battered sedans.

Scruggs takes out the keys to his blue and white Ford Ranger. "Was that it?" he says. "There anything else?"

Whicher takes out his own keys. "Couple names have come up."

Scruggs stands by his truck.

"Possible identities," Whicher says. "For the female victims at the Channing Ranch."

"The hell from?"

"INS. Looks like it might be a couple of Mexican working girls. Out of Piedras Negras."

Scruggs eyes him. "They missing?"

"Miguel Carrasco talked to police in Piedras Negras." Whicher leans against his Chevy. "Could be a chance to confirm IDs, get something solid."

Scruggs doesn't answer.

"If Doctor Schulz re-examined the bodies..."

"She won't."

"If we could get access to records from Piedras Negras..."

"We're not investigating their deaths."

Whicher looks out over a field of young sorghum. "If credible ID emerges, the law says we have to check. Where the deceased are unidentified."

"I know the law."

The younger marshal stands silent by his truck.

"We're not investigating those victims."

"There's still Saldana? Webb coroner could test for toxicology?"

"When's the last time you went home?"

"Couple nights," Whicher says.

"I want you to go on home, now. This business here," Scruggs says, "running through a crowd of folk at a horse fair. Gun in your hand. It's an over-reaction."

A Peterbilt rumbles by, sun catching the twin chrome stacks.

"You need to step back," Scruggs says. "You need to take my advice on this." He pulls open the door of his truck. Climbs in, starts the motor. "I'll see you in Carrizo Springs tomorrow. Just as soon as I'm done in court."

Whicher nods.

"Don't be worrying on Merrill Johnson. We'll find his ass. The guy's in business, he's public property." Scruggs yanks the door closed. Rolls the window. "Go on home." He backs out, steers to the exit of the gravel lot.

Whicher watches him onto the county road. Till he's entirely out of sight.

Hidalgo County, TX.

Dusk. A road headed east through Hidalgo County, into Willacy. Twenty miles to the coast, the Gulf of Mexico. Harlingen and Brownsville to the south.

A knife band of light cuts the horizon in Whicher's rear-view. One last call. After Scruggs left, that was all it was going to be.

Two quarters into the payphone at the diner. A call to Laredo—the rail freight yard.

According to the manager at the rail yard, the man on Whicher's list—by the name of Jose Talamantes—worked a bunch of different places. Tonight, the Harlingen yard.

From the highway, Whicher sees the road signs for Raymondville and 77 South.

He flips the blinker.

Pushes down harder on the gas.

⅄

An hour later. The Harlingen switching yard is a mess of ugly warehousing, mesh fences, a two-lane running parallel with the tracks.

It's pitch dark, apart from working lights. A diesel switcher pushes flatbeds up an assembly rail.

Jose Talamantes had been at Laredo the night somebody took a swing at him.

The marshal steps out, locks the truck, checks the Glock at his hip. He starts to walk out into the dark, across the barely lit waste ground.

The site is fenced but cut with access roads, barriers raised, red lights winking—anybody could get in.

A screech of steel splits the air as he reaches a line of hoppers—pale dust caked to their chutes.

Three lines over, empty box cars sit motionless. Doors wide, a black void inside.

The hoppers are thick with dust—some kind of chemical. Maybe lime. The diesel switching engine slows, its light shining on the track from up high on the cab.

The driver leans from a window, shouting something at the crew on the ground.

At the edge of the yard, glowing cigarettes mark out groups of men part-hidden by the lines of freight. They're hunkered among derelict sheds. Whicher thinks of Alfonso Saldana—picked up in Brownsville a year back. Brownsville was only twenty miles south. Saldana could have jumped off a place like this, ridden a bus back—looking for the big university. A reason for the death of his son.

He steps along the track by a row of hoppers. They're the same as Laredo, painted up the same, Spanish words stenciled on their sides.

The crew in a yard like this must know what was going on—illegals riding loads.

He takes out his marshals badge, watches a man checking on a coupling. Thinks of the Hispanic that swung at him; cropped hair, canvas jacket, steel-toed boots.

The locomotive moves at walking pace—a worker following behind on the track. He carries a flashlight, a two-way radio. He's Caucasian, slender—with a goatee beard.

"*US Marshals Service*," Whicher calls out. He holds the badge up high.

The man sees him, raises his light.

"Looking for somebody name of Talamantes. Jose Talamantes."

The man points at the locomotive.

"He's here?"

"Up on the switcher."

Whicher follows the slow-moving engine.

He waves at the driver—a black guy dressed in coveralls.

The driver slows, drops the revs to idle.

The marshal grabs a hand rail, mounts the locomotive's steps.

"*What you want?*" The driver calls down.

"US Marshals Service—looking for Jose Talamantes."

The driver screws up his face.

"*Talamantes*," Whicher shouts. "*I need to see him.*"

From the front-end platform of the locomotive another man steps into view. Hispanic, short haired.

"Your name Talamantes?"

The man nods, face caught suddenly in the train's forward light.

It's not him.

It's not the man that attacked him.

Whicher stands with Jose Talamantes by an empty stretch of access road. Talamantes is older than the Laredo guy. Same short hair. But the face is different, the features sharp.

"I'm working a homicide investigation."

The man smokes a thin cigar. Saying nothing.

Whicher adjusts his hat. "You work nights as a supervisor, according to the manager at Laredo. Six nights back, I was attacked there—in the yard."

There's a flicker in the man's face.

"You were working—according to the roster."

"Rail yard's not a good place at night, man." Talamantes looks around the darkened waste ground.

"The guy that came at me was packing a wrench. Real big thing. Like he was working."

"Trespassing, I'd say."

"You got no idea? No idea at all?"

Talamantes puffs on the thin cigar. "Maintenance crews come and go, man. It could have been anyone."

Whicher takes out the pack of Marlboros. "What's going on here?" He lights up, points the cigarette at the switching crew.

"They're making up loads. Assembling for outbound."

"Headed where?"

"North. Chicago, mainly."

"Chicago?"

Talamantes nods.

Whicher takes a hit off the cigarette. "You know a man name of Merrill Johnson? Freight man, customs broker."

"Maybe."

"He come here?"

"Brokers come around yards." The man smokes his cigar.

Whicher studies him. *Talamantes,* a guy on a list—no reason to seek him out, except for that name. "Tell me something? Are you related to somebody name of Raul Talamantes? Works for Border Patrol."

The switching engine piles on revs, drawing up to a line of hoppers. Agent Raul Talamantes had had the bodies removed, it'd changed everything, right from the start; no ID was recovered, potential evidence got destroyed. How much of everything was down to him?

Jose Talamantes looks at him. "It against the law? Being related?"

The locomotive edges up, engages, starts to push.

Talamantes blows out smoke. "Raul's a cousin. Why you even want to know that?"

The marshal only stares at the long line of freight inching forward. Screeching, rolling, clacking on the steel rails.

CHAPTER 30

Zavala County, TX.

He'd slept in his own bed a few scant hours. The apartment in Laredo numb and black. He'd showered, changed. Lit out in the pre-dawn silence.

Past the airport, the breakfast joint served him huevos rancheros and refried beans. Corn tortillas. Stewed coffee. He'd finished up and hit the road.

Two hours later parked at the foot of a driveway—the nagging feeling is stronger than ever. A sensation building, same as right before they sent him overseas. A point approaching—fork in the road. *Something final set to change.*

He stares at the concrete deer grazing in a barren yard.

A station wagon's parked in front of a one-floor house. He walks up to the door, knocks hard. Steps back. Hears a female voice, muffled.

The lock turns, the door starts to open.

Lindy Page is in a bagged-out top and jogging pants. She stares a split second, tries to slam the door shut.

He jams his boot into the gap.

"They let me out already." She stares at him, eyes shining. "I talked with that lady deputy."

"You tell me what I need to know," Whicher says, "and we're done with this."

She stops pushing, steps out in the yard. "I wish I'd never met him." She takes a few paces, stands beneath the Mexican white oak.

The marshal follows. "I need to know about Todd."

She shakes her head.

"He worked up in Chicago one time, were you with him then? He ever talk to you about it?"

Lindy sniffs into her hand.

"Reba Williams told me Todd was working some warehouse. How'd he come by a job like that, all the way up there?"

"I don't know."

"Did he know a man named Merrill Johnson?"

Her face is blank.

"You really don't want to know who killed Todd?"

She stares at the ground.

"Why'd you run out on me that first day? At the restaurant..."

"I done told you why."

"You told me law enforcement showed up," Whicher says. "Was it a blond haired man? Wearing a suit?"

A flicker passes behind her eyes.

"You can't wash your hands of this, Lindy."

"I got nothing to say to you."

Dogs. He remembers the dogs. Three of them, farm dogs, German Shepherds.

He can hear them. Barking, coming. He steps from the truck, into the nearest barn.

The earth underfoot is hard, trampled down. No animals. The farm had no stock. He eyes the standpipe—the place had water, shelter. Isolation. *Maybe that was all it needed?*

Through the barn's open doors, he sees Zach Tutton coming through the yard, dogs out in front.

Whicher draws the Glock.

"What's going on?" Zach calls.

The marshal walks to the next-in-line barn.

Straw is on the ground. Electric lights hanging from the roof. He spots a door, crosses to it. The door leads back out to the yard—to a lean-to shelter, a plywood stall, the smell unmistakable; an outhouse.

Zach Tutton runs around the side of the barn, dogs yelping. "*What do you want?*" he shouts. "Is this a search?"

Whicher keeps on walking.

"*You come with a warrant?*"

At the house old man Tutton steps out, length of stick in his hand.

Whicher points at the German Shepherds. "Y'all get them dogs under control."

The old man moves in, stick raised. He yells at the dogs, "*Shut the hell up...*"

Zach grabs at the collar on one, the old man snatches it from him, pulling the animal toward the house. "These here is guard dogs..."

"Get 'em in hand."

The loose dogs scatter.

Zach stares. "You just searched the place. You better have a warrant..."

Old man Tutton kicks the door to the mud room, storming in.

"I came here to talk, is all. Your dogs chased me through the yard."

Zach spits in the dirt. "Real smart," he says.

Whicher fits the Glock back in the holster.

"What do you want?"

"You knew Todd Williams."

"He told me he was..."

"Working as a hunting guide, you told me that already. I want to know about Chicago. What the hell was he doing up there? Don't give me any shit, you must've known about it."

Zach bugs his eyes. "He got a job, he was working..."

"Thirteen-hundred miles away? He couldn't get a job digging ditches the end of this lane."

The young man's face is sullen.

"What was he doing? How'd he get the damn thing?"

"I don't know. It was, like, some warehouse job..."

"A warehouse?"

Zach shoves his hands in the pockets of his jeans. "They'd get freight, unload it. Same as his pa done."

"His pa?"

"He's been dead ten year. But he used to work the railroad."

Whicher scans the empty farmyard. "What's going on out here, Zach? What do you do all day?"

"The land's all rented..."

"Who do you talk to? All that radio gear of yours?"

"All kinds of people..."

"People in Mexico? People from around here? People coming through the brush?"

Old man Tutton's out of the house now—making straight for Whicher's Chevy. In his hand is a wad of notepaper.

The marshal calls over, "*Mister Tutton...*"

The man reaches the truck. He stares at the front, writing something on the pad.

Whicher moves to him. "Mister Tutton, what are you doing?"

"License plate."

"You're writing down my license plate?"

"I want your badge too, your number. Last time you came here, I called a lawyer out to Crystal City." He squints up from the notepad. "I get your number, I can make a complaint."

Whicher pushes back the Resistol.

From inside the Chevy is a static burst on an incoming call. He opens up, whips the receiver off the hook. "Whicher..."

"Marshal, this is dispatch at Dimmit County Sheriff. We have a message. Highway Patrol, in Medina County."

"Medina?"

"San Antonio area."

"What's the message?"

"They picked up somebody name of Boyd Harris. Sheriff said you'd be wanting to know."

Jug Line Harris.

"He was running?"

"All I have is they arrested him."

"Where is he now?"

"Sheriff says he's on his way down here."

CHAPTER 31

Carrizo Springs, TX.

Whicher drives twice around the courthouse square, looking for a place among the trucks, sedans and sheriff's vehicles. In a row beneath the sabal palms a pickup's taking up a space and a half. The marshal slows, blinker on—staring out the window at it, a black Toyota SR5

Maybe it's the angle of the sun—some trick of the light. He stares a long moment.

A horn sounds—he cuts his eyes to the rear-view, a truck coming up behind.

At the corner, a panel van pulls out—Whicher hits the gas, accelerating to take the space.

He shuts off the motor, steps out, locks it up. Walks fast back down the sidewalk. Stops at the black pickup under the row of palms.

In his mind's eye he sees night time, the brush—
Saldana running in a beam of light. He turns away from
the vehicle. Walks to the courthouse entrance.

The Hispanic deputy with the black-rimmed glasses
watches from behind the counter.

"Ma'am. I'm looking for Deputy Alvarenga."

The woman checks on the desk. "Processing a
detainee..."

"Upstairs?"

"I can call her, marshal?"

Whicher crosses to the back of the lobby, reaches the
stairwell, climbs the steps fast. In the custody area Benita
Alvarenga's leaning into a small desk, writing.

She looks up. "Harris is here, they just brought him
in."

The marshal moves out into the corridor.

Deputy Alvarenga steps in his path, hand out, catching
him full in the chest.

He stops.

She looks at him, flushes. "You can't go in," she says.
"Sheriff says a lawyer has to be present." She moves her
hand from his shirt.

"Is Harris under arrest?"

She nods. "He's going in front of the judge, arraign-
ment should be within the hour."

The marshal takes a half-pace back, feeling the mark of
her hand beneath his shirt. "Is Scruggs here?"

"On his way."

324

"What do we know?"

"Highway Patrol picked him up out by San Antonio. He was driving too fast. They checked his license, saw there was a stop order. The vehicle's not his, they went over it—they found an under-dash receiver."

"A radio?"

"You want to see it?"

His eyes are blank a moment.

The deputy fits the cap onto her pen.

Whicher looks at her. "The vehicle's *here*?"

Benita Alvarenga stands in front of the black Toyota. "Highway Patrol sent it down on a flat-bed," she says. "Scruggs requested it."

Whicher steps from the sidewalk into the roadway. He walks the full length of the truck. Around the tailgate, back along the curb.

"Don't touch anything," she says. "We have a crime scene technician coming out to take a look. It's registered at an address in Del Rio. I called the PD, they're going to get back."

Through the driver window, Whicher can just make out the radio receiver under the dash. He takes off the Resistol, runs a hand through his hair.

Deputy Alvarenga looks at him over the roof of the cab.

"I went out to Crystal City this morning. Saw Zach Tutton. At that farm." Whicher sets the hat back in place. "Zach told me Todd Williams was working some warehouse up to Chicago. Rail freight. He said the kid's father used to work the railroads. Maybe he knew Merrill Johnson."

She puts her head on one side.

Whicher studies the Toyota wheels—the rims marked, side-walls of the tires scuffed from rough country.

"You think Merrill Johnson might have got him that job?" she says.

"We could go ask his momma?"

She nods. "Why'd you go out to see Tutton?"

"Randell Creagan had that bunch of trailers, like he was housing transients?" The marshal looks at her. "I think they could be doing the same."

"Sheltering and harboring?"

"Zach has a bunch of radio gear..."

"That's not illegal."

"The place is walking distance from those trailers, a night's walk, a guide like Todd Williams could get 'em through. Zach maybe talking with 'em on the radio. They're getting money doing something." Whicher rubs a hand over his freshly shaved chin.

"What are we doing about the women?" she says. "Carmela Ramirez. Sara Pacheco."

A

In an annex to the courthouse building, Marshal Reuben Scruggs leans against a tall file cabinet. He reads from a bunch of faxed sheets.

Whicher scans the lobby to the interview suite—decades old plaster, light streaming in the high windows, ceiling fan stirring the confined air.

Behind closed doors in the interview room, Jug Line Harris waits with the court-appointed lawyer.

Scruggs reads aloud. "VIN number on this here Toyota matches the VIN of a truck boosted in Laredo. Three weeks back."

"It has an under-dash radio," Whicher says.

Scruggs looks up.

"What if it were mobile comms?"

"Harris broke his bail conditions," Scruggs says. "Court restricted movement to Dimmit, Maverick and Zavala counties only. He was up to San Antonio, so we've got him, we can keep him a spell. Stack up the original hunting charge, plus breaking bail, plus the stolen truck—it adds up to he ain't going anyplace, anytime soon."

At the far end of the lobby, Sheriff Cole Barnhart approaches—expanse of white shirt billowing like a sail.

Scruggs straightens.

"*Marshal*," the sheriff calls out. "I need a minute of your time."

"We're about to go on and talk to Harris," Scruggs says. "Can it wait?"

The sheriff steps in close, palm straw hat raked back on his head. He blinks once. "No, sir."

"It can't wait?"

"I had two phone calls out of Eagle Pass. Sheriff Owens at Maverick County. And Miguel Carrasco, from INS."

Scruggs eyes him.

"Both calls were about a couple of Mexican hookers."

Scruggs glances at Whicher.

Sheriff Barnhart looks at the younger marshal, expression pointed—then back to Scruggs. "The both of 'em want to know if we're investigating their deaths?"

Whicher clears his throat. "It looks like we might have identified the two women killed at the Channing Ranch."

Sheriff Barnhart hooks his thumbs in his belt loops. He speaks his words to Scruggs. "I told you day one of this investigation—we categorically will not look into the Hispanic deaths."

Scruggs juts his chin. "Criminal investigation can lead unexpected places."

"The hell it can." The sheriff rocks back on his heels. "A pair of God damn cat-house *chicas*..."

Whicher cuts him off; "What difference does it make?"

"Shit. Listen at the new guy...."

"Nobody deserved what happened in that ranch."

"The bunch of 'em entered illegally," the sheriff says. "They snuck in like a bunch of God damn criminals."

Scruggs runs his tongue around the inside of his cheek.

Whicher stops himself responding.

"The county ain't about to be held responsible. I told y'all, day one. Forget about the Hispanic victims. They could be from anywhere."

Across the lobby, the door of the interviewing room opens. A bearded man in a suit steps out.

Sheriff Barnhart spears a look at him.

The man steers his large gut into the lobby space. He looks at Scruggs and Whicher in turn. "James Schneider," he says. "Criminal defense attorney. If you gentlemen are ready, my client can see you now."

A

The interviewing room is cramped after the wide expanse of lobby. To one side of a small table, Jug Line Harris is slumped in a chair, ball cap down on his greasy hair.

Beside him, Schneider, the court-appointed lawyer, rests the arms of his light gray suit on the table top.

Marshal Reuben Scruggs sits notepad open, pen in hand.

Whicher leans against the wall, hands behind his back.

Scruggs begins the interview. "Let's start with the truck," he says. "What can you tell me about that?"

Harris looks at Schneider. He pulls his denim jacket around himself, feet shifting under the table.

The lawyer sits forward, gut straining against his shirt. He gives Harris a small nod.

"It belongs to a fishin' buddy, out of Del Rio."

"A fishing buddy?"

"Carlos, the guy's name is. Leaves it up at the lake."

Scruggs bounces the pen against the notepad.

"I look out for it," Harris says. "He lets me use it, time to time."

"Sheriff's department checked with Del Rio police," Scruggs says. "The guy on the title never heard of it."

"There must be some mistake," Schneider says.

"No mistake. Carlos Evans is the name on the title. Says he don't own a Toyota SR5 pickup—never has."

"That's all I knowed," Harris says. "It's a guy fishes. Carlos. Got a bunch of lock-ups out at the lake, man leaves it there."

Scruggs reads from his notes. "The VIN number on the pickup matches a Toyota SR5 stolen in Laredo three weeks back. What you think about that?"

Jug Line Harris opens his mouth to say something.

Schneider cuts in, "My client does not wish to answer that."

"Stolen. Not stolen. Whatever it is," Scruggs says, "we got crime scene personnel heading in to look it over. You want to tell me what you were doing high-tailing it north— in Medina County?"

Schneider speaks for him. "No comment."

"That's a straight violation of the court's bail conditions," Scruggs says.

Harris is silent, staring at his hands.

"There's a radio receiver under the dash in that Toyota," Whicher says. "What's it for?"

Harris clumps his work boots together, saying nothing.

"It's not my client's vehicle," Schneider says, "the radio has no connection with him."

Whicher looks at Harris. "You know a feller name of Zach Tutton? Or his father? They own a farm west of Crystal City."

"No comment," Schneider says.

"You don't feel like talking," Scruggs says to Harris, "you got the right. But you'll be looking at some jail time, here." He looks at Schneider. "All things considered. What with the original hunting charge…"

"A misdemeanor," the lawyer says.

"Compounded by skipping town in a stolen ride."

"Did Merrill Johnson give you that truck?" Whicher says. "Did somebody tell you to run?"

"My client declines to answer," Schneider says. "And that is a leading question."

"When crime scene examine the vehicle out there," Scruggs says, "they dig up anything related to my investigation, what are y'all going to do about it?"

"That's a supposition," Schneider says. "My client doesn't wish to answer."

"Slick as a whistle."

"We're cooperating with the interview here."

"If y'all want to cut a plea, let me give you a piece of advice."

"And what might that be, marshal?"

"I ain't a patient man."

"You feel that's something that'd be a concern to us?"

"If you're looking for a deal, you best get to it, right quick. County attorney will be wanting the view of the investigating officer. Hell on you if y'all make me wait."

⋏

Upstairs at the open window of his office, Sheriff Barnhart rests against the sill, smoking on a cigar, shoulders bunched.

Marshal Scruggs sits at a corner of the big desk, notes laid out before him.

Whicher watches from the side of the room.

The sheriff puffs on the cigar—tip glowing, clouds of blue smoke about his head. "Jim Schneider stonewalled the pair of you, that about the size of it? You get anything at all out of Harris? That little son of a bitch."

Scruggs stares down at his notes. "Nothing we didn't already have."

The sheriff shifts his weight on the sill. "Exactly where do you think he fits with this investigation?"

"He's on the periphery," Scruggs says.

"The periphery?"

"Involved..."

"But not the killer?" The sheriff looks from Scruggs to Whicher and back again.

"Not the killer, no," Scruggs says, finally. "Crime scene are coming out to take a look at the vehicle, the Toyota. It could be connected with one or more of the murders. We know it ain't Harris's truck, it don't belong to him."

"I think it's a possible for the truck I saw firing on Alfonso Saldana," Whicher says.

Scruggs looks at him.

"I think it could be the vehicle from the night."

"You got any kind of a good reason for saying that?"

Sheriff Barnhart leans into the room. "We ain't investigating Alfonso Saldana."

"Whoever shot him likely killed Todd Williams," Whicher says. "Him and everybody else at the ranch."

Scruggs lets a moment pass. He picks out a loose paper from among his notes. "Has the doc been consulted—on disinterring the Hispanic victims?"

The sheriff's face is grim.

"Did y'all ask?"

"I can tell you she took a look at the clothing those people were wearing. This toxicology thread is pretty damn sketchy, marshal." Sheriff Barnhart knocks the ash from his cigar. "Doctor Schulz reckons if any of these people were riding trains, riding freight loads, chemicals and all, there'd be plenty evidence on the clothing—just the clothing, mind. Without having to dig 'em on up."

"She rechecked the clothing?" Scruggs says.

"She didn't find a damn thing. If you want a full test for toxicology, Webb County can do it," the sheriff says. "They can do it on Saldana. If he was traveling with the group from the ranch, he'd show the same signs."

"We don't know he was traveling with them," Scruggs says.

"You mean Webb County wouldn't buy it either?"

Whicher looks at the sheriff. "We have possible IDs for the victims. We're obliged to check, there's a legal obligation."

"We can't access a God damn thing," the sheriff says. "No photographs, no dental charts. We can't get finger prints, palm prints, nothing on ante-mortem medical conditions—no alerts for missing persons. We can't get shit."

Scruggs studies the sheriff from his position at the desk.

"I want to know about Harris," the big man says. "How's he in this? Let's hear it."

"Harris's name came from Sheriff Owens, in Eagle Pass," Scruggs says. "Somebody in the PD passed it on. We were looking to arrest Randell Creagan, nobody seemed to know the guy, the police department in Eagle Pass came up with Jug Line Harris. An associate."

"Harris admits knowing him," Whicher says.

"There's a good chance this Toyota was stolen by Randell Creagan in Laredo," Scruggs says. "Even if it turns out the truck has no direct connection to any of the murders, the fact Harris was driving it ties him in with Creagan pretty good."

"And that's it? That's all you got?" Sheriff Barnhart's nodding to himself at the window.

"What's that supposed to mean?" Scruggs says.

The sheriff fits the cigar to his lips, snatches it away. "The only man y'all have picked up is Harris, and he's not it. He's not a killer."

Scruggs cuts him a look.

"Or, are you saying he is?"

"No. We're not saying that."

"The only other name I'm hearing is some customs broker. Merrill Johnson. You think he's the killer?"

Whicher levels his gaze on the sheriff.

"Neither one of them killed anybody. Is that right?"

The man's words like a cold slap.

Sheriff Barnhart steps from the open window. "This thing's gone about far enough..."

Marshal Scruggs stands. "There something on your mind, sheriff?"

"You bet your ass there is. I want this inquest transferred."

"Say again?"

"It stays federal—hell, it can stay with the Marshals Service. But I want it transferring. Y'all are getting nowhere, pissing up a rope."

Scruggs stares at the big man.

"It's turning into a God almighty mess. Western district can take it on."

"Does Marshal Lassiter know about this?"

"Quint Lassiter agreed to come down, talk it over..."

"You already talked about it?"

"Jim Gale's on his way from LA, he's the local man, I should've give it him, the first place."

Scruggs steps to the sheriff.

"Marshal, you been in court in Laredo most every day of this investigation."

"That's not an issue…"

"Meanwhile, your deputy's arrested a waitress from a Mexican grill in Crystal City—plus Jug Line Harris, a semi-literate field guide. Neither one of 'em have made a blind bit of difference. And now y'all want me to authorize digging up a bunch of Hispanics. I told you day one, not to go there."

"We go where we need to go," Scruggs answers.

"You need to get the hell out of my office," the sheriff says. "That's where you need to go now."

⅄

Whicher follows Scruggs down the stairs, moving fast, no words.

They stride along the polished corridor, reach the back office. Scruggs steps in the room. Whicher waits at the threshold.

Benita Alvarenga looks up from the desk.

"You know about this?" Scruggs says. "Marshal Lassiter? The sheriff calling him down here?"

Nothing registers on her face.

"Yes or no?" Scruggs barks.

"I don't know what you're talking about," she says, heat suddenly in her eye. "I was about to tell you crime scene have arrived. Meg Wheeler—she's outside."

Scruggs turns. He grunts at Whicher. "Let's move."

They step out along the corridor, Scruggs pushes open the rear door.

Outside, the glare of sun is blinding.

Across the square, a van's parked alongside the Toyota—its rear doors wide.

"I'm taking this to District," Scruggs says, "Buddy Riggins can throw me the hell off a case, damned if anybody else will."

A female scene tech is dusting the Toyota truck for prints. Meg Wheeler's short, round-faced, with auburn hair. Dressed in khakis, an open-necked shirt.

Scruggs stops, turns. "This whole damn thing with Saldana, the rest of them Hispanics—it's a can of worms, sheriff knows it. We keep shoving the damn can beneath his nose." He takes out his badge.

The scene technician's holding a camel hair brush between blue-gloved fingers.

"I'm investigating officer," Scruggs says.

She taps the ID clipped to a pocket. "Officer Wheeler," she says. "There was no information, I was just getting started." She points at the velvet black powder spilling down the window of the truck.

"If Randell Creagan's prints are on this," Whicher says to Scruggs, "we got Jug Line Harris nailed."

"You get done with prints," Scruggs says to the woman, "can you run a check for blood?"

"I got Luminol, plus a UV lamp. That's not about to work in these light-levels."

Across the street, at an empty store, three Latino boys sit watching from the shade.

"What's the story on the vehicle?"

"Stolen in Laredo," Scruggs says. "Possible link to one or more homicides."

Whicher eyes the driver window. "Can we run a check for gun shot residue?"

"Difficult. Definitely not out here."

Whicher points at the under-dash radio receiver. "Try lifting prints off of that thing. I think it might've been receiving short-wave."

"I can give it a shot." Officer Wheeler reaches for a two-inch print card from a pack laid on the roof of the cab.

"If we know who was using that radio..."

Scruggs looks at him.

"I think that kid at the farm might have been hooked up with this. Zach Tutton. I think he might have been their radio man..."

⋏

For ten minutes, Meg Wheeler works the Toyota pickup. In the palm shade, Whicher smokes a cigarette, Scruggs silent, arms folded.

Across the street the three Latino boys watch beneath the awning of a store.

Whicher glances at the courthouse, the upstairs office window.

Carmela Ramirez. Sara Pacheco. Alfonso Saldana.

Besides the three of them, two more victims, *campesinos*, country boys. Unmourned.

Scruggs studies the younger marshal from beneath the black brim of his hat.

Whicher takes a long hit off the cigarette. "Can we take a walk?"

Chapter 32

Half a block from the courthouse, at the roadside eatery, Whicher buys coffee, passing a cup to Scruggs. He lights a cigarette off the still-lit end of the last.

"You fixing to smoke yourself to death?"

Whicher stares down the block at store-front law offices, loan companies, banks. "I spoke to Lindy Page this morning," he says. "Drove out to Crystal City. Before you came in. I think she was telling the truth."

Scruggs looks at him.

"I think somebody in law enforcement told her not to talk to us."

The older marshal takes a pull at his cup of coffee, eyes hooded.

A semi rolls along the street, compressed air hissing from its brakes. Whicher waits for it to pass. "I think it was Dane Vogel," he says.

"Lindy Page tell you that?"

Whicher takes a draw on the Marlboro. "Dane Vogel followed me, yesterday morning."

Across the street at the Western wear store, a man steps out, hat box cradled beneath an arm. He stares at the two unfamiliar men—suited, unsmiling. The weight of the sky upon them.

"I went out to where Saldana was shot," Whicher says. "Before I met you at the horse fair yesterday."

"What the hell for?"

"It's where a man died. There hasn't even been a regular search."

The wind scours dust along the cross-town highway, swirling spirit dancing in the air.

Scruggs looks out across the street. "You never mentioned this yesterday. You're telling me Dane Vogel followed you?"

At the courthouse, Deputy Alvarenga steps out, hand to her brow.

She scans the square, starts across to Meg Wheeler at the pickup.

Scruggs steps into the roadway.

Whicher follows his boss over the street. He glances at the sheriff's window—sensing the big man looking down.

Alvarenga spots them, she calls out; *"Sheriff's asking to speak with you, marshal..."*

Scruggs turns for the main entrance.

Alvarenga heads for the rear door, color at her face.

Whicher crosses to the forensics van.

Officer Wheeler watches him. "Trouble?" she says. "Everybody's spring seems like its wound a little tight." She turns back to working a brush above the door handle of the truck.

Across the street, the Latino boys sit eating from a paper bag of churros.

"Some pretty clean prints," she says. "Three, at least."

"Three?"

"We'll need to move to an inspection bay if we're looking for blood or gun shot residue." She angles her head at the door. "We're talkin' trace evidence, honey. Microscopic..."

"Three distinct sets of prints?"

"I can call for a tow vehicle? Homicide investigation, it ought to be okay..."

The door of the courthouse flies open. Scruggs is out again, hat down.

"*I want to move this*," Officer Wheeler calls out. She steps from the Toyota, holding the jar of powder.

Scruggs's eyes are gimlets.

"I want to move to an inspection bay," she says. "You want me to check with the county? Or will the Marshals Service pick up the tab?"

"Move it, do it. Put it on the federal tab." Scruggs turns to Whicher, stabs a finger at the blue and white Ford Ranger at the end of the square.

Whicher throws down the cigarette. Follows Scruggs to the truck.

"Jim Gale's flying in from LA," Scruggs says, over his shoulder. "Sheriff Barnhart had the balls to ask me to meet with him, you believe that? *Meet Gale.* Brief him. Then hand him the God damn reins..." He rips the keys from his pocket. "You'll have to do it. I told the sheriff I'm going the hell up to Houston. I'll take it to Buddy Riggins. I'm going up right now."

"Sir, can't it wait?"

"Hell it can."

"What about Vogel?"

"Screw Dane Vogel." Scruggs jams the keys in the lock. He snatches open the door.

Whicher's throat is dry. "There's something you need to know..."

"If I want to know what the God damn FBI are doing, I'll ask Gerry Nugent..."

"I don't know if Houston even know about this..."

Scruggs turns. The skin at his face mottled with anger.

"Dane Vogel's running some kind of investigation."

"You want to get the hell out of my way?"

"He's investigating US Marshals Service."

"He's doing *what*?" Scruggs stands one foot in the truck the other still on the sidewalk.

"Yesterday, he practically accused me of disturbing a crime scene."

"What the hell are you talking about?"

"The site of Saldana's murder—he said I could be trying to dispose of evidence."

Scruggs's mouth works, silent. He shakes his head, body taut.

He pulls himself into the driver seat of the Ford. Locks out his arms on the wheel.

"Let me see if I got this straight." He stares out through the windshield. "I got a sheriff trying to throw me off a case for bringing up the names of two dead hookers. My deputy's being followed by an FBI internal affairs agent. And you're telling me US Marshals Service is under investigation?"

"Sir, it was me found out the names of those dead girls."

"It was Miguel Carrasco. At INS."

"No, sir."

Scruggs twists his head around. "You told me your damn self—it was Carrasco."

"I crossed into Mexico. Piedras Negras, night before last. I found out."

The older marshal's knuckles are yellow-white on the steering wheel.

"Vogel knows I did it, he had me followed."

Scruggs stares at the backs of his hands. "You know what a jurisdictional boundary is?" His voice is tight in his throat.

"Sir, I know."

"You employ illegal means it's inadmissible. You screw the whole thing up..." He sits, stares out through the windshield—eyes alive.

"I'm supposed to stay quiet, Vogel thought he had enough on me..."

Scruggs doesn't respond. The muscles in his face flex, working beneath the skin.

Whicher takes off his hat. Now that it's out, there's no point holding back. "I think a lot of things are wrong with this case," he says. "I think the women at the ranch could've had ID—maybe the men too. I think they could've had ID—and it was taken from them."

A dry bark of sound catches at the back of Scruggs's throat.

"The bodies were moved, no justice of the peace, nothing done right. You said so yourself..."

Still his boss won't look at him.

"If Dane Vogel's investigating the Marshals Service, I think it's 'cause of Jim Gale. He was there, close by, he had free rein. The guy's on a shooting charge in LA. Plus, I found his number in Creagan's apartment—the day right after Creagan was killed."

Scruggs's arms finally flex from rigid—his shoulders slump.

"He tried to get to Harris, soon as we started looking, Gale went after him."

His boss cranks his head around, puts out his hand, eyes shining. "I want your badge. I want your gun."

Whicher looks at him.

"You're off the case. Suspended from duty."

The younger marshal stands numb on the sidewalk.

"Go the hell home. Be there when I call." Scruggs turns the ignition. The motor fires up under the hood. "Badge and gun."

Whicher reaches in his jacket pocket. Fingers touching the leather holder.

"I'm driving this truck to Houston," Scruggs says, eyes flat. "This thing is all over."

CHAPTER 33

Scruggs's blue and white Ford Ranger reaches the intersection—it pulls out fast, tires catching on the hot road. It chops a lane, turns for 85 east. Whicher watches it down the highway, heart thumping in his chest.

He spins around. Surveys the square.

Meg Wheeler's dusting the inside of the Toyota for prints. She's kneeling, shirt stretched across her back. *She's seen nothing.*

The three Latino boys watch, dark-eyed.

He turns for the courthouse, head down, walking fast.

At the main door he pushes into reception, crosses the lobby, reaches the stairs.

In the corridor, Benita Alvarenga's approaching.

"I'm signing Harris out. Into my custody." Whicher hits the stairs, starts to climb.

"Wait," she says. "Where do you want to take him?"

"*Out,*" he barks back.

The marshal reaches the landing, hears her footsteps coming up behind. He turns. "I'm a federal law officer, I can take custody of a prisoner."

"I didn't know about any of this. About Sheriff Barnhart, about Lassiter..."

"I never said you did."

"Is Lassiter taking over the investigation?"

"Right now, it's ours."

She shakes her head. "I can't let you have him."

"You can't stop me. I'm taking Harris to the Channing Ranch."

"What for?" Her eyes are hot beneath the line of her brow.

"I want him to see where five people were shot to death. And stand there tell me nothing, like I'm shit for brains..."

Her hand moves to her hip. "We take a cruiser."

"We do what?"

She pulls out a set of keys. "We take a car from the county pool. Harris stays in my custody."

"We?"

"The three of us. I'll drive."

⋏

Jug Line Harris is handcuffed in the back of the sheriff's department cruiser—chained to a D-ring in the floor. Whicher sits alongside him. Benita Alvarenga at the wheel.

Harris stares out the window at the south Texas brush.

"You know this country," Whicher says.

The man doesn't answer.

"You and Todd Williams used to hunt it."

Benita Alvarenga slows the cruiser as the track worsens.

"Only thing Todd was good for was right here," Whicher says. "Cutting out. Vanishing."

The land is covered in thorn scrub and mesquite—the brush menacing, a physical presence.

Whicher sees the outline of a ruined building. It sits beneath a bleached out disc of sun.

The track curves around a line of catclaw and guajillo. They pull up at the rear of the ranch.

Alvarenga cuts the motor, steps out, opens up the rear door by Harris.

Whicher releases the chain from the man's wrist. "Go ahead, get out."

"What for?"

"Step out of the vehicle," Alvarenga says.

Harris grunts, moves his arms, chain rattling to the floor. He leans forward, swings out his legs. "I ain't going in there."

"Sure you are." Whicher steps out, scanning the crumbling ranch.

"I don't have to do squat..."

The marshal puts a hand in the small of the man's back—pushing him forward to the empty doorway.

At the threshold, Harris locks out his legs.

Whicher raises a boot—pushes him forward.

"Get the hell off of me..." Harris staggers inside.

Deputy Alvarenga glances at Whicher—a look of warning in her eye.

The marshal points to the ground inside the house. "You knew Todd Williams. A week ago he was laying face up, right there. With a bullet in his head."

Alvarenga takes a pace into the broken room. "Why'd you run out, Mister Harris? If you've nothing to do with any of this?"

Harris stares at his boots.

"You knew Randell Creagan," Whicher says. "He's dead, too."

"I ain't got nothing to say."

"You and Todd were hunting guides. You know this land, you used that to work *coyote*. Was it Randell Creagan hooked you in?"

Alvarenga tries to catch the man's eye beneath the ball cap.

Harris stares at the dirt.

"Take a look here." Whicher steps to the back wall. "You look, God damn it." He points a finger at the floor.

Harris screws up his face.

"This," Whicher says, "right here. Is where two young women died. Twenty-something years old, they crossed a river, Todd Williams brought 'em here." He looks at Harris. "This is the place he used—to rest up, after crossing. Am I right?"

"I don't know what the hell y'all are talking about."

Whicher moves across the room. "Here," he says, "in this corner, I found a kid shot to death. Out in the back, I found another guy. Somebody killed him trying to get away."

"Take me back to my cell..."

"I'm in the middle of my own country." Whicher stares at the blood stains on the wall. "How does it look like this?"

Jug Line Harris raises his cuffed wrists. "Y'all take me back..."

"Somebody chained Randell Creagan to a freight train."

"It ain't nothing to me..."

"You know a man named Merrill Johnson, a huntin' man? Did Johnson ever come out here? Or to the river camps? To Lake Amistad?"

"No, no—*I don't know...*" Harris clamps his mouth shut. "I want my God damn attorney."

From the cruiser is the sound of a call, the radio crackling.

Alvarenga eyes the marshal. "I need to get that."

Harris steps forward, "I'm walking..."

The deputy draws her pistol, "Stay right where you are."

Whicher catches hold of Harris. He takes him out of the building, stands him up against the wall.

Alvarenga moves to the cruiser, picks up the radio call.

Whicher leans in close to Harris. "Tell me about Gale?" he says, under his breath. "Five minutes after I busted you hunting javelina, Jim Gale showed up."

"I want Schneider, I want my lawyer..."

"Gale was supposed to bring you in two days back."

"The hell you talking about?"

"Was it Gale told you to skip town?"

Alvarenga steps from the cruiser. "That was dispatch. Your boss is looking for you—he called the sheriff's department." She holds up the radio transmitter. "You want to call?"

Whicher turns to Harris. "You ran out to San Antonio..."

The man's head drops between his shoulders.

"You were running for your life."

⅄

Back in the courthouse in Carrizo Springs, Benita Alvarenga locks Jug Line Harris in a cell.

In the office, Whicher finds a note from Meg Wheeler. She's moved the Toyota, left a number to call.

He shoves the note in his jacket. Searches out a list of contacts from the file cabinet, pulling out a sheet of paper from the back of a folder. He writes down an address.

On a shelf above the cabinet is a law enforcement directory. He takes it down, flicks through the pages to the San Antonio section. He eyes the phone on the desk, takes out a cigarette, lights it. Lifts the receiver. He dials the number, listens to it ring.

A woman answers, "FBI field office, San Antonio."

"US Marshals Service. I need to speak with an agent named Dane Vogel, is this the right office?"

"Yes, sir."

"Name's Whicher. It's an urgent call."

"I'll see if he's in the building."

The phone switches to hold.

Whicher smokes the cigarette, stares at the floor.

At the other end of the line is a faint click.

"Vogel?"

He can hear breathing.

"Is that Dane Vogel?"

"What do you want?"

"Merrill M. Johnson. Do you know him?" The marshal jams the phone between his jaw and shoulder. "Do you know where he is?"

"Why are you calling?"

"Is Merrill Johnson part of your investigation?" Whicher takes a pace around the office. "If you know where he is, you better bring him in, now." He feels a lick of rising anger.

"You're telling me what I need to do?" Vogel says.

"You had Creagan under surveillance. Are you watching Johnson?"

"I'm about to put the phone down..."

"Scruggs knows. He's on his way to Houston to see District Marshal Riggins. I got Jug Line Harris in Carrizo Springs. And you have about two hours till the southern district Marshals office is all over your ass."

"You told him?"

"I'll tell you something else—your number one suspect is flying in from LA as we speak."

"What the hell are you talking about?"

"Pick up Merrill Johnson," Whicher says. "If you know where he is, do it now."

"You listen," Vogel says. "Do nothing. Nothing more. If you do, I'll indict. Understand me. I'll press charges..."

Whicher's hand is at the phone cradle.

"If you screw this up any more than you already have, I'll press for the absolute maximum..."

"Bring in Johnson. Before Gale gets in." Whicher chops off the call.

⚓

The road into downtown Eagle Pass is alive. Whicher pushes the Chevy through the early evening traffic, gunning fast along the tight lanes.

At the river, people are everywhere—cars parked double by the Mexican supermarket. He hits the intersection by the liquor store, crosses Main, powers into a narrow road, scattered housing, cut-down trucks.

He pulls over at the house with the Trans-Am in the yard. Jumps out, climbs the steps to the porch. Knocks hard at the door.

"*Eric. You in there?*"

He knocks again, harder. Tries the door—it's unlocked.

"*Eric?*" He pushes it open. "*It's Whicher...*"

He steps inside, in the kitchen—crosses to the living room. Eric's flat-out on the couch, TV on, no sound.

"Wake up..." Whicher puts a hand to his shoulder.

The man's eyes open—blurred, red, his face bloated. "What time is it, man?"

"Five-thirty."

"Is Karen here?"

"I don't think."

Eric pushes up on an elbow. Head sagging. "What you doing here?"

"You have a gun?"

His friend stares from the couch.

"I need a gun. You have one?"

"What the hell are you talking about?"

"Yes or no?"

Chapter 34

Maverick County, outside Eagle Pass, TX.

A caliche track rises into low hills—cactus, scrub, a rock and gravel wasteland. In the rear-view of the Chevy, Whicher sees the town of Eagle Pass below. Eric Kessler watches from the passenger seat.

In the cup holder is a tan, saddle-leather holster. Ruger revolver inside. Six-inch barrel. Stainless steel.

The sun is low, air dense with heat, tires raising dust up the long grade.

The name at the foot of the hill matched the name pulled from the file cabinet. The land is rising to a plateau—choked with greasewood and mesquite.

Eric sits forward. "Last time I seen you look like that, you were fixing to shoot somebody."

Whicher doesn't answer.

"Day before we started the ground offensive in Iraq. That's the look you were wearing."

Letting Eric ride had been a mistake—a deal for the Ruger.

His friend buttons the dash lighter. Pulls a pack of cigarettes from his shirt. "Want one?"

"No."

The lighter springs back. "What kind of trouble you in?"

"I'm driving my truck up the side of a hill."

Eric touches the lighter to the cigarette. He cracks the passenger window. Super-heated air blows in the cab.

Whicher thinks of taking out the revolver, giving it back. Turning the man out.

"Karen's leaving me." Eric takes a pull at the cigarette, blows smoke. Puts a boot on the dash.

"That how come you sleep till five?"

"I drink. I don't stop."

"You think, or you know?"

"I know she's cheatin' on me."

The marshal cuts a look at his friend beside him. "She has a bank account," he hears himself say. "At the Southern Surety. In Eagle Pass. You know about it?"

Eric doesn't answer.

"Been paying a life insurance company. Westland Life. Started paying February of last year. The date kind of jumped out at me..."

Eric lets his boot slip from the dash.

"I guess if you'd been killed, out in Iraq…"

Neither man speaks for a long moment.

"I was looking at bank records. I saw it. I didn't know what to say." Whicher glances at him. "I'm sorry."

Ahead is a gravel wash running sideways down the hill. Pieces of twisted brushwood lie scattered in it, boulders, mud-washed stones. The marshal steers on looking at a line of black persimmon, the roof of a property. He drives another fifty yards to a dirt track meeting the caliche.

Where the paths join, a steel post is mounted with a wooden sign. One word painted on it, black over white.

The word reads; *Gale.*

⋏

He wouldn't be there—the flight from LA was three hours, landing six-thirty. He'd take time to get back, maybe stop.

At the end of the track, the house sits facing east across a plain. In the shade of the trees is a half-ton GMC pickup.

Whicher scans the site fast—to the north, black persimmon form a dark barrier. The house is unfinished, split-level—wood-frame, deck at the side. He kills the motor. Picks out the holstered Ruger.

Eric looks at him. "You better not shoot anybody with my gun."

Whicher climbs out, unbuckles his belt, threads an end through the back of the holster.

"I'm serious man, what the fuck?"

The marshal refastens the belt.

Eric starts to climb out.

"I need you to wait here."

The two men exchange a look.

"If I hear shots..."

"Get on the radio." Whicher turns, crosses the flat ground.

He squats at the rear of the GMC truck. Holds up a hand to the tail-pipe, the metal's hot. He takes a backward glance at Eric. Passes a hand over the Ruger—rosewood grips, six-brass jacketed rounds, .357 magnum.

He steps to the house, to a deck of rough-sawn boards. By a new-built rail a box of tools is open. He stands in the fading light, heat radiating from the bone-hard land. Through a glass insert in the wall, he sees a shape move.

The door opens. The six-five frame of Jim Gale steps out.

His back is turned to Whicher—he's bareheaded, dressed in jeans, a work shirt, boots splattered with paint. In his right hand is a claw-hammer.

"Marshal Gale..."

The man rocks, spins on his heel. He stands wide-legged. "God damn. What you doing here? I just flew in from LAX."

"Came to tell you something."

Gale raises the claw-hammer. Points the shaft at a cable looping from a pole. "I got a phone. You could've called."

"I'm done waiting."

A hard look crosses the man's face.

"Jug Line Harris is in a cell in Carrizo Springs," Whicher says. "You were going to pick him up."

Gale looks blank. "I was going to pick his ass up—in California?"

"I could've done it—if you would've called. Instead of that, Highway Patrol got him. He was up to San Antonio, running..."

Gale stares, head to one side. A strange light in his eye. "Think you got yourself a killer?"

"I heard LA County is looking to charge people from the Marshals Service. Account of the riots?"

The big man hooks a thumb into his jeans. "That little pissant hearing?"

Whicher eyes him.

"Everybody was cleared."

"They say a lot of shooting went on." Whicher thinks of the ranch, of standing among bodies, none of them long dead. Everybody in the ranch was shot with nine millimeter ammunition. Like the bullets from his service-issue weapon, his own Glock; the Marshals Service gun. "Two days I've been waiting on Harris. Man would've been long gone, we got lucky."

"You mean to say something by that?"

"The day Randell Creagan got scraped off a rail in Eagle Pass—they sent me out to search his apartment. I found your number. Why would Creagan have a number for you?"

The big man juts his chin. "You have an idea, son?"

"Next day, at Lake Amistad, I tried to pick up Jug Line Harris. I show up, you're already there."

Gale opens his mouth to speak. He closes it, runs a hand through his fine brown hair. "You been sitting on that for five days..." He cracks a dry laugh. It dies in his throat.

"I finally arrested Harris, you showed up at Carrizo Springs," Whicher snaps a finger and thumb. "Like that. Every time I want to talk with him, you're there..."

"Watch your mouth, son." Gale cuts a glance across the desert scrub, jaw tight.

"You know a guy name of Merrill Johnson?"

The big man's gaze stays on a spot out in the brush.

"Or Dane Vogel? Works for FBI."

Gale finally turns to face him. "You come out here fixing to do what?" He takes a step forward, hammer swinging.

From behind is a sound—both men turn, Eric's stepping up on the deck. Gale stares at him, then back at Whicher.

"Whatever y'all came to do, you best do it." Gale steps closer. "Else get the hell off of my property—before I throw your ass down this God damn hill..."

CHAPTER 35

In Eagle Pass at the river, Whicher pulls up by the Trans-Am. "I need you to step out now..."

"Whatever you're thinking of doing," Eric says, "you got to slow it on down."

The marshal puts a hand to the Ruger. "You want your gun back?"

"It's not about the gun."

A car rolls by on the lane. Whicher stares at its tail lights. "I think this guy maybe knew about the people crossing—the people that were shot."

"You think he's on the take?" Eric sits forward.

"In LA there's talk of law officers shooting people—Marshals among them."

A hundred yards from the house is the river—the Rio Grande, the line. Whicher thinks of borders, friendly ground, enemy ground.

Limits, rules of engagement.

᛭

Zavala County, TX.

Forty minutes later, dusk. The yard at the Tutton Farm is dark. At the door of the house, a figure's standing—holding a flashlight. The beam sweeps onto the windshield of Whicher's truck, blinding.

The marshal squints through his fingers, drives to the side of the house, window rolled. "Get the damn light off of me."

Old man Tutton shouts above the noise of the cir-cling dogs. "*What the hell you doing here?*" He switches out the light.

"I want Zach. I want to know about the radio gear." Eyes adjusting, Whicher sees a shape between the man's hands—a black, fluted cylinder—a telescopic sight. It's not a flashlight the man's holding; it's a rifle fitted with a hunt-ing light. He feels a snap inside his belly, pulls the Ruger. "I want that gun...."

Tutton steps back. "I don't have to give you squat."

The marshal flings the driver door open, raising the big-frame revolver. "Call off the dogs..."

Tutton's rooted—the dogs bristling.

"You lay that rifle in the truck bed. And get Zach."

"You come out here threatening me?"

Whicher cocks the hammer.

Meets the man's eyes full.

⅄

Carrizo Springs.

At the Dimmit County Courthouse, Deputy Hagen studies the rifle laid across the reception counter. Remington 700. A jacklight. A scope. A two-point sling. Zach Tutton and his old man stand in front of the main desk.

Benita Alvarenga races down the stairs in back.

"I need two cells," Whicher says.

She takes in the scene. "What charge?"

"Sheltering and harboring."

Her eyes cut to the rifle.

"Plus accessory to first-degree murder."

Tutton senior spins around; "What did you say?"

Whicher ignores him. "I think this could be the weapon. The rifle used to shoot Saldana." He turns to Hagen. "There an evidence room?"

Tutton's face is ash. "What're you talking about?"

"I want Meg Wheeler to have the rifle, soon as she can come get it..."

Tutton cuts in, "That there's a hunting rifle, nothing but..."

Zach Tutton's shifting from foot to foot, white as a sheet.

"District Marshal Lassiter's on his way in," Alvarenga says. She reaches to a set of keys. "I have to brief him on behalf of the sheriff..."

"I have to go," Whicher says.

"You can't go...."

"I have to get to Creagan's place, that bunch of lay-up trailers."

She stares at him.

"I want everything—all the evidence we have..."

"What the hell am I supposed to tell him?"

"Get the defense lawyer. Get Schneider, or get somebody else. All of these people are talking. They're talking tonight."

Dimmit County, South of 277.

Off the highway, the brush is dark—first stars showing. Brady Iverson's sketch is on Whicher's lap. Picked out in the edge of the truck's hi-beam is the group of shacks. He checks the map, slows—peering along the Chevy hood. Ahead, the line of scrub dips to the clearing in the brush. He steers the truck to the dirt spur, swings in, lighting up the group of three trailers.

He brakes to a stop. Draws the big revolver.

The clearing's empty—just a scatter of shoes and rags, plastic water bottles. He cuts the motor, searches out a flashlight. Steps down from the truck, eying the wall of brush.

"*US Marshal,*" he calls out. "*Policía...*"

No sound comes back.

He moves to the nearest trailer, mounts the cinder block step. Rips open the unlocked door.

Flashlight and the barrel aligned, he scans the interior space—thin mattresses, piles of trash. No faces.

He steps in, the smell of stale sweat rancid. In the flashlight beam he sees a pile of clothes—rags, filthy shirts. The white gray dust is on them, the fine red powder.

He grabs a bunch of shirts, jumps from the trailer. Bundles them all on the seat of the truck.

He hurries to the second trailer.

Inside it's the same—dark, no faces. He grabs a handful of clothing, backs out, dumps it in the Chevy.

He runs to the last trailer.

He opens the door, mounts the step. Inside, something moves at the edge of his vision. On the back wall a shape is moving. A shadow, arcing, shifting sideways.

He spins around—stares through the grime on the window. A light is out there. A light along the track.

He steps to the door, snaps out the flashlight, jumps to the ground.

He can hear a motor. He crosses the clearing, backing into the brush.

A vehicle's slowing—lights flaring through the high mesquite. He thinks of Gale. Thumbs back the hammer on the Ruger.

The vehicle's starting to turn in, braking. It's a truck.

The driver door opens, a man gets out. Shorter than Gale, lighter.

The marshal stares at the man's back, the tilt of the hat. The truck's a K5 Chevy Blazer. The man turns, searching—one hand shielding his eyes from the head-lights.

Whicher takes a step forward. It looks like Lassiter—Marshal Lassiter. Lit up, super-real in the beams.

"God damn, army. Where you at?"

Whicher moves from the edge of the clearing, releasing the hammer, holstering the gun. "Right here."

"I've been driving around circles, about to give it up. I called Carrizo Springs, Benita Alvarenga told me you were headed out in the brush. The hell is this?"

"Some kind of camp…"

"She told me where to get off the highway—I couldn't find a God damn thing…"

"I think it's some kind of lay-up point."

"You mean for wets?" The headlights cut beneath the brim of Lassiter's hat. He steps to the truck, kills the motor.

Whicher looks around the clearing at the battered trailers.

"Scruggs called me." Lassiter stands by his vehicle. "I'm headed out to Eagle Pass. To speak to Jim Gale."

Whicher nods. "He tell you?"

"Some, he told me. I wanted to hear what you have to say."

The younger marshal stares at the glare of truck lights. "I think Gale knew one of the murder victims."

"That's what the man said."

"I found his number in Randell Creagan's apartment."

"You done what?"

"The day I searched it," Whicher says. "The day Creagan was found in Eagle Pass."

Lassiter folds his arms.

Neither man speaks. The air in the clearing is heavy with the smell of brush, of desiccated earth.

"Lawman knows the low-life," Lassiter says.

"I think he knows one of the suspects."

The district marshal gives a low whistle.

"Harris," Whicher says. "The man's scared to death. After what happened to Creagan and Williams."

"Buddy Riggins likely won't release the case," Lassiter says.

Whicher looks at him.

"I'm not sure we'd even take it. But I want you clear on one thing; Gale is Marshals' business. You keep your mouth shut. Hell, you ain't supposed to be workin', Scruggs done told me he took your badge."

"I think I found a murder weapon. Tonight. A rifle. Used to shoot Alfonso Saldana..."

Lassiter stares out at the line of dark mesquite.

"Let me check the last trailer," Whicher says. "Then I'm done." He snaps on the flashlight. Steps fast to the third trailer, climbs inside. At the far end he spots a pile of jeans and shirts, filthy with the colored stains. He picks out a few pieces, stashes them under an arm, breathing shallow, backing out.

At the edge of the clearing, Lassiter has a gun in his hand, a squared-off semi-automatic.

A sensation pricks Whicher's skin.

"Something's out here," the man says.

The brush is black, still.

"Dogs, maybe."

"Could be people," Whicher says.

"You get everything you wanted?"

The younger marshal nods.

"I got to go talk to Gale."

"I ride out with you?"

"Your ass is suspended," Lassiter says. "Gale's too, as of now."

CHAPTER 36

Carrizo Springs, TX.

Benita Alvarenga stares at the ball of filthy-looking rags in the evidence room.

Whicher dusts off his hands, glancing at Tutton's hunting rifle. "Did you get a hold of Schneider?"

"I can't get a defense attorney like that."

They step out of the room, she locks it. They set out down the corridor.

"The Tuttons say they have a lawyer, in Crystal City..."

"You can't get hold of him?" Whicher says.

"Nobody's picking up."

Their footsteps are loud in the long dim space.

"I want to see Harris."

"Can't do it," she says. "Not without a lawyer."

They reach the door to the office.

She catches his arm. "Deputy Hagen took a call from Scruggs. A second call. While you were out. Did you call him yet?" Her eyes search his face.

He pulls loose, steps inside the office.

Laying on the desk are two black and white photographs. Enlarged shots, copies of ID.

Benita Alvarenga stands in the door. "What's going on? With Scruggs?"

Whicher stares at the grainy images on the desk, throat tight. "What the hell are these?"

"Police in Piedras Negras sent them up."

Names are written along the edges of both pictures. Two young women, the younger, Carmela Ramirez, the girl with the broken necklace. The elder, Sara Pacheco— the second woman from the Channing Ranch. "This is them..."

"They were reported missing."

"Reported?"

"Yesterday."

The girl from the bar. *Lucila.* She must have done it.

"Carmela Ramirez is from Coahuila. Sara Pacheco from Nuevo León. Both states border with the US." Alvarenga looks at him. "They didn't come up on any freight load."

The marshal stares at the pictures.

"Is Lassiter taking this?" she says. "Him and Gale?"

He doesn't answer.

She picks up the photo of Carmela Ramirez. "Miguel Carrasco thought you ought to have these. He said Lassiter hasn't been around since the sweep, why bring in somebody else?"

Whicher looks up from the desk.

"What?"A frown crosses her brow.

"He was around that day?"

"I'm just saying what Carrasco said. Lassiter called, wanted to know if any of the Hispanic victims had been ID'd."

Whicher pushes himself out of the chair.

"I want Harris."

"We can't. I told you..."

"Put him in an interview room, we're not breaking any law. Let him claim the fifth. I talk—he listens."

꙳

Jug Line Harris slumps in the denim jacket, one hand on the bill of his cap. Hair covers half his face, he sits staring at the little table.

"You're headed one place," Whicher says.

The man doesn't bother to look up.

"A jail yard." The marshal lets a moment pass. "You broke bail, you ran out on the court. Highway Patrol stopped you in a stolen vehicle. There's not a chance you walking a second time."

"Get my damn attorney."

"Only thing you got to do is listen," Whicher says. "You ain't here to answer questions." He takes off the Resistol, places it on the table.

Harris stuffs his hands into his jacket.

"The hunting charge, they'll convict." Whicher takes out a Marlboro. "Handling stolen property—the same." He lights up. "I got a crime scene tech working that Toyota. We found the gun. The rifle."

Harris is still.

"Remington 700, fitted out with a scope. Big light on it."

"I got nothing to say."

"I got it locked in the evidence room. Is it yours?" Whicher takes a drag. "Want me to show you?"

Sweat is on the man's skin now. Sweat and the smell of fear.

Jug Line Harris is locked back in the holding cell. Zach Tutton occupies the seat in the interview room. Deputy Alvarenga stands at the door.

"Is it your rifle?" Whicher says.

"No comment."

"It belong to your old man?"

Zach sits forward, elbows on his knees.

"Those barns you got out at the farm," Whicher says. "They fitted out for wets to sleep in?"

"They ain't fitted out for nothing, they're for animals."

"That how you see them?"

Tutton's mouth opens. Closes.

"You had the Miranda," Alvarenga says. "You have the right to remain silent. If that's what you want."

Tutton spears an angry glance at her.

"Merrill Johnson," Whicher says. "You know him? I told the FBI to pick him up. They get a hold of him, my guess is, he'll let everybody swing. You included."

The young man sits back in his chair—face turned to the wall.

"We're testing for gun shot residue in a stolen Toyota. Pretty fancy radio receiver under the dash. You wire it in there?"

"Any decent auto mechanic could wire a radio in."

"Reckon we'll be able to lift prints. You wearing gloves—when you fixed it in?"

Tutton throws back his head. Stares at the ceiling.

"We find your prints—or your call frequency, stored in the memory? How you going to explain it?"

"Get me a lawyer..."

Whicher shakes his head. "We're all out of time for that."

⚓

Back on the upper floor of the courthouse, Deputy Alvarenga opens the cell door for Zach Tutton. Whicher hustles him inside.

"How long am I going to be here?"

Alvarenga takes off the cuffs. "We'll get you arraigned when the court is in. Not before."

"You can't just keep me here."

"Wrong. That's exactly what we can do."

From the next cell, something strikes against the door, noise echoing in the corridor.

"What the hell's that?"

"Harris," Alvarenga says. She snaps the handcuffs to her belt.

Whicher steps out. She closes the door to Zach's cell, locking it.

Harris is banging and kicking, shouting—his voice muffled, no making out the words.

"He losing it in there?" Whicher says.

She turns the key to open up.

"Let me go in first," he says.

Harris is on the other side of the door, ball cap on the floor, jacket off, his face wild.

"Back the hell up..."

⅄

Harris stands beneath the ceiling light, wired. "I'll talk."

"You want to talk?"

"We make a deal..."

"You mean a plea?"

"I don't know what the hell it is."

"We can't use this," Alvarenga says.

"I talk, you make the judge go easy..."

"None of it will be admissible."

"I want my lawyer. I want Schneider."

"I already told you," Whicher says. "We can't get him."

The man's hands fly up, yanking at his hair. "Y'all are going screw me over..."

"You want to deal, you got to testify."

"I cain't just sit here. I cain't do this no more." He crashes on the side of the cot, eyes darting around the cell.

Whicher looks to Alvarenga. She's staring at Harris.

"It was Randell. God damn *Randell*."

For a moment nobody speaks.

"I was with Todd, out at the ranch. Randell shows up..."

Alvarenga turns to Whicher. "We need it on record."

Harris looks to the marshal. "He went stone fuckin' *in*sane crazy. He comes in driving like a madman, shouting out, *'we got to get rid of 'em'*. He takes out a pistol, shoots both the girls."

"Creagan?" Whicher says.

"Fuckin' Randell."

"Creagan shot everybody?"

"Them other wets, them boys, they tried to jump him—he just kept on shooting. One of the wets grabs a hold of Todd—he's messing his pants, the wet gets a hold on him, Randell's firing, he hits Todd. Right in the head."

Benita Alvarenga steps back.

Harris rocks on the cot. "Todd ends up on the ground, one of the wets is dead, the other two ran out. Randell shoots one of 'em..."

The *campesino* draped across the wall.

"The other boy was too fast. He got out. He made it out. Randell grabs a hold of Todd's rifle..."

"It was Todd's?" Whicher says.

"Shit, I don't know, he had it with him. It had a light, Randell grabs it, gets in the truck, goes to chase the man down..."

"What did you do?" Alvarenga says.

"What do you think? I got in my truck, got the hell out."

"Why shoot the women?" Her face very still.

"Jesus Christ." Harris grabs his head. "I don't know..."

"Randell Creagan shot everybody?"

"That's the God's honest truth."

Whicher feels his pulse climb. "What about Jim Gale?"

"Who?"

"Marshal Jim Gale."

The man looks at him, eyes shining. Face blank.

⋏

Gale's number won't answer. Lassiter's not picking up the radio calls from dispatch. Whicher slams down the phone.

Benita Alvarenga grabs it from him.

"Who're you calling?"

"Sheriff Barnhart, he needs to be here, this is out of hand..."

"Call Schneider again, get a defense attorney." The marshal pulls out the Chevy keys.

"What the hell are you doing?"

"I have to go out there."

"I'm supposed to keep a lid on this? You need to be here when the sheriff gets in."

"Keep everybody locked up..."

Her eyes burn him.

He steps from the office, doubles down the corridor, pushes open the rear door to the square. Wind's sawing at the palms. Noise of traffic is in the air.

He reaches the truck—wrenches open the door. Fires it up, gasses it from the curb.

At the intersection the stop light's on red. He barrels through.

Forty minutes. Forty minutes he can be there.

He guns the Chevy down the road, overtaking a truck.

North end of Eagle Pass, then up the hill. From the highway, he can skirt town, head for the track. He pushes down on the throttle pedal, noise of the V6 rising.

Creagan.

At the side of the road is a brick church, he swerves avoiding a turning car.

Creagan shot everybody.

Ahead is a roadside panel, a sign for the highway. He takes the spur down to 277. The road dark, empty.

He floors out the gas, speed climbing. Glances in the rear-view, at Carrizo Springs falling behind.

Night covers the surrounding brush. How many out there right now, wets, *mojados,* tramping through the scrub?

Running. Running where? The land's empty, featureless—
a wasteground, save for places like Creagan's trailers.

He stares through the windshield—breath caught in his
throat. At the corner of his eye is the radio, back-lit on the
dash. He picks up the receiver, presses down, sends a call.

A burst of static. "Dispatch. Dimmit County Sheriff."

"This is Marshal Whicher. I need to speak with Deputy
Benita Alvarenga."

"Switch to channel two, non-emergency."

The marshal buttons over the channel switch. He stares
along the highway, engine humming, tires loud against the
road.

The radio lights up. "Alvarenga..."

"Did you give Marshal Lassiter directions? Out to that
hunting concession?"

"Say again?"

"The trailers, Creagan's trailers—did you give Lassiter
directions?"

Another burst of static.

"No."

"You didn't?"

"You'd already headed out, he telephoned, I told him
where you went."

"You have a copy of Brady Iverson's map?"

"No, I told him roughly—that you went out, that you
were headed to those trailers, off of 277. Off the highway..."

He holds it in his mind—the cold thought passing
through him. "Alright. That's all I wanted."

He grips the wheel.

Switches out.

✦

Up the long grade the truck wheels bite in the caliche. Whicher peers above the headlights—trying to make out the first sign of Jim Gale's place.

Petrified wood lies stark in a gravel draw. The posted sign to Gale's property is up ahead.

He swings in on the track, lighting up the hill. At the house is a truck—Lassiter's K5 Blazer, no sign of Gale's pickup.

He thinks again of the feeling—at the trailers, Lassiter prowling, gun in hand. He pushes the thought aside—so far, he's been wrong about everything.

By the line of dark trees, he pulls up, shuts off the motor. He steps out, crosses to the raised deck, lights showing from the house.

At the front door he knocks hard. *"Anybody in there..."* The sound of his voice strange in the mute dark.

He tries the door—it's unlocked. He steps into a hallway. The house bright, silent. *"It's Whicher, anybody here?"*

He moves fast through the rooms—they're unfinished, strewn with pieces of timber, electric cables, cans of paint. He checks the phone—it's working. In the kitchen he smells food, sees half-eaten enchiladas. He pushes through a screen door, steps out in back.

In the dark clearing, he moves to the Blazer. He touches the front grill—it's warm.

He runs back to his truck, climbs in, hits an overhead light. He searches out a map. *Where would they go?*

South is the bunch of trailers. There's Creagan's place in Eagle Pass. West is the border, the river, then Mexico. East on the map there's nothing but empty scrub.

No vehicle passed him coming down the hill.

He traces a finger upward on the map. Nothing out there, a drainage cut the only feature marked. Two miles north is Elm Creek. His finger stops.

He holds the map close to the dome light.

A rail line. Group of lines. Running up the back of Elm Creek.

He feels his heart rate quicken. *Rail.*

He fires up the Chevy, sticks the truck into drive, turns around. Dumps his foot on the gas.

At the track he heads up the grade, tires spinning, ripping dirt.

The hill plateaus into flat scrub. Then barrels into a down slope—the Chevy bouncing, starting to shake.

The hi-beams pick out something—an earth bank blocking the track.

He hits the brakes, the truck goes light. He skids, comes off the pedals, lets it roll. Then brakes again, stopping the truck in a cloud of dust.

To one side of the track is a drainage canal. The earth bank is man-made—big as the truck. No way around.

He jumps out, sees wheel marks chewed into the side of the bank. He scrambles to the top, to crushed stone and hard pan stretched out.

Steel tracks disappear into the dark.

He can just make out the backs of warehouses. He starts to walk.

Looking north, rail lines glint, box cars stand motionless. Whicher crosses the track, enters a small yard—a group of metal-sided warehouses.

An unpaved road leads to the line of unlit buildings. He circles around, walks the track side, re-enters the yard looking for vehicles.

There's no security, no barrier on the road.

At one warehouse, light shines from an office window by a metal service door.

He steps to it, tries the handle—it opens. He draws the Ruger, moves inside.

He's in a block corridor, low-power light. He stands a moment, listening for any sound. The office is deserted— he can see through an open doorway. He moves into the warehouse, smell of diesel fuel, plastic and oil.

Piles of crates are stacked high—he sees pallets, a forklift.

At the far side of the warehouse, Marshal Lassiter's standing, gun in hand. He stares at Whicher. "Jesus, army, it's you..."

The marshal stands rooted.

"Gale's outside. What're you doing here?"

"I came up. To the house..."

Lassiter slips his gun back in his holster.

"Nobody was there," Whicher says.

Lassiter steps around a stack of crates. "We did a bunch of talking. I told Gale I was suspending him—he says he has to show me this place."

Whicher scans the inside of the warehouse.

"Reckoned he found something y'all overlooked—this here yard. Private loading yard..."

"That's what it is?"

"According to Jim."

"He never mentioned it."

Lassiter pushes back his hat. "We got here, he flat out went for me."

Whicher feels the weight of the big revolver in his hand.

"I coldcocked the son of a bitch."

An A/C unit on the roof kicks in, droning sound filling up the dead space.

"I saw light inside the place," Lassiter says. "I thought to check."

"Where's Gale?"

"Outside. Cuffed." Lassiter jabs a thumb over his shoulder.

Whicher takes a pace, backing into the corridor, stepping out into the yard. He moves fast to the rear of the warehouse, Gale's half-ton truck is parked behind.

He moves to it. The big man's slumped at the wheel. Whicher opens the door.

Gale twitches—his face is turned to the side, eyes half-shut, blood running from his nose.

His cheek is cut. His hands are cuffed through the steering wheel.

He grunts, tries to focus on the younger marshal. Tries to speak, the words slurred, "He brought me out...to kill me..."

Whicher feels the sweat on the rosewood grips of the Ruger.

He turns, sees Lassiter—out of the building now, walking up behind the warehouse, along the rail line.

Gale struggles to sit up. "He shot Creagan." He spits blood from his mouth. "Lassiter shot him..."

From the far side of the yard is the sound of a motor— a vehicle approaching on the unpaved road.

Lights turn shapes over the blocks of buildings. Lassiter stands motionless on the track.

Gale grunts, "I think he's meeting Johnson..."

Whicher steps from the truck, into cover behind the warehouse side.

The vehicle's close now—somewhere on the frontage of the yard.

Gale calls out; *"Him and Johnson chained Creagan to that freight load..."*

The district marshal steps from the track, moving in behind the warehouse, no gun, his hand empty. He looks at Whicher; "You believe his shit?"

Whicher listens to the sound of a car engine, tires rolling over asphalt.

"You want to check that out, army?"

"If that's Johnson," Gale calls, *"he's got no reason not to kill you..."*

"Jesus Christ," Lassiter says. "You watch Gale, I'll see who it is." He steps past Whicher, draws the Glock from the holster. At the corner of the warehouse, he pauses. Edges out.

Whicher moves up to the corner, takes a half-step from the side. Over Lassiter's shoulder he sees a vehicle, a sedan—slowing to a halt.

A lone man steps from the driver seat. Headlights shining at the warehouse office.

He's wearing a long coat, a duster, a pinch-front hat. He steps to the back of the vehicle, opens the trunk. In his hand is something that looks like a pistol.

"Freeze," Lassiter shouts. He steps forward. *"US Marshal..."*

The man turns from the car, gun arm rising.

Lassiter fires five shots in quick succession—the noise deafening.

The man at the car staggers back.

Lassiter moves in.

Whicher stares down his iron-sight.

The man lies spreadeagled, hat gone, face caught in the tail light. Whicher makes out the metal-frame glasses—it looks like Merrill Johnson.

"Marshal," Whicher calls out.

"He had a weapon..." Lassiter calls back. He kicks the gun from the man's hand, puts a boot in his side—the man doesn't move.

Whicher turns to Gale in the half-ton truck.

"He kill him?" Gale's staring, trying to see.

Lassiter steps away from the car, from the man on the ground. He moves up the side of the warehouse.

"That's the only man could take him down..."

Lassiter calls to Gale; "*That why you brought me out here— you son of a bitch?*"

Gale breathes, "You got to do something..."

Whicher turns to Lassiter. "Marshal—put away your weapon."

Quint Lassiter shifts his weight onto one foot. "That guy would've shot me..."

"Marshal Gale's under control. I'm asking you to holster your weapon now."

"Son," Lassiter says. "Don't talk out your ass."

Whicher levels the revolver on the district marshal. Heart beating like a trip-hammer. He looks through the rear sight. "I won't ask a third time."

Lassiter cocks back his head. A grin splits his face. "Bring it down, army. Holy shit. Alright. If you're spooked, I'll put it away."

The sound of a shot explodes in the night air.

Whicher stares down the sight of the Ruger, ears ringing. The hammer's still up.

He can't feel a hit.

Lassiter's legs go from under him.

Whicher ducks right, Merrill Johnson's on the ground, holding up his gun arm, clutching at the pistol.

Whicher fires twice. The man jerks.

Both men lie inert in the yard.

EPILOGUE

Carrizo Springs. One week later.

In the White Star Cantina, Whicher sits smoking on a
Marlboro Red. On the table is a long-neck bottle—ice-
cold, condensation beading in the heat. It's early evening,
the place half full—Hispanic Americans, field hands, construction workers. Beside the bottle is a tin ashtray. He
flicks the cigarette. Checks the door.

Alfonso Saldana. Todd Williams. Randell Creagan.

Carmela Ramirez. Sara Pacheco.

Two more, unidentified. Non-documented, Hispanic
males. Last, he thinks of Merrill M. Johnson. And District
Marshal Quinton Lassiter.

He stares around the room, taking in the bar, thinks
of another; *Viajero,* in Piedras Negras. He raises the bottle.
Takes a long pull.

La zona. Everybody went there. From way back, Eric
said. Great and the good.

Quinton Lassiter had been one of them.

Whicher's gaze settles on his draft report—inquest notes compiled for Dimmit County Sheriff.

Scruggs had lifted the suspension; District Marshal Riggins had him do it. But nothing broken had been fixed.

Lassiter.

At twenty, Quint Lassiter had been in Korea fighting a war. By twenty-five, stationed in Germany with 2nd Armored. Holding back the communist east.

Borders—always at the front line. *Always into the Enemy.*

By '57, Lassiter was in the Marshals Service, on the border with Mexico. A line crosser. Like Whicher himself.

He pictures the man in a '50s Chevy—cat houses, pretty girls, easy money. Mixing with the twilight people.

Quint Lassiter made money all kinds of ways on the border; no drugs, no guns, nothing to get on any federal radar. Just a word in the right place, either side of the line. Thirty years on, married, a family, he was a big noise. Friend to everybody—Merrill Johnsons of the world included.

But times were changing.

Carmela Ramirez.

The girl with the broken necklace.

Carmela left her home in Sabinas, Coahuila. For two years in Piedras Negras, she was practically Lassiter's own girl, his private property.

She asked her *tío rico*, her sugar daddy, to let her come live in the states. She'd live someplace near San Antonio, he could see her all the time.

He told her no. He meant it.

But Carmela Ramirez had her own ideas.

Whicher gazes out the window onto the street. Cars roll past the dust-streaked store fronts, cars and trucks, the sidewalks empty. At one corner of the bar room, a group of Hispanics bet on a pool game. A guy sinks four off of two rails, only calling three. Shouts start up, the player flips the bird. Whicher takes another sip.

Carmela Ramirez. A girl like her, working *la zona*, it took her no time.

It took her no time to hook into the *coyotaje*. No time to hook up with a bunch of *campesinos* looking to make the trip north. She could surprise her sugar daddy, show up, what was Lassiter going to do? He probably thank her for it, no time. Didn't she always make him thankful?

She talked a girlfriend into going with her. *Sara Pacheco.*

Whicher taps the ash from the end of the cigarette. Runs a knuckle up the side of the bottle.

For days, Quint Lassiter couldn't find her in Piedras Negras. He asked his friend Merrill Johnson to try.

And Merrill Johnson had obliged.

Merrill Johnson knew everybody. Not just in freight, in all the trade along the border. *Brinco* people included; *pateros*— boat men, guys making river crossings, with wets.

One of the boat men in Piedras Negras said he knew of a group making the trip with two young women. They were crossing downstream, out in the brush. Across the river, a *norteno* would get them through. The *norteno's* name was Williams.

Todd Williams from Catarina—Merrill Johnson knew him.

He knew he worked with Creagan.

They'd likely come up through the Tutton land.

A half hour passes. Whicher buys another beer. The bar-keep is a woman, middle-aged, bee-hive hair, a smoker's face. Whicher takes the beer back to the table, lights an-other cigarette. He'd quit. He told Eric he'd quit. But Eric had to quit too, go see the professor down in Brownsville. That was the deal.

Him and Karen finally split. Eric said he was alright, it didn't come as any surprise. The army looked like be-ing the next thing to go from his life—they were talking about a medical discharge. Only thing anybody could see to do.

From the corner of his eye, Whicher sees the street door open. Benita Alvarenga walks in. She's wearing uni-form, olive pants, tan shirt, her hair pulled back. She walks to the counter, all the men in the place turn to look.

She says something to the woman at the bar. Then crosses the room to Whicher's table.

"I get you a drink?" He stands, pulls out a chair.

She nods at the bar. "Got it." She sits.

He looks at the uniform she's wearing. "Figured you might be about done..."

"We have a lot going on," she says. "Did you bring the inquest notes?"

He gestures at the folder on the table.

The barkeep brings a can of diet soda, a glass, a napkin. Benita Alvarenga takes a sip, eyes dark, feline.

"I was thinking," he says.

She glances at him.

"I don't know. Dinner?" He clears his throat.

Her eyes cut away.

Neither speaks for a moment. He takes a hit off the Marlboro. Feels the hint of color at his face.

"Miguel Carrasco called," she says. "He's been doing a lot of asking around."

Whicher taps his cigarette in the tin ashtray.

"He has the best informers. He's hearing Johnson was making money from wets riding loads he brokered."

Whicher nods.

She flicks an eyebrow. "Looks like you got that right."

"Plenty I got wrong."

She puts a hand on the folder of notes. "You talked to Gale?"

Jim Gale.

Gale had seen enough. Year on year he'd seen things, noticed things. He'd started looking for something on Lassiter. Couldn't get what he wanted.

He started talking to fences, snitches, giving out his number to the low-life. Pimps and racketeers. The likes of Randell Creagan. FBI caught wind of something going on, something bad in the district. Suspicion fell on the Marshals Service. Dane Vogel had been the result.

Everything Whicher saw, he saw it backward.

Benita Alvarenga swirls the ice in her glass. She picks up the folder. "You get it all figured out?"

Whicher gets a shot of whiskey and the taco plate at the bar. He orders rice and black beans, pico de gallo, stewed chicken.

She won't eat.

"Miguel Carrasco says it was him called Lassiter." She sips her drink. "The sweep was short-handed, he thought of Jim Gale, thought to clear it with Lassiter first."

He meets her eye over the table.

"That's how come Lassiter heard about it," she says. "All of those people might still be alive."

Whicher chews on a mouthful of chicken. "If *la migra* got a hold of Carmela Ramirez, she'd likely sing. He would've known that."

"So he came down."

Whicher nods. "He called Merrill Johnson. Had Johnson call the Tuttons."

"They're co-operating?"

"Moving them to Huntsville scared the shit out of them."

"Sheriff says they'll go accessory to murder."

Whicher takes a knock of whiskey. "Way it breaks." He puts down the glass. "Tutton told Johnson the wets were headed up in groups, in relays. Todd Williams getting them to the Channing Ranch—Jug Line Harris from the ranch to

Creagan's trailers. From there, they'd move up to the farm. Quint Lassiter drove out to the trailers—nobody was there..."

"They were still at the ranch?"

"He didn't know that. He drove to the Tutton place, they told him the wets were on the move—but Zach could radio. So Lassiter had Zach radio Creagan, to tell him— 'get rid of the girls'."

Benita Alvarenga looks at him.

"He probably never meant 'kill them'. He probably only meant; 'take 'em back'."

Whicher finishes up the plate of food. He runs a fork around the last of the black beans, the pico de gallo.

"Creagan lost it," he says.

"You believe what Harris said about him?"

"I believe him. He started shooting, didn't stop."

She shakes her head.

Whicher looks around the bar room; filling up with the evening crowd. Guys like Creagan, working guys in ball caps and battered Western hats. "Jim Gale was pressuring him..."

"Did Gale tell you that?"

"He had Creagan take his number, he was riding him pretty hard. He reckons Creagan was a part-time snitch."

"As well as a car thief. And *coyote?*"

"Scruggs thinks FBI in Houston knew him. They won't confirm. But they might've been trying to get him to turn federal witness. You think about it, Laredo court were charging him, FBI putting in a squeeze. On top of that, a US Marshal, Jim Gale is on his back."

"You think he just cracked?"

"He's out in the brush, the middle of the night, running *mojados*. Zach Tutton radios, tells him to get rid of the girls. God knows what was said..."

She looks at him.

"They're never going to admit it was anything more. The death house is up in Huntsville," Whicher says. "State execution unit. I'd think they'd be mindful of that."

Alvarenga sinks an inch in her chair.

"Creagan shot everybody. Plus Alfonso Saldana—from the truck. Harris ran for his life. The Tuttons say Creagan searched the bodies at the ranch, took anything that looked like ID. Then drove to the farm, told 'em what he'd done. Quint Lassiter was there. He shot him dead."

The marshal's gaze settles on the empty plate. Amber light of whiskey on the table.

He walks her out. Benita Alvarenga. Into late evening sun on West Alamo Street.

She holds the folder of inquest notes. Something in the way she stands—as if reluctant to leave. "Meg Wheeler says she can't prove that Remington 700 was fired from the Toyota."

"Zach admitted it was theirs." Whicher shrugs. "He saw it in Creagan's truck, he'd loaned it to Todd. He grabbed it back—never knowing Creagan shot a man with it."

Alvarenga looks off down the street toward the turn for the courthouse.

Whicher buttons his jacket over his gun. "Zach says Merrill Johnson came out to the farm. Lassiter and Johnson took Creagan's body out to Elm Creek in the stolen Toyota. We think they picked a load headed for Mexico in the morning. Johnson must've picked it."

"Except the body fell off a mile down the line..."

He stands. Looks at her.

She glances at the folder. "Sheriff better have these."

"I call you sometime?"

She doesn't look up.

"I mean..."

"I know what you mean." She raises the folder. "I only came for the notes."

He stands awkward in the suit and hat.

"And maybe to tell you something. That last day, the whole time you were suspended—you had no right to do any of the things you did. But you didn't say a damn thing..."

He doesn't answer.

She looks him up and down. "You got the guy, you probably figure it all worked out."

"Listen..."

"You could have cost me my job. That's really all I need to know."

✦

Laredo, TX. Two days later.

Whicher pulls in to the truck park in downtown Laredo. It's near eight in the evening, stock trailers lined up in the lot. He cuts the engine, pushes open the door. The smell of beasts strong in the air.

Vic Delossantos from Border Patrol is walking along the side of an open-slat trailer.

Working a clipboard, talking with one of the truck drivers is the APHIS vet—Hannah Scott.

Delossantos spots the marshal. He crosses the expanse of pitted asphalt, last of the day's heat radiating.

Whicher steps from the truck.

"You got my message?" Delossantos says. "You could've come see me in the morning."

The marshal watches Hannah Scott at the row of trucks. Sandy hair, freckles. Blue polo shirt and cap.

"This whole thing, man. Lot of people got shook up." The Border Patrol agent looks at him sideways. "I heard Jim Gale's running for Lassiter's job. Up in San Antonio."

"I heard the same."

Delossantos screws up his face. "How about you?"

"We get done with the inquest, I'll be leaving. Transferring. Northern district."

"I'm sorry to hear that."

They stand a minute watching horses move inside the transports, tails flicking, stamping feet.

Hannah Scott's finishing up with the driver.

"You said you had something for me?" Whicher says.

"Not me. Hannah. The vet. It's about Brownsville, the university."

"She wanted to see me?"

"I'll let her tell you, man." Delossantos reaches out his hand. "Northern district. You know where?"

"Abilene. Lubbock, maybe."

The Border Patrol agent places a hand over the marshal's as they shake goodbye. Then turns back to the waiting line of trucks.

Hannah Scott fits a top to her pen.

Whicher spots a bench in a park off the lot—scorched grass, a line of palms stretched along the river bank.

The vet takes a loose strand of hair from her mouth, stepping over, clipboard beneath one arm. "Evening."

He nods. "We take a walk?" He takes out the pack of Marlboros. "You smoke?"

"Nope."

"Didn't think."

They walk across a loop road to the little park. Sit at a bench facing the water.

Downstream, Convent Avenue Bridge spans the Rio Grande, cars and trucks stacked solid.

"So, Vic tell you?" She puts the clipboard on her lap. "It's about that man. Trying to find out about his son."

From his jacket, Whicher takes a book of matches from the White Star Cantina. He lights the cigarette. Shakes out the match.

"Vic was pretty upset," she says.

Whicher smokes. Stares at traffic on the bridge.

"About the little boy, I mean. About the father. He asked me about it a few times." She pauses. "I told him we see it a lot."

On the Mexican bank of the river, a mass of trees shimmer in the wind.

"Fatal birth defects," she says, "in horses. The same as NTDs."

He glances at her. Takes the cigarette from his lips.

"Neural tube defects," she says. "In human births. I told him what I know. He wanted me to talk to you."

Upstream, upriver, red steel trusses of a railroad bridge span the water. A freight load on it, creeping north.

"There's been studies in the horse world. Animal medicine's a separate world from human medicine," she says. "Except, of course, it really isn't."

At the far side of the park, a lone Hispanic kid turns on a cinder court, shooting hoops at a rim with no net.

"We see NTDs every year toxic mold gets into the corn harvest."

The marshal meets her gaze.

"Stillborn foals," she says. "The white matter of the brain is liquified: We know what causes it—it's the corn mold."

"Ma'am?"

"Fumonisin. It's a toxin in unprocessed corn."

He shifts on the bench. "I'm not any kind of science major..."

"It's a naturally occurring mold." She lays her hands on the clipboard. "Some years it's worse than others. But any year the toxin level is high, all livestock are taken off feed containing corn."

"You're saying that's what causes it?"

"There's a glut of corn, it goes cheap, places like Mexico, anyplace people want cheap food. Like unprocessed corn to make tortillas. Not the store-bought kind—the raw ingredients."

Whicher stares at the parched grass in the park, an image in his mind; the woman at the painted shacks by Creagan's trailers. Grinding corn in a bowl.

"If a pregnant woman ate it," the vet says, "the effect on an unborn child would be the same as on an unborn foal."

He twists his head to look at her. "The folk at the university know this?"

"Human health and animal health." She shakes her head, crosses one leg over the other.

He smokes in silence.

She stares out over the river.

The kid on the court runs, shoots—hits the backboard.

"But you think it's been passed on," Whicher says, finally. "This information?"

"It'll be somewhere in the bottom of a drawer."

From the corner of his eye he sees the railroad bridge. Trains had nothing to do with it, with the kid getting sick, the mother riding freight, breathing chemicals. *How many things could a man get wrong?*

The catch of animals is strong in the air. He thinks of horses sent down to the knife; people dying to come up. Stillborn kids in a hospital. Rotten feed.

He takes off the Resistol. Sets it down on the crown.

She stands, turns to go. "I don't suppose it changes anything," she says. "Vic just wanted me to tell you." She spreads her hands. "I guess it didn't really matter..."

The river moves in the channel, toward a waiting ocean. He watches the water's surface, sun dancing—points of brilliant light. Across the city, the noise of traffic drifts in the air, a flow of moments, lives entangled, intertwined.

He hears her footsteps as she walks away. Throws down the cigarette, sets the hat on his head.

"It mattered." He speaks his answer to the wind.

The kid on the court has gone.

No one hears him.

"It mattered," he says.

Made in United States
North Haven, CT
04 May 2023

36215807R00243